C000181984

Summer
Cake
at the Cosy Kettle

BOOKS BY LIZ EELES

THE SALT BAY SERIES
Annie's Holiday by the Sea
Annie's Christmas by the Sea
Annie's Summer by the Sea

THE COSY KETTLE SERIES
New Starts and Cherry Tarts at the Cosy Kettle

A Summer Escape and Strawberry Cake at the Cosy Kettle

LIZ EELES

bookouture

Published by Bookouture in 2019

An imprint of StoryFire Ltd.

Carmelite House
50 Victoria Embankment
London EC4Y 0DZ

www.bookouture.com

ISBN: 978-1-78681-671-9
eBook ISBN: 978-1-78681-670-2

For Suzie, a true northern goddess

Chapter One

I love it when The Cosy Kettle is busy. There's something about the soft hiss of the coffee machine amid the gentle buzz of conversation that hits me right in the heart – which is surprising for a fairly unsentimental person like me.

But nothing beats being alone in the café at the end of the day, when the coffee machine has fallen silent and rays of golden summer sunshine are slanting across the whitewashed walls. I look around me, at the tables with their pretty pink cloths and the strands of colourful bunting looping from the ceiling, and smile. This place has changed so much in such a short time.

Only a few months ago, where I'm standing was a dingy storeroom in the back of a small-town bookshop. And now it's a warm and welcoming space, decorated with paintings by local artists and a shelf of gleaming copper kettles. It's been transformed – rather like me. Though my transformation from unambitious forty-something wife to confident small-business owner is still a work in progress.

I pull the door of the café closed, walk through the bookshop and step outside onto Honeyford High Street. June sunshine is turning the Cotswold stone around me a glowing butter-yellow and I'm struck again by the town's beauty. I noticed it the first time I came here, just before I took on the bookshop. And the tiny stone cottages and grander gabled buildings, with hills rising behind them, still take my breath away.

Talking of which… after locking the door of the shop and pocketing the key, I tentatively sniff. Country air is invigorating. Usually. Unless the wind is in the wrong direction and the sickly sweet scent of manure is wafting off the hills. It makes me wince but the locals don't seem to notice the occasional pong that drifts through the town.

I mentioned the smell once to eighty-year-old Stanley, who's a regular Cosy Kettle customer. But he laughed and accused me of being 'a namby-pamby city girl'. So now I just suck it up – so to speak – and trust that my olfactory cells will soon become blunted. Stanley's are obviously long dead after being exposed to eight decades of countryside aromas.

Fortunately, this afternoon's air carries nothing more than pollen and a hint of honeysuckle. So I take a long, deep breath before walking past the stone arches of the market house, towards my car.

Tourists are wandering nearby, with their camera phones pointed at the ancient buildings that line the High Street, and I wonder if they assume I'm a local who belongs here. Or if they also see a namby-pamby city girl who's trying to fit in?

'Excuse me, ma'am,' says a stout man in baggy shorts, in a drawling American accent, 'I'm Ted and this lady is my wife, Linda. Would you mind taking a photo of us together, right here?' He points at a brass plaque, on the front of the Pheasant and Fox pub, which reads: *Sixteenth-century coaching inn, once visited by Oscar Wilde.* The plaque is almost obscured by purple verbena cascading from a huge hanging basket, and Ted gently pushes flowers out of the way before handing me his phone.

'Of course I don't mind.' I put my shoulder bag down on the pavement and snap several pictures as he and his wife point at the plaque with toothy grins. 'Hopefully at least one of those will be OK.'

'Thank you,' says Ted, taking back his phone and nodding as he scrolls through the photos. 'Good job! These will be a perfect memento of our visit. You're so lucky to live here, in such a truly special place.'

I don't actually live here. My home is a two-bedroom flat above my husband's restaurant in Oxford. But I don't let on as Ted and Linda wave and wander off.

I walk on, chuffed that Ted and Linda assumed I belonged in Honeyford – right up until I catch sight of myself reflected in a shop window. Nope, I still look like a namby-pamby city girl to me.

Callie, Stanley's granddaughter who helped me set up the café, always looks effortlessly casual and at ease with herself. But I rarely seem to get it right. Today, my fitted green dress and matching jade shoes look over the top for a small country bookshop and café – as though I'm trying too hard to be the boss and to convince myself that I know what I'm doing.

Ah, well. I push my sunglasses up my nose and run a hand through my dark shoulder-length hair.

The good news is that business has picked up since we opened The Cosy Kettle at the back of the shop. Even Malcolm, my often-critical husband, has grudgingly admitted that maybe me taking on the shop wasn't quite such a disastrous idea after all. At first he warned me the shop was a mistake, over and over again, before I decided to plough the money left to me by my parents into this 'business opportunity'. That's what the agent called it: 'an amazing business opportunity that rarely becomes available'. Malcolm called it 'a big black money pit that no one in their right mind would touch with a bargepole'.

I think that was when I decided to go for it.

I love Malcolm, I admire his ambition, and I've always supported his restaurant ventures, even when he's overstretched himself and they've gone slightly tits up. But now I'm over forty myself, I've been feeling little tremors of… something. Panic? Boredom? Rebellion? Possibly. Or maybe it's just my own ambition scrabbling hard to get out.

Whatever the reason, those tremors pushed me to swallow my fear and become a bookshop owner. And things *will* work out because, quite frankly, I couldn't bear asking Malcolm to bail me out. He's a good man and we've been married pretty happily for over twenty years. But he does have a tendency to say 'I told you so'.

To be honest, I feel proud of myself for taking a chance on Honeyford Bookshop and The Cosy Kettle. I've found out what customers want and ordered in a wide array of books and, though it's been tough at times, it's been fun. I'd never say this to Malcolm because he wouldn't understand, but I've felt more alive over the last few months than I have done for ages. And that's why I'm determined to do all I can to become a proper part of this close-knit community. Even if I have to toil long hours, wear jeans to work and suppress my sense of smell forever.

My car, parked next to the war memorial, is like an oven when I open the door. The sun has been beating down on it all day, the steering wheel is baking hot when I slide into the driver's seat – and the whole vehicle smells of cheese. What is it with Honeyford and eye-watering whiffs?

When a quick search reveals Malcolm's ripe trainers under the passenger seat, I wrap them in a carrier bag and dump them in the boot. He must have left them in my car after I picked him up from the gym a couple of days ago. Though quite why he's suddenly started weight training after years of avoiding any exercise is a mystery.

I did wonder if he was having a midlife crisis but he assured me everything was fine when I gently asked him about it. Then he went off on one about some bloke at the gym who hogs the running machine, so I changed the subject. *But maybe it's something I need to keep an eye on*, I think, as I pull out into Weavers Lane and head for Oxford.

The journey takes less time than usual because the traffic's not too bad when I get to the city outskirts. And when I reach our restaurant, The Briar Patch, I spot a perfect space for my car nearby. The gods of city centre parking are smiling on me this afternoon.

The back door of the restaurant is propped open with a crate of potatoes to let a breeze into the steamy kitchen, so I walk straight in.

The first thing that strikes me as odd is the low-pitched giggling. It sounds like Malcolm – but Malcolm doesn't giggle. He sniggers at jokes sometimes, and does the occasional snort when something funny takes him by surprise. Coffee came down his nose once when he was watching Michael McIntyre. And he's been known to guffaw – usually at reruns of ancient sitcoms.

But in all the years we've been married. I've never once heard him giggle.

The second thing that strikes me as odd is that the sound is coming from the restaurant's cold store – a small room that houses meat, fruit and veg. I start walking more quickly. Maybe Malcolm's accidentally shut himself in and the giggle is really a strangled gasp from my frozen husband? Maybe he's been trapped in there for hours and is dying of hypothermia?

That's strange; the door is ajar. I wrench it open, bowl into the room, and stop short.

Malcolm is not dead. At least, not yet.

My husband is in what can only be described as 'a clinch' with a petite blonde whose corkscrew curls are winding down her back. His hand is resting on her pert backside and his mouth is open so wide he looks like he's eating her face.

This is something I'll never be able to unsee. The image sears onto my brain as my familiar, contented life shatters into a million pieces, like china hitting concrete.

'What the hell is going on?' I gasp.

Malcolm has come up for air. He wipes his hand across the back of his mouth, which is red with transferred lipstick, and his grey eyes open wide with alarm when he spots me.

'What are you doing here? You don't usually get home this early,' he splutters as though it's my fault that my world is currently crashing down around my ears.

I don't do or say anything. I can't because my body seems to have suddenly seized up. And my shallow breaths hang white in the chilly air as I push down a rising feeling of panic. This can't be happening. Not to me and Malcolm. We're an ordinary married couple, living an ordinary life. We have our ups and downs – who doesn't? But we love each other. Don't we?

The woman rests her forehead against his chest for a moment before turning around. But I already know who she is. Marina works here at The Briar Patch as a waitress. She's young enough to be Malcolm's daughter – far younger than me, and skinnier, with long legs, big blue eyes, and lips that look like someone's taken a bicycle pump to them.

I'm so stupid! I should have guessed.

Images from the past few weeks start running through my head. Marina's hand brushing Malcolm's leg; the two of them, heads bent together, sorting out food orders. She even laughs at his terrible jokes, for goodness' sake. It was obvious!

But I didn't see it because I trusted Malcolm and thought he loved me.

'Flora, I'm sorry you saw me and Malcy – us – like this,' says Marina, her cheeks flaming against her white-blonde hair.

Malcy? No one calls my husband Malcy. He'd throw a fit if I called him Malcy. And are they really an 'us'? We're an 'us' – me and Malcolm. How can my husband be an *us* with someone else?

'Marina, you'd better go and make sure the menus are on the tables,' says 'Malcy'. He glances nervously at a row of meat cleavers hanging on the wall beside me, as though I might suddenly lose control.

She pouts at him. 'Really, Malcy? Do you want me to leave?'

When my husband nods, she wrinkles her pert nose, picks up a bunch of purple freesias that are on the floor at her feet, and brushes past me in a cloud of overpowering perfume. The heavy door bangs behind her and I hear the dull, disappearing clip of her high heels.

Malcolm and I stare at each other as a hanging animal carcass swings back and forth between us. It's not the most romantic of locations but then Malcolm has never been a romantic man – something I should have realised when he proposed over a takeaway vindaloo. To a sheltered eighteen-year-old with parents who considered spaghetti bolognaise to be foreign and adventurous, it all seemed rather exotic at the time.

'We can't talk in here,' says Malcolm. He strides towards me and grabs my hand, but I snatch it back.

'So it's OK for you to snog your staff in here but you can't have a conversation with your wife?'

I haven't used the word 'snog' since I was a teenager, and my voice sounds shrill and high-pitched. I don't sound like me at all.

'Not so loud, Flora. You'll embarrass yourself,' says Malcolm, almost pushing me out of the door. Freddie, who's in the corner of the kitchen prepping the veg, glances up before going back to chopping carrots into tiny orange batons.

How much does Freddie know? How much do all the staff know? Am I the butt of bawdy in-jokes or pitied as the wronged wife? I expect they've all been discussing me: 'Poor old Flora. Her husband is fooling around with younger women and she doesn't have a clue.'

Is it women plural or just nubile, oestrogen-soaked Marina with her stupid corkscrew hair?

Malcolm grabs my arm and pulls me out of the kitchen and through the restaurant which will be opening in half an hour. Marina is in the corner, near the bar, polishing glasses in a frenzy. She carries on scrubbing the spotless crystal and doesn't look up as we rush past the tables and start climbing the stairs to our flat.

Living above the 'shop' isn't ideal. Our home has a lingering smell of fried onions and fish wafting up from the kitchen below. But being so close to his business means Malcolm doesn't have far to stagger to bed when the restaurant closes, and I can help out in the evenings, even when I'm knackered after a day in my bookshop and café.

Malcolm slams the door to the flat behind us and pushes past me. 'I think I need a drink,' he announces, heading for the kitchen.

I wander into our light, bright living room, feeling dazed, and perch on the windowsill. Below me, in the narrow street, shoppers are scurrying along in shirtsleeves and I spot the blue of the river in the distance. Students are wandering along arm in arm and there's a buzz of conversation from people sitting outside a nearby café. How can everything around me look the same when my life is suddenly so different? I take a deep breath, close my eyes and rest my forehead against the cool window as pain and sorrow threaten to overwhelm me. What happens to Flora Morgan now? A frisson of fear stirs in my soul.

'Here you go, you'd better drink this.' As Malcolm shoves a glass at me, liquid slops onto my dress and soaks through to my skin.

Good grief, it's a large glass and it's filled to the brim with – I give it a sniff – gin. He may as well have given me the bottle with a straw. I carefully place the drink on the painted white windowsill, untouched.

'Go on then. Say it!' says Malcolm, gruffly, pacing up and down the rug we bought together in Habitat.

My husband is sweating. Usually he takes great pride in his appearance and is immaculately turned out. But damp patches are spreading under the arms of his blue cotton shirt. He stops pacing and stares at me while I try to put my feelings into words.

'How long has this been going on?' I manage, eventually. I must sound like every wronged wife in the history of infidelity.

'How long has what been going on?'

'Your affair with Marina, obviously. Stop treating me like an idiot, Malcolm.'

'I wouldn't call it an affair. That's a very loaded word.'

'What would you call it then?'

Malcolm blinks rapidly. 'I don't know. It's just a… a dalliance.'

'A dalliance?' My laugh sounds hollow. 'So did you dalliance Marina into bed?'

'Now you're just being ridiculous,' puffs Malcolm, knocking back a slug of whisky from his brimming tumbler, and avoiding answering the question.

When he steps closer to the window, I notice that the subtle stripes of grey at his temples have disappeared. He must have dyed his hair!

No wonder two of my best white towels have mysteriously disappeared and he'd cleaned the bathroom when I got home a few nights ago. I was so pleased at the time – I thought he was coming round to the idea of the bookshop and trying to be helpful. But it turns out he was just covering his tracks.

I cover my face with my hands and listen to the ticking of the clock on the mantelpiece. The clock was left to me by my parents, who never really got on with Malcolm. They made an effort but he was always too busy to spend much time with them and always seemed slightly distant when he did.

When I look up, Malcolm has resumed his pacing, up and down in front of me.

'Go on, then, what else do you want to say?' he says, puffing out air like he's giving birth. 'You'd better get it all out.'

'She's so young, Malcolm. You're old enough to be her dad, for goodness' sake. And she works here. Were you so desperate you had to hit on the staff?'

'I wasn't desperate,' says Malcolm, jutting out his bottom lip. 'I'm sorry, Flora. I really am. But, at the end of the day, it's your fault.'

He stops pacing as my mouth drops open.

'What on earth are you talking about? How can you kissing Marina be my fault? I didn't force you to stand there with your hand on her backside and your tongue down her throat.'

'There's no need to be unpleasant, Flora.' Malcolm runs his hands through his dyed hair until it's standing up on end. 'It's that damn bookshop and café of yours. You're there all the time and, even when you're home, you talk about nothing else. It's all books and coffee, this, and Callie and Honeyford, that.'

'That's not fair, Malcolm. You bang on endlessly about the restaurant.'

'That's different. The restaurant is my career. The bookshop and café are your…'

'My what?' I say, standing up and daring him to finish his sentence.

Malcolm's mouth turns down at the corners. 'Your hobby, Flora. And a damned expensive hobby at that.'

'Hobby?' Ooh, I've gone all high-pitched again, and Malcolm takes a step back. 'I'm working fifty hours a week to get my business on a good footing. You work at least that many hours here in the restaurant, and I don't complain.'

'Because it's a different thing entirely. Look, I'm not trying to say my work is more important than yours. Not really. But it's hardly a career, is it – selling books and coffee in a tiddly little town where the locals are weird. You belong here, with me. Not with them.'

'The people in Honeyford are not weird.'

'Really? What about that old bloke who ties himself to stuff?'

I should never have told him about Stanley's protest which involved chaining himself to a tree he wanted to save from being axed.

Malcolm rubs his stomach as though he's been punched. 'And what about that nervous goth girl who scuttles about in the café?'

'Are you referring to Becca? She suffers from anxiety but she's come on leaps and bounds since she started working in The Cosy Kettle. She's brilliant and kind, and I couldn't cope without her.'

Picking up my glass, I take a huge swig of gin and wonder why we're talking about my job, rather than Malcolm's infidelity. He's always been rather good at manipulating situations to his advantage. He's always been rather good at manipulating me, I realise, as the small tremors I've been feeling recently start building into a swell.

'So what are you going to do now?' asks Malcolm in the truculent voice he uses on the rare occasions when he's unsure of himself.

It's a fair question but I don't know the answer. Not yet. What *do* people do when the person they trust and rely on most in the world turns out to be deceiving them, and everything suddenly becomes shaky and unreal?

'First, I need you to tell me exactly what's been going on.'

I pull my shoulders back because the truth is going to hurt. Though not as much as the 'truth' I'll make up if Malcolm doesn't fill in the blanks. I'm already imagining Marina rubbing her lithe young body along my husband's as she whispers 'Malcy' in his ear.

Malcolm sighs and tugs his shirt away from his damp armpits. 'It's the age-old story, Flora. I felt neglected and Marina took advantage of the situation and threw herself at me.'

'Marina took advantage of *you*?'

'Sort of.' Malcolm has the good grace to look embarrassed. 'OK, I was flattered when she flirted with me and I let things get out of hand. I admit that I made a mistake and I'm sorry, Flora. I really am. But, let's face it, this could turn out to be a good thing – a wake-up call that brings us closer together.'

He moves towards me and places his hand on my arm. His fingers are hot and clammy on my bare skin.

'I thought we were close already,' I say, pulling my arm away. 'You've been deceiving me, Malcolm, and that's the hardest thing to take. The lying has to stop if our relationship has any chance of surviving this, so I need you to be completely straight with me now.' I draw in a deep breath and swallow loudly. 'Have you and Marina slept together?'

'Absolutely not,' he says, shaking his head vigorously. 'I've been a fool, Flora, but I would never betray you like that. You have to believe me. I got fed up with not seeing so much of you and I was weak and kissed Marina a couple of times. But you're the only woman for me. You must know that.'

He tilts his head to one side and opens his eyes wide, like he does when he's trying to be sincere. And I so want to believe him. I want to believe that throwing away two decades of shared history over a few foolish kisses would be ridiculous. My life has been intertwined with his for so long, I've forgotten what me minus Malcolm is like.

He was almost a decade older than me when we first met in a nightclub that had sticky carpets and a faint aroma of vomit. He was confident and ambitious, while I was shy and insecure, and he completely bowled me over. We fell in love quickly and I went straight from my parents' house to Malcolm's; we were married a couple of years later. I'm forty-two years old now, and I've never lived on my own. Is that a bit pathetic?

'Come on, Flora. What do you think?' urges Malcolm.

'I don't know what to think about any of this. I feel so shocked and hurt.'

When my anger evaporates and tears start dribbling down my cheeks, Malcolm steps forward and puts his arm around me. He smells of sweat but I bury my head in his chest anyway and sob. He feels so solid and familiar and safe. As my sobs turn into shallow gasps, a hair on his shirt is sucked into my mouth. *Urgh.* When I pull it from my lips, it's long, blonde and twisted like a corkscrew.

'How am I supposed to trust you, Malcolm?' I break away from him and drop the hair, which spirals down onto the rug.

'I've told you the absolute truth,' he insists. 'It was just a stupid kiss. That's all. I promise. You're the only woman for me, Flora.'

His eyes meet mine, imploring me to believe him. I usually end up doing what Malcolm wants, partly because I can't be bothered to argue and partly because I don't normally mind. But, this time, I walk past him into the bedroom without a word and shut the door. I need time to think.

It's only when I'm sitting on the bed that I realise my hands are shaking. I lie back against the pillows and try not to look at the wedding photo in a polished wooden frame on my bedside table. Malcolm promised to love and honour me, not a twenty-something blonde who was probably still in nappies on my wedding day.

I try to empty my mind and get some perspective, but images of Malcolm and Marina keep coming. His big hands on her tiny waist; her head against his chest; his mouth latched onto hers as though he's sucking the life force out of her. *Love, honour and betray.* Reaching out my hand, I give the back of the photo frame a hefty whack and it falls, face down, with a clatter.

Malcolm's obviously in the wrong. He's a big fat cheat. But am I also at fault, for taking on the shop and café against his advice? I close my eyes and bite down hard on my bottom lip. Was I kidding myself when I thought I could have something in my life that was my own?

In the end, I must have fallen asleep because, when I open my eyes, dark shadows are tracked across the bedroom floor and the background hum of rush-hour traffic has disappeared. Beneath me I can hear the sounds of a busy kitchen – saucepans banging on the hob, the metallic ring of knives falling onto tiles, and the urgent tones of our highly strung chef, Pierre.

For one blissful moment, I think the last couple of hours were a dream and everything's as it should be. Malcolm's downstairs in the restaurant, all handsome and efficient in his suit, and I'll join him in a moment to help with anything that's needed. But then I spot our wedding photo, face down, and reality hits me in the heart. I feel horribly sick, as though the betrayal has solidified into a lump in my stomach. Pushing myself up on the bed, I pile the pillows behind me, and take slow, deep breaths.

Life was good in Yorkshire, where we ran a city restaurant for several years. Well, Malcolm ran it and I helped out in the evenings after the daytime office job I took on to boost our income. We felt a part of the community and I had friends I could go out with to the pub or cinema.

Down here in the Cotswolds, I've been so busy I've not had time to make many friends. There's Callie, of course, who I 'inherited' when I took over the bookshop. She'd already been working there for a couple of years and proved to be a total godsend. I couldn't have sorted out the shop or set up the café without her. But she's younger than me and we don't have enough shared history to be the kind of friends who share their lives, warts and all. In any case, she's loved up with Noah, her old boyfriend who's moved back into town, and my woes might burst her happy bubble.

Hey, Callie, you think your romance will last forever, but just you wait. Look at me, over forty, heading for perimenopausal, and cast aside in favour of a younger model.

Honestly, I've never felt this alone. Not even when I spent birthdays on my tod because staff shortages in the restaurant meant Malcolm had to work at the last minute and cancel our plans.

I pick up the wedding photo and run my finger over the couple smiling back at me. Malcolm looks suave and assured, standing on the steps of the register office in his blue suit, but I look slightly self-conscious in my knee-length white dress. Mum and Dad were hoping I'd marry in church and I wouldn't have minded, but Malcolm said a register office would do just as well. He was already saving money to open his own restaurant and baulked at the extra expense of a church wedding, even though Mum and Dad said they'd cover what they could.

What would my parents think of my marriage going up in flames over a couple of stupid kisses? Would they blame me for *getting above myself* and thinking I could run my own business?

I stretch and pad into the empty flat. The restaurant comes first with Malcolm so he'll be down there right now, working side by side with Marina and hopefully fighting off her rabid advances.

It's the betrayal of trust that hurts the most.

I wander into the bathroom with its matching basins and pat cold water on my puffy eyes. Have I let myself go? Is that why my husband is kissing a younger woman in the cold room?

I stare at my pale face in the mirror and sigh. I'm not a raving beauty – I've never been pretty-pretty like Marina – but my violet eyes and black hair mean I'm striking. I rub my hands over my face and brush my hair with hard, brisk strokes. I look as though I'm recovering from a nasty bout of flu, but I need to go downstairs and sort out this mess.

The restaurant isn't busy, Mondays rarely are, though business is picking up as long summer days draw more tourists to beautiful Oxford. Three couples are eating, placed near the window so we look busier than we are. And two women in short skirts are drinking cocktails at the bar and laughing at a joke. But there's no sign of Malcolm. Or Marina.

When I walk past the bar, Johnny stops pouring vodka into a sugar-rimmed glass and gives me a sympathetic smile.

Oh God. They all know.

I quicken my pace and scoot through the kitchen, which is bless-edly quiet this evening. Pierre throws regular hissy fits about… well, everything. He reckons it's because he's a brilliant creative luminary, while I reckon it's because he's a spoiled drama queen. But his cooking is to die for so we put up with his volcanic eruptions.

Tonight, he's quietly pan-frying fish while Freddie, in the corner, is prepping another mountain of veg. Malcolm is nowhere to be seen, but the door to the back yard is slightly ajar and I can hear the low murmur of voices.

As I get closer, I realise that one of the voices is Malcolm's. Is it wrong to eavesdrop on your husband? It can't be worse than snogging a girl young enough to be your daughter behind your wife's back. I creep to the door and peep through the crack. Malcolm is outside, puffing on a cigarette though I thought he'd given up smoking ages ago. I'm beginning to think I don't know my husband very well at all.

'You've just got to keep your head down for a while,' says Malcolm, before taking another drag on his cigarette. The tip of it burns red in the courtyard gloom.

'How can I keep out of sight when I work here?' says Marina, stepping out of the shadows. 'Are you ashamed of me, Malcy?'

'Of course not. It's just that Flora's upset right now and it's best to let things settle down. She's had a shock.'

'Why did she come home so early?' whines Marina. 'Do you think she suspected something and came back early on purpose? I told you I lost an earring yesterday but you just ignored me. Flora probably found it under the bed and put two and two together.'

Malcolm's reply is drowned out by blood pulsing in my ears: he lied to me. Malcolm and Marina have slept together. And worse than that – if anything can be worse than your husband cheating on you and then brazenly lying to your face about it – they did it in our bed. The bed I slept in last night.

Of course they did, you idiot, says the voice in my head. *Malcolm's hardly likely to turn down the chance of getting his end away with a young woman who's smoking hot, rather than hurtling towards hot flushes.*

I stumble away from the door and through the restaurant. Johnny calls out to me from the bar but I carry on walking. The man I trusted most in the world has deceived me, and the future I saw stretching ahead of us has disappeared. But at least there's no dithering now about what happens next.

Standing in our bedroom, with our biggest suitcase open on the bed, I start throwing things in. The last time we used this case was when we went to Venice for a second honeymoon to celebrate twenty years of marriage. How ironic that it's now being used as our marriage ends.

In go a few changes of clothes, toiletries, make-up, a framed photo of my parents, underwear, and the box of tissues by the bed. I'm going to need those. Last of all, I pack my pyjamas. As I smooth them into the top of the case, I wonder if Malcolm lost interest in me because of them. They're sleeveless and pretty with pale blue butterflies picked out across grey satin, but no one would describe them as sexy. When exactly, I wonder, did I decide it was too cold at night to sleep without PJs?

'This is not your fault, Flora,' I say out loud, closing the lid of the suitcase and snapping the locks shut with a satisfying clunk. This situation is Malcolm's fault, rather than mine for not sleeping naked.

Hauling the case off the bed almost gives me a hernia. Wow, I thought the boxes of books delivered to the shop were heavy. This feels like a case of lead weights – it must be the shoes. I open the case, take out my trainers and ankle boots and throw them into a corner of the room. Sandals will be fine for this time of year, and who knows where I'll be by the time autumn starts painting the leaves gold and rain clouds bunch over the hills?

When I drag the case down the stairs, it thuds on every step and takes a chunk out of the skirting board at the bottom. As I wheel it through the restaurant, which is busier now, people look up from their meals and stare at me. Marina also glances up from the bar where she's serving a customer and her baby-blue eyes open wide.

'Flora?' Malcolm is suddenly at my side. 'What are you doing?' he hisses, giving a wide, toothy grin to everyone in the restaurant.

'What does it look like, Malcy? I'm leaving you.' That came out rather loudly but I don't care.

'Keep your voice down!' Malcolm follows me to the front door and almost shoves me through it into the narrow pedestrianised street that fronts the restaurant. He's desperate to keep up appearances, even as his marriage collapses around him.

It's a warm evening and people are sitting at tables outside the bistro a few doors down. Young couples are laughing and gazing into each other's eyes. They think their love will last forever. Poor deluded fools.

One young woman glances up from the ice cream she's sharing with her boyfriend and stares at me.

'Look where you'll end up in twenty years' time,' I call out, before turning my back to hide the deep blush I can feel rising up from my neck. Blimey, one emotional upset and I've morphed from a sensible bookseller into a woman who shouts at random strangers in the street.

'What are you doing and what's going on?' says Malcolm, stepping in front of me. 'I know you're upset but this is totally over the top. Don't throw away all we've worked for over one stupid kiss.'

'What about the earring?'

Malcolm looks pale in the street light that's reflecting off the restaurant window. 'I don't know what you're talking about,' he blusters.

'Oh, I think you do, Malcolm. It was under the bed.'

'You found an earring there?' he splutters. 'It must be one of yours.'

'It's not. It's Marina's.'

Malcolm's swallow is more of a gulp. 'There's a good explanation.'

'Which is?'

'Um.' I can almost hear the cogs in Malcolm's stressed brain whirring. 'Marina came up to the flat to tell me we were out of… butter and I was sitting on the bed tying my shoelaces so she came in and sat by me for a minute and that's when her earring must have fallen out.'

If his story wasn't so pathetic, I'd laugh. When I take a step forwards, Malcolm's hands move to cup his genitals, as though I'm about to knee him. It hadn't even crossed my mind, though in the circumstances…

'Come back in, Flora,' pleads Malcolm, glancing around to see who's watching. A couple sitting in our restaurant window are agog. 'We can talk about all this inside. There's no need to be so dramatic.'

But I shake my head. I just need to get away.

'Where will you go?' Malcolm calls after me as I wheel my case along the paved street. The wheels are catching on the stones and making a terrible racket. Great, I've shouted at strangers and now I'm broadcasting to the whole street that I'm leaving my adulterous husband.

'Flora, you're being totally ridiculous.' Malcolm's words float through the heavy summer air as I turn the corner and walk towards my new future.

Chapter Two

After parking my car next to Honeyford's weathered stone war memorial, I sit for a moment with my hands on the steering wheel. The town square is quiet at this time of night at the beginning of the week. The parking spaces are mostly empty except for a lone Corsa parked under the tall beech tree that stands outside the butcher's. In front of me, the arches of the medieval market house are shadows in the gloom and its honey-gold stone looks grey.

Honeyford is just as I left it a few hours ago. In many ways the town is much as it has been for centuries. *But I'm different*, I realise. My busy married life in Oxford suddenly seems unreal and I feel more grounded here, surrounded by a dark sweep of ancient hills.

After heaving my case out of the boot, I wheel it along the High Street towards my bookshop. There's a tiny cottage squeezed between the post office and Amy's sweet shop and I glance inside as I trundle past. An elderly couple are sitting hand in hand on the sofa as the blue light from a TV flickers across their faces. That's how I thought Malcolm and I would end up – watching reruns of *Inspector Morse* together in our old age.

I bite hard on my lip to stop the tears that are threatening to fall and I hurry past the pub with my head down, in case any of my customers spot me. At the shop, I let myself in and flick on the lights. The usual smell of ink, paper and coffee hits me, along with a sense of organised chaos. There are piles of books everywhere and, at the back of the shop, Callie's hand-painted sign for The Cosy Kettle hangs above the café door.

I've achieved a lot in the short time since I took on this business. I've gained new customers and new confidence in my abilities, but now I'm contemplating what I've lost.

I wander into the café, open the back door to let in some air, and sit at one of the tables. Callie's beloved coffee machine is gleaming silver in the corner, near the burnished copper kettles that once belonged to Stanley's now-dead wife. The cake counter is sparkling clean and empty, ready for tomorrow's delivery of delicious treats.

The last time I was here, earlier today, I was Flora Morgan, shop and café owner, and Malcolm's wife. Now, I'm not sure who I am. The ginger cat that's often in the café garden darts inside and starts winding its way round my legs as I gently lower my forehead onto the table and start to sob. I cry until my nose is running and my head is hurting and I feel totally wrung out. Then I pick up the wriggling cat and bury my wet face in its fur as I consider my options. Walking out was the right thing to do, but what the hell do I do now?

Turning up with a sob story on Callie's doorstep at – I check my watch – quarter past ten isn't really on. And it would be awkward, what with me being her boss. She might feel obliged to find me a bed for the night. There's a new boutique hotel in Honeyford, but it's expensive and I need to save my money right now – plus, my story would be all around the town by tomorrow lunchtime. And I don't think I can bear the locals wandering into the bookshop to see how I'm doing. So, there's really only one thing for it…

One step at a time, I haul my case up the wooden stairs at the back of the shop and fumble across the bare bricks for the light switch. My fingers find it and harsh white light almost blinds me. A bare bulb is swinging overhead, illuminating an attic room and a small door leading off into a tiny cubbyhole that holds a toilet and a cracked basin. Old, empty boxes are piled up in one corner and, beneath a small window, there's a battered leather chair and an ancient put-you-up bed. Ruben, who ran the shop before me, left them when he handed over the store. Apparently, he used to slip up here for an afternoon nap and leave Callie in charge.

When I pat the thin mattress, a puff of dust rises into the air, but it'll do for tonight. I pull a fleece blanket out of the case, ball up a jumper as a makeshift pillow and take a couple of puffs of my inhaler, just in case. Then I switch off the light, lie on the bed and gaze out of the grimy window.

A full moon has risen and is casting silver beams across the grubby room. A humungous spiderweb is glowing silver in the corner, and I pull the blanket over my head until only my nose is poking out.

Images from the last few hours play out in my mind, like a record that's got stuck. Malcolm and Marina locked in a steamy embrace, Malcolm swearing that he'd only ever kissed her, the lost earring that I never found. Round and round they go, until my head feels as though it might split in two. I don't think I'll sleep but I eventually fall into a fitful doze.

I wake to see early morning light slanting across the dusty wooden floor. I ache all over when I stretch, and a fresh wave of misery hits me as I remember last night all over again. A glance at my muted mobile shows that Malcolm has called half a dozen times and left several text messages.

The first reads: *Where are you? Let's behave like adults about this.*

I delete the rest without replying, which probably isn't particularly mature but, right now, I don't care.

The water's freezing when I fill the basin and have a wash, and the fleece blanket is a rubbish substitute towel, but I'm downstairs and ready to open the shop before eight o'clock.

I spend the next ten minutes completing an order from yesterday that I should have done before I went home. If only I had stayed to do it, I wouldn't have walked in on Malcolm and Marina, and I'd still be blissfully unaware of what was going on. Would that be better?

'Hello. You're in early,' says Becca, poking her head around the shop door. 'I'm going to the newsagent to get milk for my muesli and I spotted you were open already. Do you want anything? I can…' She trails off and narrows her green eyes as I rub a hand over my face. I've slapped on some make-up but I must still look pretty rubbish.

'I don't think I need anything, thanks. And there's no rush to come in because the café's still closed. I was just up early this morning and thought I'd get ahead with things.'

'If you're sure,' says Becca, slowly, flicking her purple fringe out of her eyes.

Her hair changes colour so often, it's hard to keep up. It was a startling shade of emerald green when we first met, after she had a panic attack in the shop. Callie took Becca under her wing and got her to help with setting up The Cosy Kettle. The rest is history – Becca now manages the café while Callie spends most of her time running the coffee house at Honeyford's boutique hotel. Though she still helps me out sometimes.

Becca is still standing in the doorway. She swallows. 'Um, I'm not trying to intrude or anything but is everything all right?'

'Absolutely fine. I just didn't sleep too well,' I say breezily, looking back down at my computer screen. Discussing my marriage problems at work is a no-no. And the last thing I want is people feeling sorry for me.

'OK. I'll be in soon then.'

Becca wanders off along the High Street, but is obviously not convinced. She's back to open the café before nine o'clock and, though she doesn't quiz me any further, steaming cappuccinos and thick slices of my favourite strawberry cake are placed in front of me at regular intervals throughout the day.

'Just in case you're sort of, you know, thirsty and a bit hungry, maybe,' she gabbles, a flush spreading across her cheeks before she scuttles back to the café. She's as sweet as the cake, which is chock-full of fruit from a local strawberry farm.

I gulp down the drinks – caffeine is essential after a night on Ruben's put-you-up – but only manage a few mouthfuls of the delicious sponge. There's a whole shelf of diet books in the shop, but it turns out that all you need to lose weight is marital trauma – The Cheating Husband Diet.

There's no sign of Malcolm. I texted him back after his twelfth message, to say I wasn't coming home, and I haven't answered any of his phone calls. I doubt he'll turn up and make a scene here, but I jump every time someone comes into the shop.

'Got any horror?' calls a middle-aged man across the shelves, as I'm shoving my phone back into my bag.

'We have a selection at the back of the store.'

He wanders off and starts running his finger along the Stephen Kings, all the while glancing at me and scowling until the hairs on the back of my neck start to prickle. He either thinks I look a fright or he's about to shove a book up his jumper and do a runner. I really hope it's the former because I'm in no mood to chase him along Honeyford High Street and through the tiny lanes that criss-cross the town.

As though he can mind-read, the man walks over with a paperback and thumps it down in front of me.

'Lovely weather,' I say, feeling guilty for doubting his good character, but he only grunts as he hands over his money. I try again: 'Are you in the Cotswolds on holiday?'

He nods, shoving his change into his jeans pocket.

'Have you come far?'

'It depends if you think Leicestershire counts as far.'

Bit rude, but I plaster on a smile. 'It is quite a way. Did you find everything you wanted in here today?'

I regret asking the question the minute it's out of my mouth. My customer is in a right mood and champing at the bit to vent about something – probably anything – and I've just given him the perfect opportunity.

'I did not,' he sniffs. 'I thought your horror selection was very poor, with nothing out of the ordinary at all. Frankly, it was disappointing.'

I take a deep breath to try and stifle a yawn. I'm so tired but I doubt Mr Angry would take kindly to me yawning in his face. 'I'm very sorry to hear that,' I say, calmly. 'We're a small bookshop and can only stock a certain number of titles, but I'd be happy to order in a specific book for you.'

'How is that going to help me when I'm here on holiday?'

'We could possibly get it in tomorrow.'

'That's still too late,' barks the man. 'I'll get my book elsewhere but you need to tell the shop owner that you should expand your range.'

OK, knackered or not, I'm starting to feel annoyed now. Most people who come into my shop are lovely, but the occasional customer can be challenging. And it's just my luck that I get a grumpy bugger on today of all days.

'I *am* the owner,' I tell him, pushing his book into a paper bag with more force than is necessary.

'Really? That's surprising.'

I'd like to think he's surprised because I look far too young to have such a responsible role. But his expression, which screams bulldog chewing a wasp, tells me otherwise. I must look really rough today.

Before my addled brain can come up with a suitably withering reply, the man grabs his book and stalks out with his nose in the air.

I sigh as the door bangs shut behind him. Overall, today is shaping up to be a total bust. The publishing rep I was expecting this afternoon cancelled at the last minute, customers have been few and far between, that last bloke was a rude idiot, and I'm half-asleep with the prospect of another night on Ruben's lumpy mattress.

'All OK, Flora?' shouts Stanley, who belongs to The Cosy Kettle's afternoon book club. He's been in the shop, browsing, for the last ten minutes.

'Fine, thanks,' I call back, grateful that Stanley didn't hear my exchange with Mr Angry and feel obliged to wade in. Because that's just the kind of gung-ho thing he'd do.

'Coolio.'

Stanley carries on flicking through a book on extreme sports, which will strike fear into Callie's heart. She already spends loads of time reining in her grandfather's more extreme ideas. Last week he announced he was planning to trek the Inca Trail and bungee jump off a dam in Switzerland. This week, if the book's anything to go by, he's set his sights on cave diving and heli-skiing.

I'm picturing him leaping in Lycra from a helicopter, like a bald James Bond with wrinkles, when Millicent bowls into the shop. Oh dear. Millicent, who also belongs to the book club, is nice enough but could never be described as soothing company. She tends to barge her way through life in her purple gilet and sturdy shoes.

'No Callie in today?' she asks, nodding at Stanley.

'Afraid not. She's busy at the hotel coffee house.'

Her face falls, making me feel very second-best. Everyone loves Callie, who's lived in Honeyford almost her entire life. They got behind her when she set up The Cosy Kettle for me, and they're still supporting her now she's running the hotel's upmarket coffee house.

Millicent sniffs. 'Ah well, I suppose you'll do, Flora.'

Gee, thanks.

'I was passing so thought I'd check if my book had arrived yet.'

'I'm pretty sure it came in this morning.'

'And yet you didn't let me know.'

'Sorry. Today has been a bit… trying and I haven't properly sorted out the delivery yet.'

Millicent's face softens and she leans towards me. 'Is everything all right, Flora? You're looking a bit peaky, if you don't mind me saying.'

'I've got a bad headache, that's all.'

'Do you get them regularly?'

'Yeah, I guess.'

'HRT!' Millicent suddenly booms across the shop. 'My friend Marigold swears by it and says it's done wonders for her headaches. You should give it a go. We ladies of a certain age need all the help we can get.'

'Ladies of a certain age'? Just how old does Millicent think I am? I know I'm not looking my best today, but still. My mood dips even lower as I contemplate the double whammy of being passed over by

my husband for a younger model shortly before being mistaken for a menopausal fifty-year-old. This week truly sucks.

'Colonic irrigation,' says Stanley, wandering over. 'I read it's good for detoxing the body so I'm thinking of giving it a go. That might help.'

'It's just a headache,' I say, faintly, as Millicent screws up her face. She's obviously imagining Stanley just as I am right now. And it's really not helping my head at all. I reach quickly under the counter and flick through today's delivery of books until I find Millicent's biography of Stalin.

'Here you go. I hope you enjoy it.'

'I'm not sure *enjoy* is the right word but I'm sure it will be educational. Thank you, Flora.'

Millicent has only just left the shop, with her new book tucked under her arm, when a loud crash echoes through the shop. Good grief, what now?

'Can you keep an eye on things?' I ask Stanley, who's wandered off and is now nose-deep in a novel. 'I'd better go and check that out.'

'Sure thing, hun. You mosey on down to the caff and eyeball what Becca's dropped before I sling my hook,' says Stanley, who regularly mangles slang in his bid to be down with the kids.

I hurry through the shop and step into The Cosy Kettle. Today's last remaining cakes and pastries are under glass domes on the counter and the room is thick with the smell of rich coffee beans.

All is as it should be – apart from a muddle of smashed crockery on the floor, a spilt latté splattered up the wall, and two slices of carrot cake lying icing-down on the concrete. Becca is on her knees picking up shards of china and a tall man with dark hair has the hand of a small boy who's looking sheepish. They came into the shop about five minutes ago and made a beeline for the café.

'What the hell is going on in here?'

That came out sharper than I meant it to and the boy flinches away from me. The café is empty, thank goodness, apart from him and the man, who I presume is his father.

'It was an accident,' says the man, equally sharply, frowning until his dark eyebrows almost meet in the middle. 'Caleb, my son, jumped up and knocked into the tray. He didn't mean to.'

A flash of burnished copper catches my eye. Caleb did more than smash china that will be expensive to replace. He also knocked two of the old kettles from their shelf, and they're damaged. The large dents look like wounds in the shiny metal and for some reason this, more than grumpy customers or abrasive Millicent, makes me feel close to tears.

'For goodness' sake,' I sigh, picking up the kettles and placing them back on the shelf. 'He's damaged these as well.'

'As I say, it was an accident and we're very sorry.'

'Well, he really should have been more careful.'

Straight away, I wish I could take the words back when Caleb shrinks behind his father. His pale skin looks almost translucent under his mop of fair hair, and his blue eyes are enormous.

I step forward to calm the situation but the man shakes his head. 'Caleb has just been to the doctor because he isn't feeling too well and we came in here for a treat. We'll pay, of course, for any damage.'

My protestations that this really isn't necessary are waved away by the man, who grabs his son's hand and pulls him forward. 'Apologise to the lady, Caleb,' he says, his dark brown eyes meeting mine.

'Sorry,' murmurs the boy, pink spots flaring in his pale cheeks. The man pulls the boy's head into his side as though he's trying to protect him, which makes me feel terrible. I don't have kids myself and I tend to avoid them – I never coo over babies in prams or strike up conversations with youngsters. But I've never frightened a child before, especially not a sick child who's just been to the doctor.

'That's all right,' I say, soothingly. 'It was an accident and I hope you'll soon be feeling bet—'

The man cuts me off by pulling a twenty-pound note from his pocket and placing it on top of his table, with its bright pink cloth. 'This should cover the damage,' he says, coldly.

'There's really no need,' I protest, but he's already put his arm around Caleb's shoulders and is guiding him out of the café.

Becca gets to her feet with a sigh and wipes coffee-stained hands down her floral apron. 'It was definitely an accident. He just got a bit overexcited when he saw the milkshake.' She dips the toe of her Doc Martens into the yellow froth that's snaking its way across the floor.

'I know, and I didn't mean to be sharp with him. But we can't afford too many breakages.'

I still sound like a right grumpy old bag. Becca, who always seems a bit nervous when I'm around, nods and goes behind the counter for a dustpan and brush, while I start piling broken crockery into a tottering pile of shards. Concrete is an unforgiving surface and clumps of sheared glass glint at me from beneath nearby tables. As I scrape up squashed cake with a jagged piece of china, I feel wrong-footed and mean. The boy should have been more careful, but he's only a child, and I hate that he looked scared. I know I'm having a bad day but I shouldn't have taken it out on a kid.

I sigh, wishing I could rerun the last five minutes. Millicent is right; it is a shame that Callie's not here. She'd have dealt with the situation with her usual calm good humour. She still helps out in the shop occasionally, and the new arrangement at the hotel coffee house is for the best, but I miss her, even more than I thought I would.

Standing up, I walk swiftly out of the café and through the shop. Pushing the front door wide open, I step outside and stand on the pavement to get some air. It's baking hot today and there's no breeze coming off the hills to cool the town.

The man and his son have just reached the end of the High Street and they disappear after turning into a lane that leads down to the river. They didn't look back and I don't suppose they'll ever return to the café. It's a shame because I really can't afford to lose customers – and I'd like to give Caleb another milkshake, on the house.

I lean back against the door frame and drink in the scene around me. Immediately, my shoulders sink down from my ears and the tension that's plagued me all day starts to ease. Honeyford is so ridiculously pretty, it never fails to make me feel better, whatever sort of day I'm having. Sunshine is glinting on the shop window and its display of seaside-themed books, with scattered sand and a soft-toy seagull. Callie's the one with the artistic flair but I think I've made a fair stab at the display – and hopefully it will bring in more customers to the shop. It's even more important that my business does well now I might be on my own.

I've done my best to turn things around. I've made some changes in the store recently which have gone down well with customers – a couple of comfy chairs for people who are browsing, a wider variety of books, better lighting at the back of the store and, of course, the café.

It's been exciting to veer off from my familiar life into unknown territory. Or at least it was until yesterday, when my life took a turn I never expected. I wanted to step out from Malcolm's shadow, not step away from him completely. Is that what I'm going to do – step away from my husband and not look back? Because whatever Malcolm's been up to, the thought of being without him forever makes my heart hurt. Closing my eyes, I take in a deep breath of summer air, tilt my face towards the sun and let Honeyford work its soothing magic on me.

Chapter Three

By Wednesday morning, my violet eyes have matching circles beneath them and my skin looks chalk-white against my dark hair. I grab my blusher from my handbag and dab a touch of colour onto my cheeks, trying to ignore a woman with long silver hair who's staring at me from the biography section. I can feel her eyes on me as I peer into the blusher compact's tiny mirror. What is she doing?

When I glance up, she catches my gaze and holds it. Her hair is loose down her back, and she's wearing wide black linen trousers and a long burgundy tunic made of loose-weave cotton. Around her neck is a huge chunk of amethyst on a leather thong. Give her a black hat and a broom and she'd pass for the local witch.

'Can I help you?' I ask as she strides over. I've seen her in the shop a few times but she's only ever browsed and had the odd cup of coffee. I think she runs a shop further along the High Street. Callie would know. She knows everyone around here.

'Is everything all right, dear?' The woman tilts her head to one side and raises her hands in front of her. Then she circles them around my head, as though she's polishing the air.

'Everything's fine, thank you,' I say, taking a step back. 'Are you looking for a particular book?'

'I'm Luna. And you are?' asks the woman, ignoring my question. She lowers her hands and extends one towards me. Her long fingers are covered in chunky silver rings.

'I'm Flora. I run this shop.'

'Flora, that's a nice name. Did you know that Flora was the Roman goddess of flowers and spring?'

'I did not know that.'

Her skin feels rough and warm when we shake hands, and she holds onto my fingers for a beat too long before narrowing her amber eyes.

'I can see your aura, you know,' she says, leaning forwards as though she's sharing a secret. 'It caught my attention the last time I was in here, but it seems rather dimmed today. Your colours are muted.'

Great, just what I need right now – a New Age customer. Talk of auras and crystals and general woo-woo stuff sends me running for the hills.

Ah, it suddenly clicks! This must be the woman who runs Luna's Magical Emporium, just down the road from my bookshop. I've never been in because the window is full of gleaming gemstones, books about angels, and dreamcatchers, which are so not my thing.

'Yes, your aura has definitely changed shade since I was last in here,' she informs me, running her fingers over the amethyst around her neck.

'What colour is it now, then – black?'

Luna frowns. 'This is no laughing matter, Flora. Your aura was a beautiful sky blue with orange edges but now it's smoky grey and flecked with imperfections. There's a lot of negative energy surrounding you right now.'

'There's not much energy at all,' I say, stifling a yawn. Ruben's old put-you-up is the most uncomfortable bed ever.

'Something's happened to you recently,' continues Luna, closing her eyes and swaying slightly. 'Something terribly traumatic.'

'Not really.'

'Your aura never lies.'

Bloody aura, I think, grumpily. *Broadcasting my secrets to every hippy who comes in.*

'You look tired, dear,' says Luna, and she suddenly sounds so much like my mum that tears fill my eyes.

'I'm not sleeping too well,' I gulp, blinking rapidly.

'What's happened?' When I hesitate, she leans forward and puts her hand on top of mine. 'You can trust me, Flora. I'm very good with secrets and matters of the heart.'

'My husband and I are having problems. He's been having an affair with a younger woman and I've left him.'

The words come tumbling out before I have a chance to stop them. I'm spilling my guts to a complete stranger in the middle of the shop and anyone could come in at any moment. *Get a grip, Flora!*

Luna gives my hand a squeeze and a deep line appears between her eyebrows. 'I knew it! A trauma triggers a shift in the energies that surround us and that is reflected in one's aura. Are you staying with friends who can support and replenish you?'

'Mmm.' I nod, biting hard on my lip, but Luna keeps on staring, her hand still on mine. It's crazy but I have the uncomfortable feeling she can read my mind. I shiver and pull my hand away as the shop door pings open.

My breath catches in my throat as Malcolm marches in with a thunderous look on his face.

'Here you are,' he says, ignoring Luna, who moves quietly away and starts browsing books nearby. 'I'm heartbroken, Flora. Absolutely heartbroken but you're not replying to my texts or phone calls. You could have been dead for all I knew.'

'Yet it still took you two days to come and find me,' I murmur.

Malcolm bristles. He doesn't look particularly heartbroken. He's wearing his favourite cord trousers and a thin mauve jumper I haven't seen before. I wonder if Marina bought it for him. It's a little tight and is clinging to the extra few pounds around his middle.

'I can't just abandon the restaurant to search for you. I thought you'd come back.'

Luna raises her eyes from the book she's holding and gives Malcolm a stare.

'What do you want, Malcolm, and why are you here?' I ask, quietly.

He turns his back on Luna so she won't hear him. 'I didn't know where you were.'

'Where else would I be?'

'Yes, I should have known you'd be in your beloved shop,' snaps Malcolm, but then his shoulders soften. 'I'm sorry you had to find out about me and Marina in that way. I should have told you.'

'Yes, you should. Or maybe you shouldn't have slept with her in the first place.'

'Keep your voice down. We don't want every Tom, Dick and Harry knowing our business,' mutters Malcolm. He steps forward as though he's about to touch me but his arms stay by his side. Maybe he'll never touch me again. A deep pang of sorrow shudders through me. Over twenty years of marriage – finished by a dropped earring that I didn't even find.

'You should come home while we sort out what's happening with you and me,' he says, quietly.

And though I'm still in two minds about what to do, annoyance zaps through me that he believes I might actually come back home after what he's done.

'Have you ended it with Marina?' I ask.

Malcolm winces at the sound of her name. 'That goes without saying. So please come home and you and I can work things out together at the flat.'

'And then what?'

'What do you mean?'

'After we've "worked things out", am I expected to sleep in the bed where you and Marina…?' I stop and gulp, unable to carry on.

Malcolm roughly pushes his hands through his hair. 'We can get a new bed, Flora, a brand new one, and put all of this behind us.'

'If only it was that easy.'

'It can be,' he urges, clasping his hands together as though he's praying.

'No, it can't be. A new bed won't change what's happened. Nothing will, which is why I need to be on my own for a while. And,' I add, swallowing so hard it feels like I might choke, 'maybe for good.'

Malcolm's face clouds over. 'You don't mean that. Are you staying with that Callie girl?'

For a moment, I'm tempted to lie but I honestly don't have the energy. 'No, I'm not with Callie.'

'Where then?' Realisation dawns in Malcolm's grey eyes and he glances upwards. 'You're not staying here, surely.'

I hesitate because I don't want to admit that I am sleeping here, with the spiders in the attic. Not when Marina has been enjoying my Egyptian cotton sheets.

'Flora is staying with me.' Luna has appeared by my side, wielding a large hardback book like a shield between herself and my husband. 'Aren't you, dear?' she prompts, giving me a slight nudge with her elbow.

'And who exactly are you?' demands Malcolm, sounding very like his grandfather, who used to intimidate the life out of me. I've never noticed the resemblance so strongly before.

'My name is Luna Purfoot and I live just outside Honeyford. How very delightful to meet you.' She holds out her hand so Malcolm feels obliged to take it. He gives it a cursory shake.

'Flora's never mentioned a Luna.'

'Does she mention all of her friends?'

'I have no idea.'

'Exactly.'

Malcolm's left eyelid starts twitching, like it does when he's confused. It twitches all the way through *Game of Thrones* because he can never follow who's killing who or why. Will Marina have the patience to explain plots to him? I wonder. Or will she be too busy watching *Love Island* and fake-tanning?

He turns to me. 'So you're living with this Luna, are you? I thought for one minute you were living here in the attic.'

'Of course I'm not. I do have some dignity left.'

Malcolm glances at Luna, who's standing with her arms folded next to me, and shakes his head. 'I've got to go.' He glances at the watch that I bought him for our fifteenth anniversary. He was very particular about the type of watch he wanted – gold, expensive and large enough to be noticed. 'Pierre is adamant that he needs a new mushroom supplier so I'm doing the rounds. He's very demanding and is running me ragged. It's hard work without you there.' He lowers his voice and leans towards me. 'We need to talk properly, Flora. When we're given some privacy. Are you sure you won't come home with me now to sort things out?'

When I nod, he gives Luna another glare before marching out of the shop.

'Hmm, he's very sure of himself,' says Luna, placing the hardback book back on the shelf. 'I don't like the colour of his aura at all. There's a vortex of negative energies swirling around him. How long have you two been married?'

I sniff back the tears that are threatening to fall, and gulp, 'Over twenty years.'

'That can't have been easy.'

'It was fine, thank you,' I reply, suddenly annoyed by this stranger involving herself in my business.

'Really?'

'Really,' I tell her, and it was – mostly. Just so long as I did what Malcolm wanted or he'd sink into a sulk. I didn't want to leave Yorkshire and move to the Cotswolds but Malcolm insisted it was the next step in his restaurant plans. The only time I've ever really gone against his wishes was when I took on this place.

I look around the shop. It's been a quiet day for bookselling, but the café has been busier. I can hear the clinking of crockery and the hiss of the coffee machine. And in spite of what's happened, I don't regret taking on this place, or coming to this beautiful part of the country.

'I presume you are sleeping here in the attic. You look as though you are. So you'd better come round to me after work.' Luna grabs one of my business cards from the side of the till, picks up my pen and starts scrawling. 'Here's my address. Have you got satnav in your car?' She smiles when I nod. 'Don't bother using it because the signal goes weird near my cottage and you'll end up going round in circles. Just follow my directions. You can park around the side of the house but watch out for my pots of petunias, and the chickens. They tend to run free and can get under car wheels.'

She passes me the card and I slide it into a drawer underneath the counter.

'It was kind of you to tell Malcolm that I was staying at your house. I'd rather he didn't know that I'm sleeping in the attic. But I'm not really going to stay at yours, Luna. Don't worry, I won't hold you to it.'

'You've got a better offer, have you?' Luna flicks back her silver hair and scrunches up her long, thin nose.

'Well, no, but I can't just turn up and move in with you.'

'Why ever not? I'm not offering you charity. I've got a spare room and could do with the extra cash, to be honest. You'll have to pay towards your board and lodging but it won't be much. And what else are you going to do? Carry on sleeping upstairs with the spiders?'

I shudder. How does she know about my fear of spiders? Last night I slept with the blankets completely over my head and woke up in a cold sweat, sure I was being suffocated. I'm thinking of picking up a net curtain and rigging up a makeshift spider net over my bed. It'll be like sleeping in a giant cocoon.

'Shall we say six o'clock,' says Luna, in a tone of voice that doesn't expect a reply. She heads for the door before I can demur and turns with her fingers on the handle.

'We follow a vegetarian diet. Is that a problem? You're not one of these carnivorous types who can't exist without a steak, are you?'

By the time I've finished shaking my head, Luna has disappeared through the door with a jaunty wave.

I take out the card and look at the address she's written down. *Starlight Cottage, turn left immediately after the elm struck by lightning on Chipping Field Lane and keep going.*

It's kind of Luna to offer me a bed, I think, sliding the card into my handbag. But there's no way on earth I'm living with a weird woman I've only just met.

Chapter Four

I follow the narrow road that's edged by a stone wall and keep my eyes peeled for a tree blasted by lightening.

My resolve not to take up Luna's offer of a place to stay lasted right until I nipped upstairs to get my cardi and spotted a spider the size of a small dog on my pillow. Netting wouldn't keep that one out – it would probably rip the fabric apart with its long legs before spreading itself over my face. Arachnid suffocation? *No thank you.*

So here I am, driving out of Honeyford, with the town in my rear-view mirror and the Berry Estate, where Callie lives, perched at its edge, high up on the hill. And all I can see around me are perfectly healthy beech trees, with sunshine filtering through their leaves and dappling on the road ahead.

Unfortunately, Luna was right when she warned that satnav would be useless. The signal vanished as I went into a dip just outside Honeyford and now, according to the display on the screen, I'm floating somewhere in the middle of a field. Luna's house appears to be off-grid.

I emerge from a tunnel of trees bending over the road and blink at the gently rolling countryside ahead of me. Just how far do I drive before turning round and having another go at spotting a zapped elm?

Aha! There, like a lone sentinel, at the side of the road, is a single blackened trunk with splintered, peeling bark. And just past it is a left-hand turn along what can only be described as a track. I take the turning and wince as my car bounces and grinds along the potholed surface. I really can't afford new tyres at the moment. My head almost hits the roof as my car lurches in and out of a ginormous hole that's so wide there's no hope of avoiding it.

What the hell am I doing, trundling along an unmade road in the middle of nowhere? I've decided to do a quick U-turn and beat a hasty retreat, back to my attic bed, when I turn a corner and spot a handsome stone cottage ahead. Oh well, I'm here now.

Smoke is curling from the chimney although it's warm today, and wild flowers are scattered across the fields to my left and right. A rabbit skitters across the track in front of me and disappears into the hedgerow, a flash of grey and white.

Luna said to go around the side of the house, and I drive carefully past huge wooden tubs of yellow and blue petunias. There's a child's bike dropped on the gravel and I manoeuvre around it. Luna must have grandchildren.

For a moment, after turning off the ignition, I rest my head against the steering wheel. A week ago I was happily married – or so I thought – and living in the middle of bustling Oxford. Now I'm contemplating moving in with a stranger in the middle of nowhere. I've gone a bit mad.

A sudden knock on my window makes me jump.

'Are you coming in then?' calls Luna, her face looming at me and her voice muffled through the glass. 'Watch out for the chickens. They'll trip you up if you're not careful. I'm sure they do it on purpose.'

I climb out of the car and stretch my legs. There's a breeze off the hills that carries with it the familiar, repulsively sweet aroma of manure. My nose automatically wrinkles in distaste.

'They're muck-spreading on the farm over the hill. It's a good earthy smell but it takes outsiders a bit of getting used to. Are you getting your case?'

I shake my head, still not sure that I'm staying.

'Maybe later then. Follow me.'

Luna leads the way between two tall stone gateposts into a small garden that's laid out with runner-bean canes and raspberry stakes. Plants are winding their way up the poles and the plots look well cared for.

'We're very self-sufficient,' says Luna, picking up a football that's sitting in the middle of the courgettes. 'Everything's organic. I don't use any pesticides, and I say thank you out loud to my plants every day for providing me with the food that I eat.'

Of course she does.

When Luna leads me around the corner, I get my first proper view of the house. I thought my first glimpse was of the front of the building, but it turns out it was the back. The real front of the house is split into an L-shape around a small courtyard and it faces a fantastic view across a green valley.

'Wow!'

'It's wonderful, isn't it.' Luna puts her hands on her hips and drinks in the fresh warm air. 'This view soothes the soul, don't you think? Whoever first built this place was very much in touch with their inner goddess.' She waves an arm at the house, which is fairly small but perfectly formed of mellow stone weathered by centuries of sun and storms. The paintwork on the deep-red door and the white window frames is flaking.

'It's a fabulous house. Do you own – I mean, do you rent…' I stop because Luna in her hippyish clothes doesn't look wealthy enough to own this place.

She smiles her mysterious smile. 'It's all mine.'

Luna doesn't elaborate and I follow her through the front door, my head brushing against a feathered dreamcatcher that's hanging from the thick stone door jamb. Two large crystals suspended from the stone are refracting rainbow colours along the dark hallway.

'They're for keeping out bad spirits and negative energies,' says Luna, leading me into the narrow passageway and closing the door behind me. 'This has been a happy home for centuries, and I want to ensure it stays that way.'

I follow her into a large room flooded with natural light; an open door in the back wall leads outside.

'Welcome to the kitchen of Starlight Cottage. Would you like some tea, Flora? I have chamomile, strawberry, or nettle and feverfew.'

I decline politely because I've never yet come across a fruit or herbal tea that I like. I'm a strong-cup-of-Yorkshire-Tea kind of girl.

'A glass of water then? It's drawn from our own well and tastes wonderful. Sit down and I'll get it for you.'

When Luna points at the huge oak table in the centre of the room, I take a seat and look at my surroundings.

Heat is radiating from a large cream Aga in the corner and there's a small fire burning in a huge recessed brick fireplace that's blackened with soot. Hanging above the flames is a bulbous black-iron pot. It's a cauldron. An actual cauldron.

'I like to cook over the fire sometimes,' says Luna, following my gaze. 'The food tastes marvellous and that style of cooking suits the feel of this room better, I feel.'

She is witchy weird. A shiver goes down my spine as she places a tall glass of water in front of me. I take a sip of the cold water and frown. This tastes different – actually, it tastes amazing. I gulp down half the glass before remembering that it comes from a well. All I can hope is that it's purified before being served to visitors. I put the glass down on the table, which is scratched with age.

'Let me show you to your room,' says Luna, as though it's a done deal that I'm moving in. 'This can be a draughty house but your room is south-facing so it gets the sunshine. Come on.'

Luna leads me back into the hall and up a narrow flight of wooden stairs. We pass several closed doors on the low-beamed landing and then she flings one open. 'Here we are. Take a look and see what you think.' She puts her hand into the small of my back and gently pushes me inside.

First impressions of my potential new bedroom are definitely favourable. The room is quite small and frugally furnished, with bare Cotswold-stone walls and dark, pitted wooden beams across the ceiling. I walk across the uneven floorboards to a small square window and look outside. There's a magnificent view across the valley. The sun is hanging lower in the sky now, casting long shadows of the trees, and in the distance there's the hum of a lone tractor making its way up the hill.

'I thought your soul could do with that view,' says Luna, coming to stand beside me. 'It oozes healing vibrations. Can you feel them reverberating through your body?'

Hmm. Not really.

Without waiting for an answer, Luna moves to a large wooden wardrobe and opens the door. A musty smell of mothballs drifts into the room. 'The furniture in here is second hand but adequate, and the bed is small but comfortable,' she explains. The quilted cover on the single bed looks home-made. 'You'll need to pay for your bed and board but we can work out what's fair.'

I turn from the glorious view towards her. 'Why, Luna? You don't know me and yet you're offering me a place in your home.'

'I'm offering you sanctuary,' says Luna, lifting her pale amber eyes to meet mine. 'That's what you need right now. Your aura called out to me and I can't ignore it. The goddesses brought us together for a reason and it's not my place to question them.'

She really is nuts but she seems harmless enough. And kind, which is what I need right now.

'What about your partner, Luna? What does he think about you renting out a room. Or she,' I add quickly, not wanting to make assumptions.

'My partner passed over a few years ago.'

'I'm so sorry.'

'Don't be. Kenneth is always with me, wherever I go. He's in the walls of this house and the trees in the garden and the mist in the valley on winter mornings,' says Luna, closing her eyes and swaying gently to a memory.

That's rather creepy. I glance over my shoulder in case the ghost of Kenneth is wafting around behind me.

'So what do you think, Flora?' Luna opens her eyes and smiles. 'Will you stay here for a while and give your soul a chance to heal?'

I take stock. On the one hand, Luna's slightly barking, with her goddesses and crystals, and there's a ghostly vibe going on in the cottage. But on the other hand, it's incredibly generous and warm-hearted of her to offer me somewhere to stay. It seems peaceful here, the view is to die for, and there must be fewer spiders in this room than in the shop's grubby attic. Plus, I need some company. I've never lived on my own before and the feeling of loneliness that's washed over me since I left Malcolm is scary.

I make a snap decision. 'Yes please, Luna. If I could stay for just a little while.'

Luna nods as though she already knew my answer and glances at her watch. 'You'd better get your case in from the car then and get unpacked. Tea is at six thirty.'

This feels like a happy house. That's the kind of loopy thing Luna might say, but there is a calmness about the place that's soothing.

I sit at my new bedroom window and gaze at the view, after unpacking my limited belongings. It's so kind of Luna to take me in and I think I'll be OK here for a little while.

The sound of a car driving around the side of the house catches my ear. Luna didn't say we'd have guests for tea and I don't really feel up to making polite conversation. But it's her house.

Sighing, I brush my thick, unruly hair into submission and put on a slick of lip gloss. Then I smooth down my work dress and head for the kitchen. At the door, I plaster on a smile and step inside.

There's a tall man standing with his back to me. He's bending over the steaming pot on the Aga and giving the ingredients a stir with a wooden spoon.

'This smells fantastic. I didn't have time for a proper lunch so I'm absolutely starving.'

His voice sounds familiar and my heart sinks when he turns around. From the look on his face, the feeling is mutual. He runs a hand through his dark hair and clenches his jaw that's faintly shadowed with stubble.

'What are you doing here?' he says, his voice hard and flat.

Luna stops chopping coriander and pauses with the knife in the air. 'Do you two know each other?'

'We met a few days ago in the bookshop in Honeyford,' says the man, not taking his eyes from my face.

'That's the bookshop that Flora runs,' says Luna, with a puzzled frown.

'I guessed as much. Caleb caused a bit of a commotion when he accidentally knocked over a tray of drinks.' As he stresses the word 'accidentally', his eyebrows shoot up into his fringe.

'Oh dear. He can be quite boisterous at times. Did he cause much damage?'

'There was no real harm done,' I say quickly, feeling acutely uncomfortable. 'I didn't realise that you know Luna.'

'Know me?' Luna gives a deep, throaty laugh and brushes strands of hair from her face with the back of her hand. 'I should think he knows me, seeing as he's my son. Flora, this is Daniel.'

Oh, fantastic! *Daniel's just called in for his tea and isn't stopping long* – please let those be Luna's next words.

Luna smiles. 'Daniel and Caleb live here with me.'

Of course they do.

She picks up her chopping board and scrapes the coriander into the pot. The aromatic smell of herbs wafts around the kitchen.

'Is Flora here for tea?' asks Daniel, with a frown, obviously thinking along the same lines as me.

'She is,' says Luna, cheerfully, 'because Flora's moved in with us for a while. Life's a little tricky for her at the moment so she's staying until she's back on her feet. I knew you'd be fine about it.'

Daniel couldn't look more horrified if I'd chucked the contents of the pot all over him.

'What? Excuse us please, Flora.' With that, he grabs his mother's elbow and steers her out of the back door and into the garden. Drips from the wooden spoon he's still holding leave a tomatoey trail across the kitchen tiles.

'What the hell are you doing, Mum?' drifts in through the back door, even though he's lowered his voice. 'Why are you moving strange people in without telling me?'

I can hear you, I feel like calling. But instead I edge closer to the door, although I know more than most that listening in to people's conversations causes nothing but problems.

'Oh, do stop making a fuss, Daniel,' says Luna, crisply. 'Flora needs sanctuary and a bit of TLC. She has nowhere else to go so I've offered her the spare room until she's sorted out something more permanent.'

'And how long will that take? You've got to stop taking in waifs and strays, Mum. I don't know Flora but I get the feeling she's perfectly able to look after herself.'

'That's where you're wrong,' says Luna, sounding cross. 'I'm experiencing waves of hostility from you, Daniel, and I don't like it. Flora is a good woman in need of support. I can feel it in my bones.'

'You and your damn feelings,' mutters Daniel.

'They've done me well so far and this is my house so you'll just have to get used to the arrangement.'

'That woman upset Caleb.'

'I doubt that, and he's a stronger child than you give him credit for being anyway. Now stop fussing or the tea will catch and burn.'

I move back from the door as the two of them troop back into the kitchen – Luna with her head high and a spring in her step, Daniel following behind with a scowl. Well, this is all going fabulously so far.

'Are you partial to lentil stew, Flora?' ask Luna, wiping her hands across her apron.

'I'm not sure I've ever tried it but it smells lovely,' I reply, not sure how much food I'll be able to stomach if Daniel is going to be glaring at me across the table.

There's a sudden clattering in the hallway and the door is flung wide open. It bangs into the stone wall with a resounding thud.

'Careful, careful!' says Luna as Caleb bowls in, his blonde hair sticking up and face flushed. He smiles broadly at his grandmother and waves at his father, but his face freezes when he spots me. He looks frightened, which makes me feel awful.

'Hello. It's nice to see you again,' I say, as brightly as I can. 'I think I owe you a free milkshake.'

Caleb doesn't move and doesn't speak.

'It's all right, mate,' murmurs Daniel, moving to stand by his son. 'She's not here to tell you off. Flora is here to have some tea.' He swallows. 'And it seems that she's going to be living with us for a while.'

Caleb's bright blue eyes flicker with alarm but he moves without a word to the table and sits down.

Luna ruffles the top of her grandson's head before dishing out four plates of steaming lentil stew. She takes blackened baked potatoes from the Aga and drops them onto the plates. Then she starts adding long green beans. She hesitates when she comes to the last plate.

'Do you like runner beans, Flora? They're homegrown and organic.'

'I love all kinds of veg.'

That's obviously the right answer because Luna nods and piles up a bean mountain on the side of my plate. The food is delicious. Who knew how tasty a stew can be without meat? But it's hard to eat and make small talk with three people you hardly know – especially when one of them dislikes you intensely and the other keeps shooting you nervous glances, like you're the Child Catcher in *Chitty Chitty Bang Bang*.

'Does your mum live nearby, Caleb?' I ask after a while, giving him my biggest smile to show I'm not really the Wicked Witch of the West.

I presume grumpy git Daniel has moved in with his mum after splitting up with his wife. I hope she's found herself a less miserable partner.

Caleb shakes his head and pauses with his fork halfway to his mouth. 'My mum's dead,' he says simply, before shovelling his food in.

I wish I was a witch right now. I'd summon up my superpowers to open up the ground beneath me and send me hurtling into the darkness.

'I'm... so sorry,' I stammer.

'That's OK. I was only little when it happened and I don't remember her much,' says Caleb with a half-smile that breaks my heart.

'It was a few years ago,' says Daniel, breezily, but there's a spark of pain in his brown eyes. 'Caleb was very small when she passed away, but we've been fine just you and me, haven't we, mate?'

When he pats his son's shoulder, Caleb gives him a lentil-y smile and nods.

I should probably leave the conversation there. Just move on to what a lovely summer we're having, or the ins and outs of Brexit. But how can I inadvertently bring up such a painful subject and then drop it, as though I don't care?

'Being a single parent must be difficult,' I say, stabbing at the beans on my plate with my fork.

Daniel shrugs. 'It has its moments but we do OK.'

'I'm sure you do,' I say, and then mentally kick myself because how can I possibly know if they're doing OK or not?

Daniel forks potato skin into his mouth and watches me while he chews.

After a while, I can't stand the silence and blurt out: 'Have you lived here with Luna for a while then?'

Daniel carefully puts his cutlery down on his plate. 'No, we moved in a couple of months ago. We needed a fresh start and Mum offered us' – he pauses – 'sanctuary for a while.'

'Just as I've done with Flora,' says Luna, patting his hand before getting up and collecting two large candles from the windowsill. She places them in the middle of the table, next to a large bowl of polished gemstones that's been calling out to me since the meal began. I'm desperate to run my fingers through the smooth, pink rock crystal and deep-red jasper.

'I've chosen chamomile for peace and rosemary for remembrance,' she says, striking a long match. Grey curls of smoke start drifting towards the ceiling and the sweet smell of herbs fills my nostrils as the blackened wicks catch alight.

Daniel picks up his cutlery but only pushes his food round his plate while Luna and I make small talk. Caleb asks to be excused as soon as he's polished off his food and runs off into the garden, banging the door behind him.

'That was a lovely meal. Thank you,' I say, pushing a small pile of leftover stew under my runner beans, so it doesn't look like so much. The food really was fabulous but my appetite is still under par. Cheating husbands plus deceased wives don't do a lot for the digestion.

Luna stares at the bulging beans and tuts. 'You look in need of a good meal. Young women these days don't have enough flesh on their bones. I blame the pressures of social media and all this constant oversharing of impossibly perfect bodies.'

With that, she gets to her feet and leans across the table to reach my plate. Her wide sleeve flaps perilously close to the candle and Daniel pushes it out of the way.

'I'll do the washing up,' I say, pushing back my chair and reaching for Caleb's plate at the same time as Daniel. When our fingers touch, we both pull back our hands as though we've been burned.

Luna looks at the two of us and smiles. 'So much buried energy! Why don't you both tackle the washing up while I do my meditation practice?' She throws a tea towel towards Daniel as she leaves the room.

'Is there a dishwasher?' I ask, hopefully, but Daniel shakes his head.

'Afraid not. My mother believes the house is a living entity that doesn't approve of anything too new-fangled. Fortunately, she draws the line at having gas lighting and an outside toilet.'

Is he making a joke or stating a fact?

'Does Luna do a lot of meditating?' I ask, stacking up pots and pans on the chaotic kitchen counter.

'She meditates for at least half an hour every day. Apparently it feeds her inner serenity.' Daniel snorts and turns the hot tap on full pelt, spraying water droplets in all directions.

'You're not into meditation then?'

'I don't have the time, what with work and looking after Caleb.'

'Your mum does seem pretty laid-back. She's quite—' I pause, at a sudden loss for words.

'Unusual? She's always been one of a kind, even before she became Luna and found her inner goddess.'

Who was Luna before her inner goddess was located? Daniel doesn't elaborate but squirts so much washing-up liquid into the water that bubbles start climbing out of the sink. They coat the plate he slides into the water and cling to the china when he places it on the drainer. He has his back to me and he's really going for it with the washing-up brush.

Luna's not the only one who can feel hostility coming off him in waves. Though, to be fair, I'd probably be annoyed if my home was invaded by someone who'd been narky to my motherless child.

'Look.' I dry a plate and place it on the table because I have no idea where it's kept. 'I'm very sorry you didn't know about me staying here and I can appreciate it was a surprise, especially after… well, what happened in the café. But Luna came into my shop this morning and her offer of somewhere to stay was all very spontaneous.'

'That's Luna all over – spontaneous and always trying to make the world a better place.' Daniel breathes out slowly and stops pummelling dirty crockery. He turns to face me, splashing water across my dress. 'So what's your sob story, then?'

'It's hardly a sob story,' I bristle. 'I've left my husband because…' I falter for a second because those were words I never expected to say. 'Anyway, it doesn't matter why. It happened a few days ago and I've been living above my shop ever since.'

'Is there a flat above the shop?'

'Nope, just an attic, with a put-you-up bed and lots of spiders.'

'Ah.' Daniel frowns. 'Contrary to what you probably think, I'm not unsympathetic to people's troubles. But I know how trusting my mother is and I don't want her to be taken advantage of.'

'I can assure you that I won't be taking advantage of anyone. I'm paying my way and I won't be here for long. It's a short-term stopgap while I find something else.'

I'm not sure that referring to his mother as a stopgap is the best idea but he doesn't pick me up on it. With a tight nod, he turns back to the greasy pots and we complete the washing-up in awkward silence. Fortunately, Caleb bowls in from the garden before I have to ask where to put everything I've been piling up, and he starts banging through cupboards and putting things away.

Figuring that my work is done, I decide to head for my bedroom but pause at the doorway and look back. How does Daniel manage being on his own? I wonder. Does he feel as scared and lost as I do right now? Um, where is Daniel?

There he is, on his knees, with his head in the saucepan cupboard. All I can see of him are long legs and – I can't help but notice – a very nice tight backside in snug-fitting black trousers.

Is that what a married woman should be noticing? I've hardly looked at another man for twenty years and now, three days after leaving my husband, I'm having lascivious thoughts about a man I don't even like. My head is so all over the place. Closing the kitchen door quietly behind me, I go upstairs to my new bedroom to have a little cry.

Chapter Five

I have no idea where I am. I yawn, in that relaxed state between waking and sleep, and stretch out my legs. But there's no reassuring warmth as my feet slide under Malcolm's legs… and no bed. My toes are poking out from under the single duvet into the cool morning air.

When I open my eyes and take in the bare stone walls, reality hits me, as it has done every morning since I left Malcolm. My marriage is on the rocks because my husband cheated and lied about it. Shock, grief and humiliation wash over me. It's a wave of emotion that's fast becoming familiar, but at least I don't have an aching back from the attic put-you-up adding to the toxic turmoil.

I stretch again and roll out of bed, my feet landing on the blue cotton rug. Sun is filtering through the thin curtains and there's an increasingly familiar smell wafting in through the open window. Yep, the farmer's definitely up early.

I wrinkle my nose, half-open the curtains and drink in what must be the best view for miles. Trees are ghostly shadows in a wispy mist caught at the bottom of Honeyford valley and, above them, grazing in pale sunshine, sheep are white dots in emerald-green fields.

I'm still taking in the glorious countryside when a child's laughter drifts upwards and Caleb runs around the side of the house. He's wearing a purple polo shirt and being chased by a black kitten that winds itself between his legs as he yells with delight. His enjoyment makes me smile and I raise my hand when he glances up and spots me. He hesitates slightly before giving me a shy wave back. Poor lad, growing up without his mum.

Caleb goes back to playing with the kitten as Daniel strides out of the back door towards his son. He's smartly dressed in a navy blue suit and his ebony hair has a slight curl from the shower.

'Hey, Caleb,' he says, his deep voice floating through the open window. 'Give your dad a hug before work. I'm just heading off.'

Caleb runs over and flings his arms around his dad's waist, the kitten following him like a dark shadow. He hugs his father tight and it warms my heart to see how much at ease with one another they are.

'You be a good boy at school and work hard,' says Daniel, stroking his son's fair hair with long fingers. He bends his head over his son's, revealing pale skin at the nape of his neck, and starts gently rubbing Caleb's back. It's such a tender moment, I can't bear to look away.

'I don't want to go to school today. Can't I stay home?' Caleb's excitement has suddenly disappeared and he sounds truculent.

'Not today, mate. I know switching schools is hard but it's not long now until you break up for the summer, so hang on in there.' Daniel glances at his watch and starts pulling away.

'I don't want you to go, Dad.' Caleb is holding on tight and Daniel squeezes back before removing Caleb's arms from his waist and stooping down to his son's level.

'Everything will be fine. Honestly. I'm always here and together we're a team. Don't forget we've got superpowers and we can face anything, right?'

When Caleb nods solemnly, I feel tears pricking at my eyes. He seems so grown-up in some ways, and yet so vulnerable beneath it all.

'Promise me you'll drive carefully, Dad?' mumbles Caleb, his lower lip wobbling.

'I promise that I always drive extra-specially carefully, and we'll both be back home before you know it.'

Daniel's head suddenly jerks up as though he can sense that he's being watched. I step further back behind the billowing curtains and pray that he didn't see me in my grey satin pyjamas. The last thing I need is Daniel accusing me of spying as well as being a sponger. I suppose I *was* spying, really. But only because I got caught up in what was happening beneath my window. Seeing Daniel and Caleb share a loving moment was so touching, it strangely made me feel both happy and unbearably sad at the same time. My emotions are so unsettled at the moment.

Daniel can't be all bad if he cares so much for his son, I decide, peeping out of the window to make sure he and Caleb have disappeared indoors. And being a single parent must be hard work. I pull the curtains fully open to let in the sunshine, and vow to give Daniel Purfoot a little more slack. We're all dealing with our own heartaches.

My drive to work from Starlight Cottage is along quiet country lanes and only takes ten minutes. This, for two reasons, is so much better than having to battle across the jam-packed centre of Oxford. It means that I don't start my day with a swear-fest that would shock a rugby team. And I also have far less time on my own to think.

It's become apparent to me over the last few days that thinking is highly overrated and only serves to makes a dire situation even worse. Trying to make sense in my head of what's happened to my marriage has led to nothing other than waves of sorrow that catch me off-guard, jagged fear that makes me sweat, and bubbling anger that keeps me awake at night.

My mind is also filled with X-rated images of Malcolm putting his back out as he tries to keep up with Marina's rampant sexual urges. And nobody wants to think about that. So I turn on Radio 2 as I drive down ridiculously pretty lanes edged by beech trees, and try to drown out my thoughts with loud music and cheerful banter. At least I'm not hungry. I often left our Oxford flat without breakfast because I was in such a hurry, but I couldn't resist Luna's home-made bread this morning.

Honeyford is awake and ready for business as I drive along narrow Weavers Lane and turn into the High Street. Cottage doors are flung open to let in the morning breeze, colourful flowers brighten grass verges, and shops are ready for visiting tourists and local customers.

Ahead of me, the medieval market house stands guard over the town. The stone floor beneath its arches has been worn into dips and grooves by centuries of market stalls and shoppers. Some of them must have dealt with heartbreak and deception and learned to live with it.

Sighing, I reverse into a parking space near the war memorial that's etched with far too many names for such a small town. *Yes, people here have carried on with a broken heart. They coped, and I will too*, I tell myself as I grab my bag from the back seat and lock the car.

I've almost reached the bookshop and Cosy Kettle when I spot a poster in the window of Amy's sweet shop that attracts tourists like bees to a honeypot. The poster is stuck to the glass in between jars of sunshine-yellow sherbet lemons, peanut brittle, wine gums and rainbow jelly beans.

Your town needs you! Take part in the 900th anniversary celebrations of the Honeyford Charter and help to put our town on the map.

Planning meeting – all welcome – in Honeyford Market House,
15 June at 7.30 p.m.

That sounds intriguing, though I doubt Honeyford really needs me – a newcomer who's never even heard of its ancient charter. What could I offer? But it's heartwarming that this community is keen to celebrate its heritage. I snap a quick pic of the poster on my phone, just in case, and head for the bookshop.

'The charter celebration? It's some dreadful community thing that's being organised by the town's heritage society,' Millicent informs me when she comes into The Cosy Kettle for our afternoon book club.

Callie set up the afternoon book club a few weeks ago – along with an evening book club more recently – and both are doing well.

'The society holds litter picks and an old-ee world-ee Christmas fayre, spelled with a "y".' Millicent raises her eyebrows to the heavens. 'I can't bear these pseudo-archaic spellings, myself. Anyway, apparently the organisation is run by a dreadful jumped-up committee who claim their events engender a community spirit.' She leans forward over her cappuccino and inspects my face. 'You're still looking peaky, Flora. Are you ill?'

'No, I'm fine – just a bit tired.'

'Are you sure that's all?' Millicent, for all her sturdy stomping around, can be irritatingly perceptive at times.

I shrug. 'There are a few problems at home but nothing I can't handle.'

Callie's head pops up. She's bent over the coffee machine, waiting for her espresso and I just hope she didn't hear me. I still haven't told anyone what's happened. Even Becca, who gave me a hard stare when she saw my car heading out of Honeyford yesterday in the opposite direction I'd be going if driving home to Oxford.

Maybe I'd have ended up telling Callie if she was still working full-time in the shop and café. But our time together has been a victim of her success at the hotel coffee house. I've got a minor financial stake in the place, so I'm pleased that Callie is running it and doing so well. But I'm always happy to see her when she pops back to give us a hand at the book club.

'Problems, you say?' prompts Millicent.

I pretend I haven't heard her, and Millicent doesn't ask any further questions. But she watches me as I pop in and out of the café while Callie hosts the book club. And, from the snatches of conversation I overhear, she doesn't lay into the poor author of the club's current thriller as much as she usually does.

Our evening book club is growing but the afternoon club is still only attended by a select few: Millicent and Becca, seventy-something Phyllis in her wheelchair, a new mum who will forever be known to us as 'Knackered Mary' – even when her baby son hits puberty, Stanley in a black T-shirt and over-tight jeans, and his elderly friend Dick, whose long white beard compensates for the lack of hair on his shiny pink head.

They're very different people, but they've gelled as a group and they look out for each other. In fact, they've gelled so well, their fortnightly book club now sometimes meets weekly, at their request. And one thing is plain – they absolutely adore Callie. But I'm not sure they've gelled with me.

To be honest, I often feel out of shape around them – kind of spiky and the wrong fit. And though I really like them, I'm not sure that the feeling is mutual.

In between serving customers in the shop and café, I track down a book on Cotswold history on our shelves and search for the Honeyford Charter. There's a paragraph about it, along with a grainy black-and-white photo of the quaint almshouses that lead down to the river.

Honeyford, a typically attractive small Cotswold town, was granted a charter in the year 1119 by King Henry I. This granted it the right to hold a weekly market in the town centre and permission to roast oxen in the town square.

The town must have hosted a lot of markets! There's still an organic market held every Friday but it's moved from beneath the arches of the market house to the Memorial Park in summer and to the town's small community centre in winter. As for oxen, I haven't seen a single one since I came to Honeyford. Sheep by the dozen, but oxen, no.

'Hey, Flora.' Callie has crept up on me and is reading over my shoulder. 'Ah, are you going to the Charter Day meeting?'

'Maybe, though I'm not sure what I can contribute, being so new to the town.' I close the book, push it back onto the shelf and turn to take a good look at Callie. She's looking fabulous in skinny jeans and a pink T-shirt, with her wavy blonde hair pulled back into a ponytail.

Callie's fifteen years younger than me but there's a calmness about her that's soothing, especially when your life is going to hell in a handcart. I take a deep breath as though I might inhale some of her peace.

'How are things with you?' I ask, though the answer's obvious – loved-up happiness is seeping from her every pore. Callie is glowing and has been since she and her old flame Noah settled their differences and became an official item.

Did I ever glow with Malcolm? I wonder. I remember being desperate to see him when he used to call at my parents' house and take me to the cinema or the pub. I thought I'd die if he ever left me and I would never have believed that, one day, I'd leave him.

'Things are brilliant,' says Callie, wrapping her arms around her waist as though remembering her last hug. 'Noah was able to leave his job without working any notice. His employer threw a hissy fit and just told him to leave. So he's back from New York now and we're both living with Gramp.'

'I heard as much. How's it going with Stanley?'

'Ah, you know.' Callie grins. 'He's delighted that Noah and I are together and he enjoys having us both around. Finn offered us a room at the hotel but Noah's happy to stay with Gramp and keep him company.'

'Was the hotel room offered free of charge?'

'What do you think?' Callie snorts at the thought of Noah's brother – the owner of Honeyford's new hotel – offering anything for nothing. 'But it's fine living with Gramp for the time being, even though he wants us to sit and watch TV with him every night. Honestly, if we have to sit through another repeat of *Midsomer Murders*, I won't be responsible for my actions. Though at least if Gramp's at home with us, he's not getting into trouble.'

'I don't want to worry you but I did spot him reading a book on extreme sports the other day.'

'Hell's bells! That's like skiing down glaciers and jumping off skyscrapers, isn't it?'

'Kind of.'

'I'll have to keep an eye on him.' Callie sighs and looks around us before lowering her voice. 'Anyway, enough about my domestic arrangements, what about you? I wasn't listening in but I overheard you telling Millicent that you're having a few problems at home. I hope you don't mind me asking but you do look a bit... stressed.'

'Oh, dear, do I look that bad?'

'No, no, you look fine. Just tired. Sorry, I shouldn't have said anything.'

'I don't mind. Actually, it's nice that you care.' I suddenly feel as though I'm about to cry and I suck my bottom lip between my teeth. I can't keep crying all the time. It's not professional.

Her eyes fill with concern and she rubs her hand along my arm, which doesn't help my self-control at all. 'Malcolm and I are having some...' I gulp, '... difficulties and I've moved out for a while. That's all.'

It's not all, and I don't want to lie to Callie, but I can't tell her the whole truth about Malcolm and Marina. Not until I've fully got my own head around it.

Callie, always empathetic to others' feelings, gets it straight away and doesn't ask for any gory details of our break-up. Instead, she gives me a sympathetic smile. 'So where are you staying?'

'I slept here, for a while.'

'You're kidding me. Not upstairs on what Ruben called his chaise longue?'

'If you mean that old put-you-up, then yes. The springs are rather... unspringy, and the spiders up there are enormous.'

'Tell me about it. I went up there once to wake Ruben and almost died when I spotted a spider the size of a dinner plate.' She grins. 'Well, a tea plate, but it was enormous. So why did you stay here and not come round to mine, Flora? You can come and stay with us now, if you like – until you get back on your feet. We haven't got a spare room but the sofa's comfy and it's plenty big enough. Noah stretches out on it and he's six-foot tall.'

Her big brown eyes sparkle when she says 'Noah'. She can't help herself, and that's why there's no way I can take up her kind offer. She and Noah are already coping with an unpredictable octogenarian; the last thing they need is a miserable mess mourning the end of her marriage. That would be a right downer on love's young dream.

'That's so lovely of you, Callie, and I really appreciate it but I'm fine. Honestly. I'm staying with Luna for a little while until I get things sorted and work out what I'm doing next.'

'I didn't know you knew Luna,' says Callie, who, Honeyford born and bred, knows almost everyone in the town.

'I didn't but apparently my aura was giving off distress signals and she came to my rescue.'

'Ha, that sounds very like Luna. She's not been in Honeyford that long and is a bit out there, but she's incredibly kind-hearted and I'm sure she's happy for you to stay.'

'Absolutely. Luna's been very welcoming.' Her grumpy son not so much, but I keep him out of it.

'If you're sure you're OK. I'm so sorry about you and Malcolm but I can see how it might happen.' Callie winces as though her words took her by surprise.

'What do you mean?'

'Nothing.' Callie's rose-pink cheeks are starting to properly glow with embarrassment. 'Just ignore me. I really shouldn't have said anything.'

'You really should,' I say, panic mounting that Malcolm might have made a pass at Callie behind my back. She's pretty. And young.

'I don't know.' Callie takes a deep breath and starts gabbling. 'You know when you imagine what someone's partner will be like and then you meet them and they're nothing like you thought they'd be? That.

Plus, you seemed different when he was around. Less like you, really. And I got the feeling he didn't approve of you taking on the shop.'

'Malcolm didn't approve. He still doesn't.'

Phew! I'm relieved that inappropriate flirting hasn't been mentioned but I'm dismayed by how Callie sized up our relationship. Is that how I am with Malcolm – less like me?

Callie glances behind her as the book club starts spilling out of The Cosy Kettle and says quickly, 'You can always talk to me, Flora, if it would help. Just remember that. And for what it's worth, I think it's brilliant that you took on the bookshop. You really should go to the Charter Day meeting too. Don't you think so, Phyllis?'

'You what?' says Phyllis, who's being wheeled past by Becca. She runs her fingers through her tight grey perm.

'I was saying that Flora should go to the Charter Day meeting and maybe get involved in the celebrations.'

'Makes sense, I suppose. If she's planning on sticking around.'

'What makes you say that? Why wouldn't I stick around?' I ask her.

Phyllis shrugs. 'Dunno. But you're not from round here, are you, so we might just be a stepping stone on your way to greater things. Like Honeyford turned out to be just a stepping stone for Elaine on her way to Brisbane.'

Poor Phyllis. Her daughter, Elaine, and her grandchildren, moved to Australia a few years ago and, though she puts on a brave face about it, she misses them horribly.

'I'm not planning on going anywhere,' I tell her, which is true enough, though I have no idea what the next few weeks will bring. My life seems to be in freefall.

'Hmm, you might as well get involved then.'

'Involved in what?' asks Stanley, who's appeared behind her with Dick in tow. He's been mainlining double espressos again and is bouncing up and down like an over-caffeinated Tigger.

'Charter Day,' huffs Phyllis. 'Flora is thinking of doing something for it.'

'That is dope, dude!' exclaims Stanley, giving me a high five.

Beside him, Dick raises a straggly grey eyebrow and slowly shakes his head. His friend's metamorphosis from an introverted octogenarian into an out-there slang mangler has been hard for him to take. But Stanley's determined to wring all he can out of life in his final years and become his true self. I admire him for that. I'd love to know who I truly am right now.

'We can all get involved and help you,' adds Mary, before giving a loud yawn. 'Oops, Callum's waking up. Gotta go before he starts bawling.'

'Thank goodness for that,' mutters Millicent as Mary wheels his buggy out of the shop, and I have to agree. That child has bionic lungs if his ear-bleeding shrieks are anything to go by. And I really can't cope with them today.

Several customers mention the charter celebrations as the day goes on and I take another look at the poster when I'm walking back to the car after work. Malcolm would say a community celebration is a waste of time but he hasn't been in touch since I refused to go home with him yesterday. So I guess it doesn't really matter what he'd say.

'What do *you* want to do, Flora?' I say out loud, before looking around to make sure no one's seen me talking to myself. Gaining a reputation as a weirdo will hardly endear me to the locals, many of whom still give me sideways glances as though I'm odd.

Truth is I feel nervous about rocking up to the charter meeting, in case some people think it's inappropriate for a newcomer and I'm intruding. But maybe going along would be a step towards proper acceptance by this close-knit community and, let's be honest, I've nothing better to do with my time.

My evenings were once filled with Malcolm bustling, Pierre yelling and the clinking of silverware against bone china. When the restaurant got busy, I'd help out, and sometimes life got too hectic. But now my evenings stretch out ahead of me, long and lonely.

Many people would envy my freedom. Knackered Mary would probably kill for an evening to herself without cranky Callum and his colic. But living in a weird house with a man who doesn't want me there, while my husband is getting up to who knows what with a younger woman, doesn't feel much like freedom to me.

Luna is home before me and gorgeous smells are wafting from the kitchen when I let myself in.

'Hi, Luna. That smells gorgeous,' I say, popping my head around the kitchen door. 'Can I do anything to help?'

Luna looks up from the pie she's just taken out of the oven and grins. 'No thanks, love. I was home before you and the tea's almost done. Caleb's letting off steam in the garden and Daniel will be down in a minute. Oh, here he is.'

Daniel ducks slightly to get through the kitchen doorway, brushes past me, and wanders over to his mother. He's changed out of his work suit into black jeans and a plain grey V-neck jumper. Dark hair flops across his forehead into his eyes and he brushes it away. Malcolm favours a short back and sides, and wouldn't approve.

'You came back then?' says Daniel, his mouth twitching at the corner.

What is it with people thinking I'm about to do a runner from Honeyford?

'Did you think I wouldn't?'

I did think about it, to be honest, and I scrolled through ads for spare rooms when it was quiet in the shop today. But all I could find were student lets in Oxford, and someone called Raymond who said he had a room to rent and was seeking 'companionship'. Raymond is probably a lovely man, but something about the advert made the back of my neck prickle.

Daniel shrugs, hooks his arm around Luna's waist and gives her a squeeze. 'Hello there, Mum. How was your day?'

'Good, thank you. I had a minibus of tourists in with auras to die for, and they bought me out of dreamcatchers. They had a very spiritual feel.'

Luna tastes the spoon she's just dipped into the pot and gives an 'mmm' of pleasure. Then she stirs it round the pot again while I try not to focus on basic kitchen hygiene. Pierre would go mad but it's either cope with the germs in Luna's warm and welcoming kitchen or spend an evening alone in a pokey attic. Sometimes braving other people's bugs is worth it, I tell myself, moving the huge bowl of gemstones off the table and laying our places.

Daniel gives me a hand and I keep my eyes fixed firmly ahead when he bends over to get plates out of the cupboard. I don't want a repeat of yesterday's backside-related thoughts that were obviously just a pathetic reaction to Malcolm's infidelity.

Tea is a fairly subdued affair. The pie is tasty, and I listen to Daniel and Luna chatting to Caleb about school. But he's pretty unforthcoming and, after mostly pushing food around his plate, he asks to get down from the table.

Luna also excuses herself after tea in order to 'commune with nature', whatever that involves. So Daniel and I do the washing-up together again, while making awkward small talk about our days.

My day mostly involved encouraging people to buy books, coffee and cake, while his appears to have involved making rich people even more wealthy. He's some sort of fancy accountant.

'I wouldn't have thought that was your thing,' I tell him as I dry plates and try not to drip soap suds on the floor. Daniel might be a whizz with figures but his washing-up technique leaves a lot to be desired.

'Really?' He raises an eyebrow, still up to his elbows in water. 'What's wrong with being an accountant?'

'Nothing. It's just that with your mum being so unusual and New Agey, I'd have expected you to be more, I don't know… creative.'

'Believe me, I can be creative with figures when I have to be,' mutters Daniel, wiping splashed water from his nose with his shoulder. When he fixes his brown eyes on me, I'm struck by just how long his dark eyelashes are. 'Tell me, Flora. Are you trying to say I'm boring?'

'Not at all.' I wouldn't dare. What looks like a brief smile flits across Daniel's face, though it's probably more of a fledgling scowl. His face would crack if he did smile, I decide, and then I berate myself for being mean. His wife died, after all. That's got to be way worse than discovering your partner is a lying philanderer.

'Flora?'

Daniel is staring at me, his head tilted to one side. Oops. I was so busy thinking about the people we've lost, I wasn't listening.

'Sorry. What did you say?'

'I said, what's happening with you and your husband?'

'Do you want to know when I'm leaving?'

'No, well, yes. But that wasn't why I asked.' Daniel starts scrubbing furiously at a casserole dish as though I've insulted him.

I sigh and shove a dry plate into the chaotic crockery cupboard. 'I don't know what's happening. He came into the shop yesterday but we didn't really talk. And I've mostly ignored his texts and phone calls.'

'Why?'

'I don't know. Maybe I'm afraid of what I'll hear, or what I'll say. I just need a bit of space first, to let things sink in.'

'You'll have to talk to him eventually.'

'I know,' I say sharply, a bit annoyed that he's poking his nose in. But I'm more annoyed with myself for being such a wuss about everything and basically running away. I'm fairly assertive in most aspects of life, but not when it comes to Malcolm.

'I was just giving my opinion,' says Daniel, with his back to me. He sounds annoyed now.

'Yeah, sorry. It's been a bit of an all-round shit week.'

'Humph,' grunts Daniel. But he turns and, rather than placing the squeaky-clean casserole dish on the draining board, hands it directly to me. I take this to be the domestic equivalent of an olive branch.

I give him a small smile and we finish the washing-up in silence that's broken only by the thud of Caleb's football rhythmically hitting the back door.

Chapter Six

The next morning, I've only been at work for half an hour when the door swings open and Malcolm strides in. He scans the shop until he spots me on my knees and marches over.

'Flora. There you are. I had to see you,' he says, towering above me.

Sighing, I slide the book I'm holding onto the bottom shelf and get slowly to my feet. My stomach's doing somersaults, like it used to when I first knew Malcolm. Only then, it was due to love and lust, and now it's due to sorrow, anger – and missing him.

I'm trying really hard not to miss Malcolm, the man who destroyed my trust and broke my heart. But it turns out it's not so easy to just stop caring about someone you've cared about all your adult life. I'm missing my old familiar life too.

'Hello, Malcolm.' I push a strand of dark hair from my eyes and take a quick look around the shop. The café's busy – I can hear the coffee machine hissing – but no one's browsing or buying books, thank goodness. Small towns thrive on gossip and I don't want to fuel the rumour mill with tales of my marital woes.

Malcolm starts shuffling from foot to foot. 'This is getting ridiculous, Flora. We need to talk. When are you coming home?'

'Is Marina still around?' I ask, folding my arms.

'She's still at the restaurant because I'd be in all sorts of trouble if I tried to sack her. Stupid employment legislation!'

'That's not what I meant.'

'OK. She's around but not *around*, if you know what I mean.' His left eyelid starts twitching as though an electric current is zapping through it.

'Not really. What exactly *do* you mean?'

Malcolm hesitates and then a flicker of relief crosses his face as the shop door tings and a young couple in hiking boots bustle in. Saved by the bell. He wanders over to the till and leans against it while I ascertain that the couple are looking for OS maps and show them the ones we have in stock.

'So how are things going in here?' he asks when I join him, as though Marina was never mentioned. He frowns when a small blonde woman comes into the shop and waves at me before heading for the historical fiction shelves. 'Who's that?'

'A regular customer. I'm slowly getting to know who people are.'

'Just as I'd expect in a little place like this,' he huffs, as though it's a bad thing. 'So you think you'll make a success of the business, do you?'

'Yes, I do. I'm getting involved in local community events and business is booming.' *Booming* is pushing it big time but, fortunately, Malcolm can't see the crossed fingers behind my back.

He sniffs. 'What sort of community events?'

'Events like Charter Day. The town's having a big celebration and I might get involved. It's to mark the 900th anniversary of King Henry the First granting Honeyford a charter to—'

'Sounds like a lot of work for very little return,' butts in Malcolm, whose eyes started glazing over at 'King Henry'. 'Will your involvement benefit the business? That's the bottom line, Flora.'

'I don't know. Maybe it will, maybe it won't. But being involved will benefit me.'

'How?'

Here goes. I take a deep breath. 'It'll give me the chance to be a bigger part of this community and to feel as though I belong here.'

Malcolm's *does not compute* expression is classic. He couldn't look more confused if I'd just told him I was giving away free doublets with every copy of *Hamlet*.

'One, you obviously belong because your shop is here. And two, why would you care whether you belong here or not? Where you properly belong is home in Oxford, with me.'

'And where does Marina belong?'

'Oh, for goodness' sake… I've already told you…' Malcolm glowers at a young man who's just come into the shop. 'It's impossible to discuss this when it's like Piccadilly Circus in here.'

'You don't seem that keen to discuss Marina anyway.'

Proving my point, Malcolm ignores what I've said and starts drumming his fingers against the till. 'So, are you coming home, Flora?'

When I shake my head, he pulls himself up tall.

'Then I may as well go and speak to you another time, when it's not so busy.'

He stalks off while I wonder just how much Malcolm really does want to talk. Every time Marina's mentioned, his mouth tightens and he goes pale. But if we can't discuss Marina and what happened, there's not much point in talking at all.

There's no way I'm going back to him. That's it. Decision made. If he can't give me a straight answer about the goings on with Marina, I'll give him one instead.

But then, at the door, he hesitates and turns back towards me. 'I know things are messed up and difficult at the moment, Flora, but I really do love you and I know we can be happy again, together, when things are sorted out. Please believe me.'

And, just for a moment, I glimpse the man I married, the man who swept me off my feet and has given me a happy enough life ever since. The man who's made a mistake. But don't we all make those? Even ginormous ones, sometimes?

The door bangs shut behind Malcolm, as my brain starts whirling again.

Three hours later, after I've worked my socks off to push Malcolm out of my mind, I realise that I've lost my key to Starlight Cottage.

The first rule of being a good house guest is not compromising the security of the property by randomly putting your key down somewhere stupid. But that's what I've done and I have to let Luna know. I'm not normally such an airhead. Malcolm insists that 'everything should be in its place' and my door key is always in my bag or pocket. But it's in neither, and Becca and I have scoured the shop and the café without success.

It crosses my mind that maybe Malcolm leaned over the counter, into my bag, and pocketed the door key as a protest because I'm not doing what I'm told. But that really is ridiculous. Malcolm can be a tad controlling at times but he's not petty.

Finally resigned to the fact that my key's gone for good, I leave Becca in charge for ten minutes and head along the High Street towards Luna's Magical Emporium. Thick white clouds are scudding across the sky today and a strong breeze is swirling the weathervane at the top of the medieval church tower. I pull my grey angora cardigan tightly around me and I wave at the local butcher, Vernon, who's selling sausages to an elderly couple.

Luna's emporium stands between a tiny newsagent's and a pretty thatched cottage with pink roses winding around the door. Her window display is a mixture of books about the 'faerie realm', a pair of pink-net angel wings, and a huge half-egg of purple crystal that's been turned into a water feature. A gentle trickle of liquid runs across the crystal and pools beneath it before being recirculated in a never-ending watery loop.

It's the kind of woo-woo shop I'd usually avoid like the plague. But its other-worldliness strikes a chord with me today, because escaping from reality feels rather welcome. I'll treat my visit to Luna's shop as an adventure.

When I push open the door, a wind chime tinkles above my head and I'm hit by a wall of sound. Pan pipes. It's definitely pan pipes.

'Flora. How lovely to see you.'

Luna stares at me over the top of a pair of half-moon glasses and points a remote control at the CD player in the corner. The pan pipes quieten down as I take in the scene. My landlady is sitting cross-legged on a huge beanbag in the middle of the cluttered shop, cross-stitching a tapestry. The fabric is bright with threads that show what looks like a nymph sitting underneath a waterfall in her nightie – not the most practical of clothing for such a damp spot.

'How are you, Flora?' Luna's smile falters and she pushes her needle into the fabric to secure it. 'I sense disruption in your force today.'

'Maybe Luke Skywalker should start firing up the X-wings.'

Luna responds to my lame joke with a puzzled frown and runs her hands over the purple chiffon scarf around her neck. She's awash with scarves today. A pale lilac one is tied around her head to hold back her silver hair, and another is looped through her waistband in place of a belt.

I shrug. 'What I mean is I'm all right, thank you, Luna. I just need to have a quick word with you.'

'All right? I don't think so and I'm concerned about you, Flora. How are your psychic energies?'

'I – um, I don't know.' It's not a question I'm asked very often. 'I think my energies are as they should be, thank you.'

I'm knackered because I'm not sleeping well, and my short-term memory is shot to pieces as the lost key demonstrates, but I don't suppose those are the kinds of energies Luna means. In confirmation, Luna raises her hands and holds her palms out towards me as though I'm a fire and she's judging the heat output.

'Your vibrations are very off. They're practically undulating, which tells me your energies are severely imbalanced right now. Even more so than they were. Have you been around your husband today?'

I nod, spooked that Luna appears to have the ability to read me like a book. Can she really see my energies swirling around me in a vibrational vortex of confusion and upset? I blow hair from my hot forehead and realise I must look distracted and bothered so it would hardly take Sherlock Holmes – or a witchy woman, for that matter – to gauge my state of mind.

'Did you go to his restaurant?' asks Luna, carefully folding the tapestry fabric.

'No, he came into the shop earlier this morning.'

'Did you invite him over your threshold?'

'No, he just called in.' *As though he owns the place,* whispers my inner voice.

Flora tuts and frowns. 'That man does enjoy encroaching on your space. He appears to have a few boundary issues.'

'That man is my husband,' I say, wearily. People seem to be forgetting this fact. I seem to be forgetting it sometimes. I feel as if I'm in limbo – a no man's land between restored marital harmony and divorce that's filled with recrimination, confusion and crying.

Luna rises from the beanbag in one fluid movement, like a cat stretching in the sunshine. She ducks to avoid a low-hanging dreamcatcher and wanders towards me as the background music changes from pan pipes to weird plinky-plonk synthesiser stuff. It has the same effect on me as nails scraping down a blackboard.

'So why are you here, Flora?' asks Luna, standing so close I notice that she smells of rosemary and lemongrass. 'You said you needed a word.'

'I'm really sorry to bother you at work but I'm afraid I've lost my key.'

Luna stares unblinkingly at me with her strange amber eyes. 'Is that all you wanted to see me about?'

'Yes. I wanted to apologise for misplacing it and, also, I can't get into the cottage without it.'

'Oh, it'll turn up with the help of a finding spell,' says Luna, breezily, as though casting spells is what normal people do. She reaches behind the counter for her handbag and pulls out a huge bunch of keys. 'In the meantime, I have a spare.'

She starts working a key off the ring while I wonder if one of Luna's spells could help me find the right way forward. Because at the moment my future is well and truly lost in a muddle of sadness and uncertainty that only gets worse every time I see Malcolm.

Luna gives me a sympathetic smile, as though she can read my mind, before handing the freed key to me. I slip it into my pocket and push a tissue on top to keep it safe.

'That's great, thank you. And I'm sorry about losing the other one. It doesn't have your address on it so no one will know where it comes from if they find it.'

'Oh, I'm not worried about burglars. The cottage can protect itself and it won't let anyone with bad intentions in,' says Luna, which, frankly, is even more weird than her talk of casting spells. She moves slowly back to her beanbag and sinks onto it. 'Talking of Starlight Cottage, how are you finding living there?'

'It's far more comfortable than the bookshop attic.' When I smile at her, Luna holds my gaze as though she's waiting for me to say something more. 'And you're right that the view from my room is very soothing.' Luna carries on staring at me with her cat-like eyes until I blurt out, 'It's just that Daniel doesn't like me living there. I don't think he likes me much at all, to be honest.'

Luna drops her gaze and waves her arm dismissively. 'Oh, he likes you well enough and you two are more similar than you imagine. My son has been hurt and he often masks his emotions.' *Not well enough*, I think, remembering his snippy comment this morning when I nipped into the shower ahead of him. Luna sighs. 'You've been hurt too, Flora, and, like him, you've been alone for some time.'

'But I was with Malcolm until a few days ago.'

'Indeed.'

Luna's enigmatic reply – a mixture of empathy and accusation – hangs in the air between us.

'I suppose I did feel a bit lonely sometimes, when Malcolm was directing all his energies into his latest restaurant,' I gabble.

'Of course.'

'But he's a busy and ambitious man and he didn't mean to neglect me. He can be attentive, kind and caring.'

'I don't doubt it. A woman like you would never have married him, otherwise.'

She tilts her head and gives me one of her mysterious smiles – the kind she uses when she's talking about her beloved goddesses. This is all getting a bit heavy for a quick chat about a lost key. A spot of deflection is required.

'Your shop's amazing, Luna,' I say, turning slowly to take in all the books and gemstones and CDs… and unicorns. There's a whole huddle of small plastic unicorns on one shelf. 'There's so much… unusual stuff in here. What got you interested in this kind of thing?'

'Oh, this and that, and I knew I had to break away from my ordinary life. Actually, that's why I admire you so much.'

'Me?' I look behind me in case someone else has slipped into Luna's emporium. 'Why do you admire me? I'm a mess at the moment – a forty-two-year-old woman with a cheating husband who's trying to keep her small business afloat. I'm the very embodiment of ordinariness.' Is ordinariness a word?

Luna smiles again. 'You've surrendered to chance by branching out with your own business and you've taken a risk by leaving your old life with Malcolm. Mark my words. It's those relatively small, courageous, out-of-the-ordinary acts that attract the attention of the cosmos.'

I'm not sure that I want the cosmos involved in my car crash of a life but I take the comment in the spirit it was offered and smile back. Luna thinks I'm out of the ordinary rather than ridiculous. She thinks I'm courageous even though inside I'm like jelly. That gives me a warm glow.

Though, thinking about it, she also reckons I'm like Daniel, which really *is* ridiculous. I spot a photo of Daniel and Caleb hanging from her key ring and I do a double take at Daniel's wide bright smile. He's got perfect teeth and he looks much more… human when he's not scowling.

'My boys are very good-looking, don't you think?' asks Luna, looking up at me from beneath her long silver lashes.

'Mmmm.' It's time to go, I reckon – before Luna starts asking me to give Daniel marks out of ten. 'I'd better get back to the bookshop because Becca doesn't like being in charge for too long, but I'll see you later back at home. Thanks for the key.' I stop at the door, with my fingers around the handle. I only have somewhere to call home at the moment because of this strange, generous woman. 'Um, Luna, thank you for taking me in when I had nowhere to go. I really do appreciate it.'

Luna winks. 'You're very welcome. It wasn't an entirely altruistic act on my part.'

I have no idea what she's talking about and two women are waiting outside the door so there's no chance to find out. I stand aside to let the customers in and give Luna a wave before heading back to my very normal bookshop.

Chapter Seven

Starlight Cottage allows me over the threshold with my borrowed key – I'm obviously free of bad intentions – and I make a start on tea. Luna's not back yet and Daniel's busy playing football with Caleb in the garden.

I'm not much of a cook, in spite of helping out in restaurants for several years, but the food is edible and Caleb polishes off a large plateful, which pleases me far more than I'd have imagined. He's so pale and skinny, I have an urge to build him up. And his little knobbly knees poking out beneath his shorts make me feel like crying, for some reason. Mind you, most things make me feel like crying at the moment.

Shortly before bed, I pad through the gloomy hallway to the conservatory in my bare feet and turn on the fringed standard lamp. Golden light floods the room, which is more a wooden-framed lean-to than an elegant space.

A sudden movement catches my eye and I spot a figure sitting in a tall armchair. 'Good grief! You almost gave me a heart attack.'

Clasping my hand to my neck, I take deep breaths to calm the fluttering in my chest. I only came in here to find my book and wasn't expecting to discover Daniel sitting in the dark, nursing a glass of red wine. For one horrible moment, I thought he was the ghost of his dad.

Grabbing my novel from the chair where I left it earlier, I start backing out of the room at speed. 'I'm sorry for disturbing you. I'll leave you in peace.'

Daniel narrows his eyes and waves his glass at me. 'Would you like a drink?'

Would I? I weigh up the Friday night opportunities available to a newly separated woman such as myself. I could head into Honeyford and check out the Cotswolds' nightlife (otherwise known as *sitting in the pub on my own*), I could read in bed for a while before crying myself to sleep, or I could have a drink with Daniel and make excruciating small talk. What a veritable bonanza of unpalatable options.

'Only I could do with the company,' says Daniel, thickly, swirling the wine round his glass. It glints in the lamplight, which is shining on his black hair and casting deep shadows beneath his eyes. He sounds so hollowed-out inside, I make a snap decision and close the door behind me.

'A drink would be lovely, thank you.'

Daniel pours me a full glass as I walk over to Luna's rickety old sofa, which is covered by a solar-system throw, and park my backside on Saturn's rings. I watch him, warily. Is he drunk?

'I'm not drunk, if that's what you're worried about,' he says, lifting one eyebrow and handing me a glass.

'It never even crossed my mind.'

I take a sip of wine and it warms my throat. I'm no connoisseur but I've been around Malcolm for long enough to recognise it as full-bodied and expensive.

'What type of wine is it?'

'A Shiraz. Do you know much about wine?'

'Not really, but Malcolm does. He did a very expensive course all about it which mainly seemed to involve him getting tipsy.'

'And Malcolm is…?'

'My husband.'

'Ah.'

Daniel settles back in his chair and sips his glass of wine while he stares through the window. The last vestiges of twilight are almost gone and the garden and the hills beyond are fading into inky blackness.

'Is everything all right?' I ask, but he doesn't reply. He just keeps staring at the nothingness beyond the panes of glass. Eventually I add, 'It's just that you were sitting in the dark.'

At that, he looks up in surprise, almost as if he'd forgotten I was there. 'It's peaceful in the dark. And I'm less likely to be interrupted.'

Point taken. He'd rather be alone after all. I stand up to go but he waves his glass at me.

'Oh, please sit down. I didn't mean you. To be brutally honest, I'm having a bit of downtime from my mother.'

'Are you hiding?'

'Something like that.' He rubs his eyes and stifles a yawn. 'She can be a bit full on sometimes, what with her positive energy and waving healing crystals over my head while I'm sleeping.'

Blimey, does she do that? Waking up to find Luna muttering incantations would finish me off. I make a mental note to wedge a chair against my bedroom door, just in case.

'She has the best of intentions, of course,' adds Daniel, with a sigh.

'I'm sure she does. She's been very kind to me.'

'Hmm.' Daniel's face is partly in shadow when he bends to refill his glass. 'She can be overly generous at times, but she's a good mum.'

'You're just not the sort of son I'd expect her to have.'

'You've already made that clear.' There's a hint of annoyance in his deep voice. 'So what exactly were you expecting? A long-haired hippy wearing Jesus sandals and smoking dope, I suppose.'

'Not exactly. Just someone a bit less…' Oh dear, I've boxed myself into a corner here. A bit less what? Unwelcoming? Humourless? Up himself?

'I think the word you're looking for is traditional,' says Daniel, with a raised eyebrow.

I nod, gratefully. 'Traditional. Definitely.'

'Mum and I have always been quite different from each other. I take after my father more. He was "traditional" too but someone had to earn the money and look after the family's practical needs while Mum was off on her flights of fancy.'

I take another slug of wine for Dutch courage and ask what I've wanted to ask for days. 'So why have you and Caleb moved in with Luna? Is it to look after her?'

Daniel, who's just taken a large gulp of wine, splutters into his glass. 'Please don't ever let Luna hear you say that! She prides herself on being fiercely independent. But she gets lonely here on her own and she loves having Caleb around. She says he keeps her young. Which is ironic seeing as he's turning me grey.' He pushes his fingers through his thick, dark hair and a few strands above his ears glint silver in the lamplight.

'You're all right. Apparently grey hair makes women look older but makes men look more distinguished.' I sniff. 'Anyway, there's always hair dye. My husband's recently started using it.'

Daniel snorts and settles back in his chair. 'Never. I haven't got a problem with looking my age. I appreciate having the chance to grow older, to be honest.' He stares into his glass as though he's seeing shadows from the past.

'How long ago did your wife die?' I ask, gently.

'Six years ago in a car accident, just after Caleb's third birthday. He was with her in the car but he escaped unhurt, thank goodness. She'd have been so relieved about that.' He continues gazing into his drink as the dark shadow of a bat swoops outside, close to the window.

'I'm so sorry about your wife. Did you say that you and Caleb moved in with Luna earlier this year?'

He looks up. 'That's right. We lived on our own for ages, near Worcester. But Caleb started having problems at school a few months ago and I'd just changed my job, so we thought we'd make a fresh start, nearer to my new office. We're here with Mum for a while until we find the right place to live.'

'What sort of problems was he having?' I hate the thought of vulnerable Caleb being unhappy at school, and it strikes a chord with me. People who say school is the best time of your life never went to my single-sex establishment. It was an all-girls' bitch-fest that only the strong survived.

Daniel sighs. 'Kids being mean. That kind of thing. Caleb's quite a sensitive soul and it badly affected him. I'm not sure that running away from it was the right thing to do. It was hard to know what to do for the best, but I couldn't bear to see him so upset.' His next two words are almost whispered. 'Not again.'

Poor lad. Only nine and he's already been through so much. They both have.

'I'm sure a fresh start will do Caleb the world of good,' I say, and then I cringe inside. That sounds like such a platitude, especially from a woman who has no idea what's best for a child. 'Sometimes an escape is for the best,' I add, lamely.

Daniel suddenly sits up straight in his chair and shakes his head as though he's ridding himself of memories. 'And what about you,

Flora? What brings you to Luna's home for the lost and lonely? You told me you'd separated from your husband. What did you say his name is – Marvin?'

'Malcolm. Yes, I walked out almost a week ago.'

'Why? Did you stop loving him?'

I'm taken aback by Daniel's direct question. He's obviously not a man who beats about the bush. I hesitate, not sure how to reply. Of course I didn't just stop loving Malcolm and I miss him horribly – his bombastic confidence, the warmth of his body at night when I roll over in bed, his awful jokes. It feels wrong that he's not by my side. But I can't bear to be with him at the moment. I'm stuck.

'I shouldn't pry,' says Daniel, sucking his bottom lip between his teeth.

'It's all right. Your question just threw me.' I take a deep breath. 'We run a restaurant in Oxford – well, Malcolm does – and I found out a few days ago that he's been having an affair with one of the waitresses, a woman called Marina. She's much younger than me.' That last bit isn't really relevant but the age gap has really got under my skin. 'Anyway, he's been lying to me so I left him.'

Humiliation washes over me. How long was I in the dark about my husband's predilection for nubile young blondes?

'He sounds like a dick,' declares Daniel.

When I splutter into my glass, wine goes up my nose. 'I suppose he is a bit. Mind you, he thinks I'm an idiot when it comes to business.'

'Why?'

I shrug and start dabbing the splashes of wine on my T-shirt with a tissue. 'I don't know. I suppose he doesn't trust me to make good decisions that benefit my business. He couldn't see the point of me getting involved in the Charter Day celebrations, for example.'

'Is that the bash to celebrate 900 years of markets that Luna mentioned the other day? I don't suppose getting involved in something like that will make you rich, but it might get you some brownie points with the locals, which won't hurt. Sometimes the whole point is just being involved.'

'Exactly!'

When I smile at Daniel, he raises the bottle and waves it in my direction. 'Another glass or three? You haven't got far to stagger to bed.'

As he moves, a lock of thick hair flops over one eye and he pushes it away impatiently. Dark curls are touching the back of his collar and I realise he looks more like an artist than an accountant. A handsome artist, tortured by suppressed creativity and lost love. Blimey, where did that come from? Has the wine gone to my head? I've hardly looked at another man since I got married. Occasional flutterings of lust over handsome actors didn't count because they were no threat to my relationship with Malcolm. Idris Elba was hardly likely to turn up on my doorstep declaring undying love, was he? But now my marriage is in tatters and Daniel is right here in front of me, all brooding intensity and floppy hair, and I can't escape the fact that he's a very attractive man. It's a good job he doesn't much like me.

'Are you all right?' Daniel leans forward and frowns. 'You're miles away.'

'Not really. Just thinking that I need to be up early for work tomorrow. So I'd better pass on the drink and head for bed.' I carefully place my wine glass on the side table, beneath the row of colourful prayer flags tacked to the wall.

Daniel nods and sinks back into his chair. 'At least a boring office job means I get Saturdays off. Though Caleb will make sure I don't get a lie-in. I rather foolishly promised to take him to football practice.'

He watches me as I stand up and stretch. There's something I need to say. 'It's not ideal, me being here, but I'm not trying to take advantage of your mum, you know. I'm grateful for the room and I'll be moving on when I know what I'm doing. Everything's a bit up in the air at the moment.'

Daniel stares at me for a few moments. 'Fair enough. It turns out we're both seeking solace at Starlight Cottage. Turn the light off, will you, on your way out?'

I flick the lamp switch and leave him drinking alone, in the dark.

The cottage is chilly and full of shadows as I get ready for bed and I'm glad to finally slip beneath the sheets. But sleep eludes me as the minutes tick by and I stare at the ceiling, wondering if the bursts of attraction I feel for Daniel are some kind of subconscious revenge. *Hey, Malcolm. Stop snogging Marina for a minute and look at me, drinking wine with a tall, dark, handsome man.* That would be a bit pathetic, wouldn't it?

I'm still awake an hour later when Daniel creaks up the stairs to his bedroom.

Chapter Eight

The whole of Honeyford appears to be going to the Charter Day meeting. Hordes of people are filing under the honey-coloured arches of the market house, climbing the stairs and spilling into the room above. Although I've arrived early, it's hard to find a seat unless I want to sit right at the front of the room – and I'd rather not. That seems a bit presumptuous for a newcomer to the town.

Eventually, I squeeze into a spare seat at the back and nod at Becca, who's just sidled in. She's dressed in black jeans and a drab grey T-shirt but she's still hard to miss with her bright hair and big green eyes. I wasn't expecting her to come along because she hates crowds – and I can't shake the feeling she's only here to support me and The Cosy Kettle. She's certainly come on leaps and bounds since the first time we met, when she was having a panic attack in the bookshop. She feels safe and at home in the café now, and she's a hardworking and loyal café manager. But I sometimes forget how anxious she can be outside work.

At first, I didn't fully understand Becca's anxiety. But I've gained new insight since Malcolm's betrayal and now I'm sometimes gripped by panic when I think of the rudderless years ahead. I thought I'd be with him until death us did part, but now, who knows?

'You run the bookshop, don't you?' asks the woman to my left, thankfully interrupting my thoughts. Her lined face is caked in powder and she smells strongly of roses.

'I do. I took over the shop a few months ago.'

She dabs her nose with a tissue before pushing it into the top of her handbag. 'Yes, I heard that Ruben had moved on. It's such a shame that the shop's no longer in his hands. He'd been a part of Honeyford for decades, man and boy.'

I don't quite know what to say to that. *Sorry for not being born here?*

'I hear you're making changes,' she continues, wrinkling her nose at 'changes' as though it's a dirty word.

'We've increased the range of our stock and opened a café with a little garden at the back. You should call in and see us sometime. I'm Flora, by the way. And you are?'

I'll never find out because a rotund man with a florid face walks onto the stage at the front of the room and the crowd falls silent.

The lady beside me stiffens. 'Have you come across Alan before?' she whispers. When I shake my head, she purses her lips. 'Prepare to be deafened.'

She's not joking. I wondered why there were still empty chairs in the front row but now all becomes clear.

'Thank you all for coming tonight,' bellows Alan, going even redder in the face. 'Most of you know me. My name is Alan and I'm the chairman – sorry, I think it's more politically correct to say chair' – he rolls his eyes at a stick-thin woman sitting to his right – 'of the Honeyford Heritage Society. We're here to talk about the 900th anniversary of the Honeyford Charter and how you can get involved.' He emphasises 'you' and points his finger at us. 'I, or rather we, want these celebrations to put Honeyford on the map and mark a major point in this town's history. As well as having fun, we're also hoping to raise lots of money to repair the community centre roof as it's in a shocking state and letting in rain. So' – he takes a deep breath – 'we're going to host a festival on the actual charter day, the third of August, which, as luck would have it, is a Saturday. Already planned are duck races on the river for the children, a community barbecue in the Memorial Park in the evening with a few fireworks, and a re-enactment of King Henry the First visiting Honeyford. I'll be playing the monarch, of course.' He puffs out his chest and carries on bellowing. 'So what else can we do? Or rather, what can you, the good townsfolk of Honeyford, contribute to the celebration?'

There's a moment's silence from everyone – we're just grateful that the shouting has stopped – and then people start putting up their hands and offering suggestions. Amy from the sweet shop suggests a treasure hunt with a confectionery hamper as the prize, Vernon the butcher offers to help with the barbecue, and Luna, who came straight from her shop and is sitting nearer the front, offers to do tarot readings. A few people start muttering at this idea but Luna sits quietly until the mumblings have ceased.

As other suggestions come in thick and fast from the people around me, Becca catches my eye and gives a little nod. She thinks we ought to be involved but I'm still not sure. Malcolm's disapproval is hard to shake and, whatever I do, I'll never match up to Ruben in the eyes of some locals. I steal a glance at the powder-caked woman next to me, whose fingers are still shoved in her ears. Plus, I'm emotionally knackered and it's probably unwise to take on more work while my marriage is in tatters. What's the point?

Suddenly I hear Daniel's voice in my head, which is rather disconcerting: '*Sometimes the whole point is just being involved*'. My hand shoots up and Alan spots me before I have time to gather my thoughts.

'That lady there, I don't believe we've met. Who are you?'

'My name's Flora and I run the bookshop and The Cosy Kettle Café,' I say, getting to my feet. 'I'm just registering that we'd like to be a part of the celebrations.'

'Excellent! So what can you offer?'

'What about…?' Jeez, now everyone's looking at me and my mind has gone blank. Their first impression of the new woman who's taken over from Ruben won't be a good one at this rate. I swallow hard. 'Details to be confirmed later but we'll run some sort of writing event during the day and, um…' Becca starts stirring her hand round and round. Is she telling me to wind things up and stop talking? As I hesitate, she mimes putting something into her mouth and chewing. Ah, what a brilliant idea!

'And, um, what?' barks Alan.

'And a Honeyford Bake-Off! We'll run a baking contest with the prizewinning cakes being sold in the café and profits going to the community centre.'

A murmur of approval hums around the room.

'Excellent!' booms Alan, nodding at the thin woman who's making notes. 'That's Honeyford Bake-Off, open to all keen cooks, and a high-profile writing event to round off the day.'

I certainly didn't use the words 'high profile'… But Alan has already moved on to someone else and, by the time the meeting ends, he's extracted promises of support from almost everyone in the room. There's something about Alan that reminds me of Malcolm – maybe it's his bombastic nature and refusal to take no for an answer. He's not as good-looking as Malcolm but, on the other hand, maybe he's not cheating on his wife.

I sigh and wonder what sort of high-profile event I can organise. It needs to be interesting, entertaining, informative and popular with local people if my bookshop and I are going to make our mark on the town. No pressure, then!

It's going to mean a lot of extra work but I don't regret volunteering to be involved. Malcolm's probably right and Charter Day won't make me any money. But as long as I don't mess things up, it'll give me a chance to make my mark on this tiny town that I'd like to be a part of my future.

Chapter Nine

It's Sunday afternoon, rain is hammering down and I'm planning to curl up in Luna's tiny summer house in the garden and lose myself in a book. Leaving Malcolm has only reinforced my view that books offer an escape to less challenging worlds.

Combine a good novel with a packet of salt-and-vinegar crisps and a cool lager, and the magic is complete. Malcolm disapproves of flavoured crisps – he says they're for people with unrefined palates – so eating them feels like a mini-rebellion.

I haven't made it to the summer house yet – I'm still in the kitchen, chatting to Luna – but I've already started on the crisps. I crunch into another one and wince as a sour, salty tang bursts onto my taste buds. I intend to make my palate as unrefined as possible. The only fly in the ointment is the fact that I don't have a novel to curl up with and read. I finished the Le Carré I was reading yesterday and I forgot to choose something else from the shop before coming home. The irony isn't lost on me – I'm a bookseller without a book.

'Not a problem,' says Luna, who's up to her elbows in flour at the kitchen worktop, when I ask if she has a book I can borrow. She puts the bread dough to one side and places her floury hands on her hips. 'We have plenty of children's books and lots of mine that you probably won't be interested in. The thrillers and suchlike are all on a bookcase in Daniel's room. You could have a look in there.'

'I'll wait for Daniel to get back,' I tell her; I'm not keen on going into Daniel's room unannounced. 'I can help you instead.'

But Luna's having none of it. 'I'm almost done here, and Daniel won't mind if you nip in and choose a book. He might not be back for ages and it's a shame to lose out on an afternoon of reading; Caleb was angling for a milkshake once the film's finished and I expect Daniel will go along with it. He's a good father.'

'I know.' I bite my lip. 'You're sure he wouldn't mind?'

'Quite sure if you just nip in and choose a book. Simple!'

Hmm. Nothing seems simple when it comes to Daniel. I find myself treading on eggshells around him – never sure what to say – and he seems to feel the same way about me. I don't think he'd approve of me going into his room uninvited. But the lure of an afternoon reading session is too strong and I'm soon loitering outside Daniel's bedroom. The door's closed and I knock, even though Daniel is miles away at the cinema. How awkward would it be if Luna was wrong and he'd just got out of the shower?

I puff out my cheeks and think of something else – anything else: book orders from this week; the tall beech tree outside the shop, which is in full leaf; Becca's newly dyed sapphire-blue hair. But it's no use. As well as registering that Daniel Purfoot can be a pain in the backside, my currently bonkers brain has also noticed that he's an extremely handsome man, and it keeps chucking lascivious images my way. Imagine if I opened the door and Daniel was inside, wrapped in a towel and still dripping. My brain would probably implode.

Pushing the image of Daniel half-naked to one side, I give the door a shove with my foot and it opens wide. Phew, the room's empty. With a quick glance along the landing, I step inside and look around. I have to admit that choosing a book isn't the only reason I'm here. I'm also curious to see what Daniel's bedroom is like. He gives so little of himself away; maybe his room will reveal more about him.

The first thing I notice is that, compared to the rest of the cottage, it's very blokey in here. Most of the other rooms are crammed with mismatched furniture, candles on every available surface and dreamcatchers hanging from beams where you're most likely to bang your head on them.

But Daniel's room is a candle- and dreamcatcher-free zone. It's relatively sparsely furnished with only a high double bed, a small pine wardrobe, a white-painted bedside table and a low bookcase. The midnight-blue quilt on the bed has silver moons and golden stars appliqued to it, and the fabric looks old and heavy. The view from his window takes in the stream at the bottom of the garden and the small clump of apple trees that Luna ambitiously refers to as her orchard. Thick dark clouds are scudding across the top of the hill.

Everything in here is very tidy – from the novels in the bookcase to the clothes hanging neatly in the wardrobe. The wardrobe door has swung open and I can see half-a-dozen shirts plus jeans and trousers hanging on rails, and a small pile of folded sweaters. They're all in muted shades of blue and grey. I run my fingers over a soft dove-grey sweater on top of the pile but quickly pull my hand back, feeling as though I'm snooping. Which, I guess, I basically am.

Guilt starts prickling at the back of my neck as I move to the bookcase and start scanning the titles. I've already read the more modern books and the older ones don't pique my interest. There's a big, black *Compendium of Witchcraft and Wizardry* but I'm feeling rather overwhelmed these days by magic and mysticism. I need something more down to earth and real. *Pick one, Flora, and get the hell out of here!*

My eye's suddenly caught by a small framed photo on top of the bookcase. A toddler is peering out of the picture – a boy with blonde hair and chubby cheeks who's sitting on a young woman's lap. The woman is pretty with fair hair swept back from her face into a ponytail. She's laughing at whoever's taking the photo and clasping her arms around the child, as though she can't bear to let him go. It must be Caleb and his mum. I peer at the picture, wondering with a stab of sorrow how long after the photo was taken she had to let him go forever.

Now I feel mega-guilty. Being in here without Daniel's permission is wrong, whatever Luna says. It's like intruding on someone's private grief. It's time to leave but, before I get to the door, I spot a pile of books on Daniel's bedside table and hesitate. What does Daniel read for pleasure? A person's choice of reading material offers a window to their soul. I'm not sure who said that – it might have been Callie – but it's probably true. Surely it wouldn't do any harm to have a quick peek?

I tiptoe to the pile and start rifling through it. There are a couple of thrillers, a biography of Churchill and the latest Robert Harris. So far, nothing terribly unexpected. The book at the bottom of the pile is face down. What will it be? I wonder, picking it up and turning it over, *The Beauty of Numbers,* perhaps, or a guide to becoming more charming?

I am very, *very* wrong. The paperback is called *Day of Desire* and the front cover shows an attractive woman with full red lips in a clinch with a handsome young man. Well, that's literally a turn up for the books! Macho Daniel Purfoot appears to be reading a steamy romance novel by an author called April Devlin. I've never heard of her.

People's choice of books often surprises me when they come into the shop – the farmer who's into obscure medieval poetry or the goth who orders a book on economics. But I'd never have taken Daniel for a reader of torrid romance. I glance at the blurb on the back of the book:

Forty-something Felicia Paulson has everything she wants in life – two lovely children, a wonderful husband and a beautiful home. Or so she thinks, until one day handsome stranger Gregor McKinley knocks on her door and blurts out a secret. A secret that will take Felicia and Gregor to hell and back, and into each other's arms.

Blimey, it sounds a bit cheesy. I'm having another look at the cover photo when the door creaks open and I almost die of fright.

'Hell's teeth!' I drop the book onto the bed as though it's red-hot. Daniel's tall frame is filling the doorway and blocking the light from the landing. 'You made me jump.'

'I do appear to have that effect on you,' says Daniel, narrowing his eyes. He steps into the room, pushes the door to behind him and folds his arms. 'What exactly are you doing in here?'

'I'm so sorry. I didn't mean to snoop.'

Daniel raises a dark eyebrow and glances at the abandoned book on his bedspread. 'And yet you were.' He crosses to the rain-spattered window, his long limbs fluid. He moves just like Luna.

'This probably looks really bad. And I'm sorry for being in here but I was looking for a book to read and Luna, your mother' – I sigh, because obviously he knows that Luna is his mother – 'anyway,' I burble on, 'she said it would be OK for me to go through the bookcase in here. To pick a book to read in the summer house. I would have waited but she said you'd be ages. Because of the milkshake.'

Daniel stands in front of the window, light falling on his sharp cheekbones and raven-black hair. He looks rather spooky, here in Luna's cottage with its old beams and low ceilings. I shudder and hope he doesn't notice.

'Surely the books you might be interested in are over there, on the bookcase, rather than by my bed?' He points at the bookshelves while, behind him, the trees in Luna's garden bend in the summer gale.

'I've had a look through the bookcase and couldn't see anything suitable. I was just leaving when I spotted the ones on your bedside table and I thought they looked interesting. I'm sorry. I shouldn't have pried.'

Daniel walks towards me, picks the book up off the bed and turns it over and over in his hands, without saying anything.

'It's not the sort of book I expected you to like,' I gabble, feeling horribly wrong-footed. Which is hardly surprising when I've basically been caught poking through his private things. *This isn't who I am,* I want to tell him – or it wasn't before my marriage imploded.

Daniel looks at me, his eyes steely. 'You seem to be very adept at judging what you think I should be like, when you hardly know me at all. What did you think would be my book of choice? Some dry accountancy textbook, I suppose.'

'No,' I protest, rather too quickly. 'Um, is it good?' When I gesture at the book, Daniel pauses and then thrusts the novel at me.

'I don't know. What do you think, seeing as you're the book expert?'

'Selling books doesn't make me a literary expert,' I mutter, grabbing the book before it falls onto the floor. 'Um, I'm not sure—'

'Not your cup of tea? Is it too lowbrow for your sophisticated literary tastes? Perhaps you only read Dostoevsky, Shakespeare and Proust.'

'Not at all.' I know I'm in the wrong but his sneering attitude is starting to grate on me. After all, it's not me who's been caught reading romantic potboilers.

I've turned to leave when Daniel speaks again. 'I'd be interested in your opinion, if you can spare the time to read it.' He sounds less certain of himself all of a sudden, which throws me. Why does he care one jot what I think about his reading material? 'You said you didn't have anything to read. And I dare say you think of yourself as open-minded.'

Did he emphasise 'think? I tuck the book under my arm and nod. 'Of course. I'll give it a go if you've finished with it.' If he's that bothered, I can quickly scan through the book, leave it a few days for appearance's sake, and then give him my opinion. Simple – though the whole thing makes me uneasy, as though it's some sort of test: is the bookseller able to adequately critique a novel?

'Wonderful,' he says, striding to the door and opening it wide. 'Now if you don't mind, Caleb and I got caught in the storm and I need to get changed, unless you're planning to stay while I do that?'

As if. It's just as well he doesn't know I was imagining him in a towel just a short while ago. Daniel stands back so I can get past him and I scoot along the landing with my cheeks burning with embarrassment, and his book of choice clutched to my chest.

A few days later, I sit sipping my coffee and turn another page. The afternoon book club will be arriving any minute and I need to get everything ready, but I'm hooked on the book that was by Daniel's bed.

My plan to read the first chapter and scan through the rest was upended just a few pages in. *Day of Desire* does not belong to my genre of choice. Give me a clever political thriller or a historical biography and I become a total bookworm. But Daniel's bedtime reading is the embodiment of why the old cliché – never judge a book by its cover – is bang on. Especially when the cover doesn't do the story justice.

To my surprise, I've been swept up in the story of a middle-aged woman trying to negotiate her own feelings when her everyday life is upended by a romantic stranger. It's a little cheesy in places and could do with another edit, but I'm taken aback by the depth and range of emotion portrayed. The writing itself is pretty good and I'm finding myself swept along by the plot.

'You look engrossed, love.'

Phyllis has come into the café, being pushed in her wheelchair by Millicent.

Did she just call me '*love*'? Members of the book club sometimes call Callie and Becca 'love', but I don't think any of them have ever referred to me in that way before. Maybe I'm growing on Phyllis. I smile at her and close the book reluctantly – our heroes are about to make up after an unfortunate misunderstanding and I'm desperate to know what happens next.

'I am engrossed, but I can get back to it later. Why don't you two get settled while Becca gets you a coffee? She knows what you both like.'

Millicent wheels the chair as close to the table as she can and takes a seat nearby. The two women have struck up a friendship even though they make a very odd couple. Widowed Phyllis, grey-haired and in her seventies with a smiley round face, looks like everyone's idea of a sweet grandmother. Millicent, in her fifties and sharp-featured, with ash-blonde hair and a philandering husband, looks like the kind of grandmother who'd smack the back of your legs.

Stanley and Dick have just wandered into the café and I give them a wave. Stanley's wearing black jeans that hang off his skinny frame and there's a chain from the front loop into his back pocket. He spots me glancing at the chain and winks. 'I'm down with the kids, Flora. Did I tell you that I'm getting a stud in my nose on Friday? A big diamanté one with scalloped edges. It's proper lush.'

Dick sighs beside him and smooths down his long white beard. He looks like a bald Father Christmas.

'Does Callie know about the piercing?' I ask. Callie's nipped into the bookshop to hold the fort while I'm running the book club but she hasn't mentioned her granddad's latest piercing plan. 'She was pretty surprised when you turned up with an earring.'

'Ah, Callie doesn't care what I get up to now she's all loved up with that Noah boy,' says Stanley. But he grins to show how delighted he is by his beloved granddaughter's happiness. 'Mind you, he's made her ill with all that kissing. She's had a rotten cold. Did you know that the mouth is one of the dirtiest parts of the human body and saliva is basically bacterial soup?'

I did not. And I wish I still didn't.

'I've tried to talk him out of having his nose pierced, silly old fool,' mutters Dick, Stanley's decades-long friend, 'but he's threatening to have a Prince Albert instead if I don't shut up about it.'

'What's that?' asks Millicent, leaning towards them. She turns ashen-grey when Stanley whispers the answer in her ear. He's incorrigible.

Fortunately, Becca brings the conversation to a close by arriving with the coffees. And we all call out a welcome to Knackered Mary when she scurries in with Callum, who's strapped to her chest in a sling. Mary sinks onto a chair, smiles at us and pushes her long brown hair back from her pretty face. She's slowly adjusting to the demands of motherhood – especially now Callum, the screamiest baby on the planet, will sometimes peacefully gum a rusk to death for five minutes.

'Shall we get on then if we're all here?' says Millicent, grumpily. But she reaches out her hand and gently strokes the top of Callum's head. And no one seems to mind – or at least they hide their disappointment well – when I say that I'll be running the book club this afternoon, rather than Callie.

As we start discussing *A Tale of Two Cities,* I look round my little group of afternoon-book-club oddballs and misfits with affection. Our evening book club is much better attended and it would make sense, in many ways, to amalgamate the two. The coffees and cakes bought by afternoon club members hardly covers our time. But I've come to realise that local bookshops and cafés are about more than profits and the bottom line. They're about being a part of the community, easing loneliness and spreading the love of literature. Though Malcolm would say I'm being sentimental.

Thinking of Malcolm lowers my mood so I try to concentrate on the *Tale of Two Cities* discussion instead. It's pretty lively, though I'm not convinced Stanley has read the book at all as he keeps referring to the Dirk Bogarde film. Millicent picks the book apart in forensic detail and declares that Dickens is 'marvellous if one can overlook his reliance on coincidence'. Phyllis states that she's in love with Sydney Carton but found the book rather hard-going and Becca murmurs that she enjoyed the story. Mary's only halfway through the book but we give her a pass because Callum has been teething.

'So I know that we're reading *Cider with Rosie* next, but what about after that?' asks Dick, who's really getting into book club now he's realised that the teacher at school who told him he was stupid was, in fact, pretty stupid herself.

'Yes, let's read something we can't put down. Something a bit less worthy,' says Phyllis. 'What about this one? You looked engrossed when we came in, Flora.' She points at *Day of Desire*, which is still lying on the table.

Millicent peers at the front cover and does a double take. 'I'm surprised at you, Flora. You've got a shop full of books and you choose to read one like that.'

Resistance from Millicent to anything other than the classics is inevitable. She always moans, even though she's enjoyed the occasional modern bestseller. Not that she'd ever admit it. She stays quiet instead when we're discussing the book and grunts rather than giving her opinion. I didn't much like Millicent at first. But I've been less judge-mental since realising that she's lonely now her kids have left home. Her husband's still around but isn't attentive – not with her anyway. It's a different story when it comes to the young PA who sees to his needs inside the office – and out, if Millicent's suspicions are right. And, thinking of Malcolm, they probably are.

'You're not being a snob, are you, Millie?' asks Stanley. 'I think we should give Flora's novel a go.' He takes the book from me and raises a bushy grey eyebrow at its steamy cover. 'I'll try anything once. Absolutely anything.' He twists his head to get a better look at the cover image.

Dick whistles softly and gives me a *what is he like?* stare.

'Huh.' Millicent sinks back in her chair, highly offended at being called Millie, as Stanley knew she would be. 'I didn't think a respected bookseller like Flora would recommend that we read this kind of book.'

'Do you know what?' I take the book from Stanley and flick through its pages, being careful to avoid the ending. 'In my opinion, you should all read this book. It's well written, the characterisation is great and the plot pulls you along. Plus it's good to read something you might never normally choose.'

'I'd never choose to read that in a million years,' huffs Millicent, folding her arms. 'What would my neighbours think if they saw this on my coffee table? They went into meltdown when the paperboy delivered

The Sunday Sport to them rather than *The Sunday Times*. Personally, I think he did it on purpose because they didn't tip him at Christmas.'

'I think reading something a bit less stuffy is a great idea,' pipes up Phyllis. 'Can you get some copies in and we'll give it a go?'

'Of course, and I can lend you my copy, Millicent, once I've got to the end, if you really don't want to buy the book. Anyway,' I add, changing the subject, 'what about the high-profile event I'm supposed to be organising for Charter Day? I presume you've all heard that we're taking part in the festival?'

'We're planning a bake-off in The Cosy Kettle,' says Becca, eyes glowing. I've put her in charge of the baking contest and she's already coming up with loads of ideas.

'And I was thinking it would be great to have an author speaking at an event in the afternoon. So we can pull people in and help to make Charter Day really special.' I grin, because the more I think about it, the more I'm looking forward to being a part of Honeyford's celebrations. 'It's a bit last minute but who could we get to speak at Honeyford Bookshop?'

'J.K. Rowling,' suggests Dick, bless him. 'Or Lee Childs.'

'It doesn't need to be someone that well known, really. Just an author of a book that people have enjoyed who can talk to us about the writing process and answer some questions,' I say, touched by Dick's faith that my little shop could pull in a big name.

'I could always ask Sebastian, I suppose, seeing as it's a good cause,' mutters Millicent, still smarting at *Day of Desire* being the club's next book of choice.

'Sebastian?'

'Sebastian Kinsley. He owes me a favour after I didn't complain too much when he vomited in my begonias.'

'As in S.R. Kinsley?' I ask, incredulously.

'S.R. who?' asks Dick, who must be the only reader unfamiliar with S.R. Kinsley's extensive back catalogue of highly regarded bestsellers, including one that's been optioned by a major Hollywood studio. I've read that Tom Hanks's people are in talks about it.

'The one and only S.R. Kinsley,' says Millicent, ignoring Dick's question. 'My husband has known him for a few years and he's come to one or two of my little soirées. I could ask him, I suppose.'

'Wow, Millicent. That would be fantastic. He'd be such a draw,' I say, grinning even more widely at the thought of such a high-profile event in Honeyford. 'Could you ask him, please?'

'I suppose so. Though you'll have to keep this kind of stuff away from him because he writes award-winning literary fiction.' She picks up *Day of Desire* with her finger and thumb and grimaces before dropping it, with a thud, onto the table. She *is* a massive book snob but, hey, she knows S.R. Kinsley so there's no way I'm going to challenge her on it right now.

'We'll also need to meet to discuss the parade,' declares Stanley. 'When are you going to start sorting that out, Flora? It'll take a while for me to pull a suitably hip costume together.'

'What do you mean?'

'Don't you know about the Charter Parade? Everyone's talking about it. Townsfolk will be marching from the war memorial to the park on the Saturday afternoon.'

'I do know about it, but the shop and café won't be taking part. There's only two of us, me and Becca – three, if you count Callie calling in to help sometimes – and we're all going to be busy sorting out charter events.'

'That won't do,' pipes up Phyllis. 'You're part of the town and you need to be involved, and fortunately you have us. The afternoon book club can take part in the parade and fly the flag for The Cosy Kettle. Can't we, Millie?' She nudges Millicent, who sniffs but doesn't say no. 'And you'll take part, Mary, won't you? And Dick?'

Mary nods but Dick folds his arms across his skinny chest. 'Only if Flora's in overall charge of the whole thing. No one wants Stanley in charge. No offence, but he's gone completely loopy since his eightieth birthday.'

'You say "loopy", dude. I say "authentic",' drawls Stanley, making a peace sign with his fingers. 'I've finally become my true self, and not before time. But it's probably best if Flora co-ordinates everything so I can devote more time to sorting out my wardrobe for the occasion.'

Taking on even more to organise right now isn't wise, but I'm too chuffed by Phyllis saying 'you're part of the town' to protest. She probably means the shop and café, rather than me, but I've still got a warm glow of belonging that blots out any concerns about what exactly Stanley's 'hip costume' might entail.

Two hours later, I've finished ordering customers' books as the clock clicks ever closer to five thirty. The door is propped open because it's so hot today, and snatches of conversation are floating into the shop when people wander past. I glance down at *Day of Desire*: it's calling to me from under the counter. I so want to know what happens, but there's no point in getting stuck into the story now, just before I head back to Starlight Cottage.

April Devlin is picked out in silver across the bottom of the cover and I do a quick search online of her name plus *author*, but nothing particularly relevant comes up, apart from a link to her book. April doesn't appear to be very hot on self-marketing. Why go to all the trouble of writing a book – a really good book – and not shout about it? Without some promotion it's likely to sink without a trace.

With a few clicks, I order some copies of her novel for the afternoon book club, and the evening book club too. Then, I add a dozen extra copies to sell in the shop. The books will take up precious shop space and Malcolm will say that taking a punt on an unknown author with no online presence is foolish. But April's thoughtful, insightful book has touched me; it deserves to be read and, as a bookseller, I'm ideally placed to champion a book that I love.

'Who cares what Malcolm will say?' I mutter, which feels rather like committing heresy after two decades in his business shadow. But times have changed and I can do whatever I like with my business. Whether it stands or falls depends on me and me alone.

Sadly, my sudden rush of confidence fades quickly while I'm switching off my computer. Malcolm can be bossy when it comes to business but he knows a lot more than me. Maybe I shouldn't have been so hasty in ordering so many copies of *Day of Desire*, but it's done now.

I slip Daniel's copy of the novel into my bag and start cashing up so I can close the shop.

Chapter Ten

There's something about Starlight Cottage that lifts my mood as I bump along the potholed track towards it. Maybe it's the mellow yellow stone surrounded by green countryside, or the smoke curling from the chimney that tells me Luna's home.

Whatever the reason, I'm smiling as I step out of my car and shoo away a chicken that scuttles over to peck at my feet. The situation with Malcolm is still a mess but there are good things in my life: this gem of a cottage, Charter Day excitement, the bookshop and The Cosy Kettle – and the kindness of strangers.

Luna stepped in to help when I was at a low ebb and I'll always be grateful to her for that. I open the back door of the car and take out the large bunch of pink and purple peonies I bought on the way home. Giving her flowers is rather 'coals to Newcastle' because the cottage is surrounded by banks of pretty primroses and cornflowers. But it's the thought that counts.

I've negotiated the front door's low-hanging dreamcatcher and almost reached the kitchen when an unwelcome thought strikes me. What if Luna doesn't approve of cut flowers? She apologised to the fruit and veg patch the other day before picking broad beans and strawberries. So she'll probably take one look at the perfect peonies and accuse me of unnecessary floricide. But it's too late now.

'Daniel, is that you?' drifts from the kitchen.

'No, it's me,' I say, walking into the room, which is blisteringly sauna-hot. Seemingly oblivious to the heat, Luna is stirring a wooden spoon around her black cauldron. The flames underneath it are sending smoke up the wide stone chimney.

'Ah, Flora. It's good to see you. Do you fancy some Mediterranean stew later, with lots of herbs?'

'Yes please. It smells delicious. You're such a good cook, Luna.'

'Thank you.' Luna smiles and pushes strands of silver hair under the trailing lilac scarf around her head. 'It's very nice to have people to cook for.'

'The cottage must have been a bit lonely when you were living here on your own.'

'Not really. I'm enjoying having people around the place again, but I've never felt truly alone here because this cottage is full of souls.'

That's just the kind of thing Luna says that makes the back of my neck prickle. The kind of thing I remember when I wake in the early hours and have to switch the light on for comfort.

'What are those, Flora?' Luna points at the peonies I've tucked under my arm. Their smell is mingling with the thick aroma of herbs that's flooding the room.

'These are for you, to thank you for being so welcoming,' I say, proffering them at her and hoping she'll accept them in the spirit they're intended.

Luna puts down her wooden spoon, scoops up the flowers and buries her nose in the deep pink and purple petals.

'They're absolutely gorgeous, Flora. Thank you so much, but you really shouldn't have.'

You really shouldn't have because you're condoning floral murder? I'm relieved when Luna starts humming as she fills a pottery vase with water and arranges the peonies. That's got to be a good sign.

I've just peeled off my cardigan, and I'm contemplating shedding more clothing, when my phone beeps with a text. My stomach lurches when I see it's from Malcolm, but I take a deep breath and open it: *Flora – hope you are well. I have exciting news. Will call into shop tomorrow. M x*

That's it. Short and to the point, though I'm not sure what that point is. 'Hope you are well' sounds terribly formal but then he's signed off with a kiss. Heaven knows what his 'exciting news' could be.

My rollercoaster mood dips and Luna looks up from her flower arranging.

'Is everything all right, Flora?'

'Yeah, fine, thanks.'

Luna wafts over in her flowing turquoise tunic and places the vase of flowers in the middle of the table. 'Why don't you go and relax in the garden until tea's ready?'

'I was going to help you get things ready.'

'I'm all organised so there's no need.' Luna takes a firm hold of my elbow, pulls me to my feet and guides me to the open back door. 'Off you go,' she says, almost pushing me outside. 'And don't come back in until it's time to eat.' Then she talks about my chakras being blocked and how steeping myself in nature will help to get my prana flowing. Or something like that. I don't really understand her but I get the gist, and she's right that her beautiful garden makes me feel better.

Ahead of me, the lawn runs towards the vegetable patch and, beyond, there are trees in full leaf and fabulous views across the valley. I settle into a shabby striped deckchair on the grass and breathe out slowly. This garden isn't always a haven of peace. Caleb's often running around with the cat or playing football with his dad, and there's often a background hum of tractors in the fields or cars on the country lane. But this evening there's only the sound of birdsong and water tumbling over stones in the stream, as the sun slides towards the hill.

It's the perfect place to relax but, although I close my eyes, my muscles feel tense. The thought of seeing Malcolm tomorrow has made me jittery. It would be so much easier if I could hate him for betraying me, but I just can't. Hating someone you've loved for over twenty years isn't so easy, whatever he's done.

I sigh and shift about in the deckchair. Luna's always going on about the benefits of meditation so maybe I should give it a go. Anything that might quieten the thoughts tumbling around my brain is worth a try. Luna always meditates cross-legged on the rug in the parlour, with a beatific smile on her face. I'd feel like a prat doing that in the garden, where anyone might see me. So I stay where I am, forget the smile, and just start breathing deeply. *In and out. In and out.* But my thoughts keep coming and they seem even louder: *Can I cope on my own without Malcolm? Will I ever feel a proper part of Honeyford? Who the hell is April Devlin?*

I don't think I'm doing this right. Should I be chanting 'Om', or something? I deliberately slow my breathing even more and I'm just starting to feel more relaxed when I hear a weird noise. It sounds like hiccups.

I sit up and look around me, but there's no one about. Ahead of me, leaves are gently rustling in a soft breeze and there's a myriad of different greens across the valley. From the palest smudge of sludgy moss-green to bright emerald. There are definitely worse places to spend a summer evening, I decide, taking in a deep breath of sweet scented air. The restaurant in Oxford will be hot and airless, in spite of the fans whirling on the ceiling.

I settle back down in the deckchair but jump up when I hear the hiccupping sounds again. They're coming from the huge oak tree that stands on the boundary between Luna's land and the farm beyond. It's only when I get closer that I notice a flash of blue in the branches and realise it's Caleb's trainer.

'Caleb, are you up there? I can see your shoe.'

When there's no answer, I'm tempted to leave him to it. He probably climbs trees all the time. But he's only little and he's a very long way up. What would his mother do if she were here?

I run my fingers across the rough bark and call up into the branches, 'Are you allowed to climb up so high? You'd better come down now before you fall down.'

The only sound is the wind rustling in the leaves, even though I can now make out Caleb's little backside far above my head.

'Caleb, answer me!' My words come out quite sharply and Caleb's white face appears through the leaves. He has red rings around his eyes, as though he's been crying, which worries me even more. If he's upset, he's far more likely to miss his footing on the way down.

'Come down now, Caleb. Very slowly, please. For me.'

After a moment's hesitation, he starts scrambling from branch to branch so quickly that twigs and leaves shower onto the ground.

'Whoa, slow down!' I shout, opening my arms wide to catch him, though he'll probably flatten me. 'If you fall, your dad will kill me.'

I definitely shouldn't have said that to a child whose mother has died. Malcolm's right when he says I'm not good with children. Adults I can cope with, but children make me nervous in inverse proportion to their size. Tiny babies absolutely terrify me. Caleb slithers safely

down the rest of the trunk and stands in front of me with his head
bent. There are stains on his Manchester City football top, and leaves
are poking out from his blonde hair. I brush them away.

'What were you doing up there?'

'Sorry,' mumbles Caleb, still looking at the floor. He gives a loud
hiccup and winces. 'I don't want to get into trouble.'

He stumbles over his words and, instinctively, I put my finger under
his chin and lift his face towards mine. He's definitely been crying.
There are red smudges on his pale cheeks, and a dribble of snot is
pooling on his upper lip. Poor lad.

'Here you go!' I fish in my pocket for a tissue and push it into his
hand. 'You're not in trouble. I was just worried about you being so high
up, and you look a bit upset.' I look around for backup, but there's no
one in the garden except the two of us. Oh, blimey. 'Why don't you
come and sit with me for a minute?'

Caleb scuffs his feet, as though that's the last thing he wants to do,
but he follows me without a word and plonks himself down next to
me on the wooden bench near the stream. There's dirt on his trainers
and a tear in his school trousers above the knee.

'Are you all right?'

'Yep, fine,' he replies, staring at the tumbling water. He dabs his
nose and hiccups some more as a crow swoops low over our heads and
lands on the fence that marks the end of Luna's garden.

'Something's obviously upset you. Would you like to talk about it?'

'Nope,' he replies, still staring straight ahead.

'Are you sure? I know I'm not your… well, you don't know me
properly. But I'd like to help if I can.'

'You can't.' When he gives a tiny, shuddering gulp, I feel so sorry
for him.

'Are you feeling ill, or has something happened at school? It'll be the summer holidays soon and you'll enjoy those, won't you?'

Caleb shrugs and kicks a stone towards the stream. It bounces on the grassy bank and plops into the fast-flowing water.

Honestly, I'm hopeless. If I was touchy-feely like Callie, I'd know exactly which words would coax him to talk. She has a real gift with people. And if I was his mum, I'd put my arms around him and get him to tell me what's wrong. But I'm no one's mum and Caleb is still wary of me. We sit in silence for a few minutes until he suddenly jumps to his feet and stands in front of me.

'Please can I go now?' he asks, still not catching my eye. He turns his foot over and gnaws at the inside of his cheek.

'Of course you can go if you want to. And I'm sorry that you're upset. Whatever's bothering you, I hope it gets sorted out really quickly.'

Caleb finally glances up and gives me a smile that's much too sad for such a small person. 'Thanks,' he mutters, before running indoors for some proper maternal comfort from Luna.

I watch him go and wonder how much having a child would have changed me and Malcolm. Maybe it would have softened my sharper edges, and made Malcolm less self-obsessed, and we'd still be together, united in our love for our child. Or maybe the stress of caring for an infant would have pushed us apart years ago. We'll never know.

Caleb picks at his tea and eats hardly anything, even though it's delicious. Luna really is a whizz with a vegetarian cookbook and a witch's cauldron, and her Mediterranean stew matches any of the posh food served at The Briar Patch.

'You all right, mate?' Daniel asks, ruffling his son's fair hair. 'You usually love Granny's stews. You're not sickening for something, are you?'

'Just not hungry,' mumbles Caleb, pushing food around his plate with his fork.

Luna holds the back of her hand to her grandson's forehead and leans forward to kiss him on the cheek. 'You don't feel like you've got a temperature, but you're definitely not right this evening. Shall I save you some food in case you feel hungry later?'

'Don't bother.' Caleb scrapes his chair back across the quarry tiles. 'Please can I go to my room now?'

Luna glances at Daniel, who shrugs. 'I guess so, if that's all you're going to eat.'

Daniel watches his son walk into the hall, puts down his knife and fork and follows him. Framed in the doorway, he catches up with Caleb, kneels in front of him and says something. I can't hear what he's saying or Caleb's reply because the washing machine in the corner has reached its spin cycle and is drumming up and down on the tiles. Cups and saucers on the worktop above it are rattling like crazy.

Caleb looks at me and then Daniel does the same and narrows his eyes, before he comes back to the table.

Oh, great! What did Caleb say about me? I'm already in Daniel's bad books for rummaging around his bedroom. And I doubt he's truly forgiven me for shouting at his beloved son in The Cosy Kettle. Daniel eats a few more mouthfuls before pushing his plate away. 'I'm going out for a walk, Mum, if that's OK? I could do with clearing my head. Save the washing-up and I'll do it when I get back.'

'Of course, love. Some fresh air will do you good after being cooped up in an office all day.' Luna places her hand on his arm. 'And don't worry about Caleb. He'll be fine.'

'I hope so.' Daniel scrapes the remains of his stew into the compost bin before leaving the kitchen. He doesn't look at me once.

I swallow a few more mouthfuls but hardly taste the food. What did Caleb say?

'Not hungry either?' asks Luna, running her fingers over the chunk of pink rock crystal around her neck. She appears to have a wearable rock for every occasion. She fixes her eyes on me and stares as though she can see into my soul. I wish she'd stop doing that – her weird stares are very disconcerting.

'I've eaten loads and the food's delicious, but I've run out of steam.'

Luna's amber eyes glint in light from the candles on the table. 'You are looking a bit peaky this evening, Flora. Just like Caleb. Maybe you could do with a walk too, to put some colour back in your cheeks. What do you think?'

Before I can reply, she stands up, walks behind me and pulls out my chair so quickly that I almost fall flat on my backside. 'Off you go. You can probably catch up with Daniel if you get a move on. I dare say he's headed off down the lane, towards Greenings Farm. Off you trot!'

'I can stay and get the washing-up done before Daniel gets back.'

'Or I can do it while you're off communing with Mother Earth. Chop-chop or he'll be out of sight.'

There appears to be no arguing with Luna when she's insistent about communing. So I slip on my trainers and jacket and head off into the summer evening. It's still glorious out here. The sun is a huge orb hanging low in the sky and the light is golden. The cottage windows are bright with reflected sunshine and a thick soup of pollen is floating in the air. I glance up at Caleb's room but his window's closed and there's no sign of him.

A walk isn't such a bad idea after being cooped up in the shop for hours. It was so busy today, I only got a ten-minute lunch break. And if I catch up with Daniel, I can let him know that Caleb was upset earlier – and try to find out what Caleb said about me to his dad.

I wander to the end of the winding track that leads to the cottage and look along the lane but I obviously didn't chop-chop quickly enough because Daniel's nowhere in sight. He's got such long legs that he walks really quickly. With a sigh, I start walking as quickly as I can, away from Honeyford and towards the farm that supplies Luna with the vegetables she can't source from her own garden.

The lane is narrow and quiet and lined with trees. A light aircraft is droning overhead and a small bird is hopping along a Cotswold-stone wall that's covered with moss. There's a smell of hot, parched earth and honeysuckle in the air. And I'm rushing to catch up with a man who thinks I'm an idiot who's terrible with kids.

I stop and squint into the distance. Nope, no sign of him. Malcolm always saunters along but Daniel obviously strides out. I puff on up the lane, almost running now, and rush around the corner, straight into the path of a dark figure who steps out from behind a tree.

'Hell's bells!' I yell, instinctively putting my hands up kung-fu style.

Daniel slowly shakes his head. 'Are you following me, Mrs Morgan?'

My heart rate starts returning to normal as Daniel tilts his head towards my still-raised hands. 'I presume you're planning to karate chop me to death.'

I lower them, feeling ridiculous. 'Will you please, for the love of all that's holy, stop making me jump. There's only so much my heart can take.'

Daniel twists his mouth into a sardonic smile. 'I'm sorry if I startled you but I don't like being stalked.'

'I'm not stalking you,' I splutter.

'And yet, here we are,' says Daniel, his eyebrows shooting up and almost meeting his hairline. He's got a point. The last time he startled me, I was in his bedroom rifling through his bedside table.

'It's Luna's fault. She suggested I should go out for a walk and catch up with you. She wouldn't take no for an answer. Something about getting it on with Mother Earth.'

'That does sound like my mother,' he admits.

'I wasn't trying to intrude on your walk, anyway. I just wanted to speak to you about Caleb.'

Daniel's face clouds over. 'Please tell me you didn't chase me along the lane so you can tell tales about him.'

'What on earth are you talking about?'

'My son mentioned that you shouted at him for climbing the oak tree.'

'I didn't shout at him like that, and I don't tell tales on anyone. I'm not a child, for goodness' sake. I saw Caleb in the tree and I thought he might fall. That was all. I wasn't telling him off. I was worried that he might hurt himself. I'm just not great at talking to kids.'

'You think?' murmurs Daniel, but his face softens. 'I apologise for thinking the worst about you. Thank you for looking out for Caleb, but he wouldn't have fallen. He's been climbing that tree for years.'

'I figured as much, but he was upset and I thought he might lose his concentration and fall.'

Daniel stops scuffing his shoes and looks up. 'What was he upset about?'

'I don't know. I did ask but he wouldn't say. That's why I was following you – so I could tell you that something's bothering Caleb, and he'll probably talk to you about whatever it is. That's all.' A silence stretches between us. 'Well, I've told you now, so I'll leave you to your walk and head for home.'

I've turned around and started walking back the way I came when Daniel calls out. 'I was walking to the lake, if you fancy walking with me.'

I stop and look back over my shoulder. 'There's a lake?'

A faint smile plays across Daniel's full mouth. 'There is. Well, don't get your hopes up because it's more of a pond really. But it's a big pond. With dragonflies.' When he moves his arm, I think for a moment he's about to hold out his hand, but he's simply brushing a smudge of dust from his thigh. 'Would you like to see it?'

I hesitate because I've delivered my message and I should head back to Starlight Cottage. Malcolm wouldn't approve of me wandering off to a lake with a handsome man. He doesn't approve of walking for the sake of it – he always takes the car.

'OK,' I reply, before I can change my mind.

Daniel waits for me to walk back to him before setting off again at a cracking pace, with me scurrying to keep up.

After a while, he veers left into a bank of trees dripping with blossom and I follow behind him. It's cooler in here, with patches of sunlight filtering through the leafy canopy. A twig under my foot cracks with the sound of a rifle shot, and two tiny rabbits shoot out of the undergrowth and across my path.

Isn't it funny how life can change so quickly? That's what strikes me as I walk along behind Daniel, with birds singing above us. Not so long ago, everything was normal. I lived with a man who ran a restaurant and my actions were largely ruled by what he wanted. In return, my life was predictable, ordered and safe. Then, I put my head above the parapet, took over a failing bookshop and opened a café. And now, only a couple of months later, I'm walking through a wood with a man who's… dangerous. Not physically dangerous. But when I'm with Daniel I feel uncomfortable and slightly out of control – not my usual sensible self at all. It's obviously best if I keep out of his way, and yet I've deliberately sought him out this evening.

But I can hardly run off now, so I put my head down and follow in his footsteps, between the trees. After walking in silence for a few minutes we emerge from the undergrowth into a large clearing. Banks of trees are reflected in a circular lake that's dotted with blooms of green algae. It's perfectly peaceful here. An oasis of calm amid the maelstrom of everyday life.

Daniel stops walking and opens his arms wide. 'This is rather grandly known by the locals as Honeyheaven Lake, though you might conclude that it's more of a stagnant pond.'

'It is rather pond-like,' I agree, shading my eyes to look at the trees growing on the opposite bank. Branches are trailing in the water and a sudden breeze sends ripples across the surface.

'How did you know that Caleb was upset?' asks Daniel, in one of the swift changes of subject I'm starting to get used to.

I brush blossom from my hair and watch as it floats to the ground. 'He looked distressed and he was hiccupping as though he couldn't catch his breath.'

'He does that when he's been crying. I could tell something wasn't right with him, but I thought it was you. Sorry.' Daniel sighs and runs a hand across his jaw, which is dark with stubble. 'I've no idea what's wrong with him. Caleb keeps things from me sometimes because he wants to protect me. It's daft really when I should be the one protecting him.' A tremor of emotion passes across his face and he turns away, as though he's embarrassed.

'Why don't we stop for a minute and have a breather in the sunshine?' I suggest, gently.

I wander over to a fallen log near the water's edge and sit down. Daniel follows and sits beside me with his arms crossed. I'd love to know more about Caleb but I don't have the courage to ask. Daniel's such a private man and I can't imagine he'd want to open up to a virtual stranger.

So we sit in silence for a while, watching electric-blue dragonflies skimming the lake, and swallows swooping and diving above the trees.

It's perfectly peaceful until I rub my fingers along the rough bark of our makeshift seat and a glossy fat beetle scurries out. *Eew!* Spiders might top my hit list of creatures to avoid but beetles come a close second.

Malcolm's used to me leaping about and yelling when anything with more than four legs comes close. He's very good at removing scary creatures. But I don't want to act like a total prat in front of Daniel, so I grit my teeth and sit still, apart from pulling my top firmly down over the waistband of my trousers – bugs crawling up my jumper would prompt a meltdown.

'How's your job going?' I ask after another couple of minutes, watching the beetle disappear into the long grass that's curling around the log.

'OK. Good, I guess. It's just a job, isn't it? I get there at half past eight and leave at half past five and it helps me to care for my son and it helps Luna to pay the bills. Starlight Cottage is a bit of a money pit.'

'I bet. I hope you don't mind me asking, but why don't you call her Mum?'

'I do, sometimes. But she likes us using her chosen name. She says it helps to distance her from her shadow self.'

'Her what?'

Daniel shrugs. 'I have absolutely no idea.' When he gives a sudden smile, his face lights up. 'She's always been interested in magic and alternative stuff. But it really ramped up after she lost my dad five years ago. She changed her name, moved to the cottage and opened the shop. She reinvented herself.'

'I'm really sorry to hear about your dad. I lost my mum a few years back and my dad at the end of last year.'

'That must have been tough,' he says, softly. 'Losing the people you love is hard.'

'Yes, it is.'

We both sit for a while, watching a duck and two tiny ducklings swim past. Their bodies leave a clear trail in the water where the algae has been pushed aside.

'What was your mum's name before she became Luna?' I ask when the silence overstretches.

Daniel taps the side of his nose. 'That would be telling and she'd have to kill you if you found out.'

I laugh. 'Muriel? Evelyn? Gertrude?'

'Does she look like a Gert?' snorts Daniel.

'Nope. She looks exactly like other-worldly Luna, goddess of the moon.'

When Daniel grins, the furrow between his eyebrows softens and he looks less fierce. 'She does. And she's happy now, which is all that matters, whatever her name is.' He looks at me sideways. 'What about you?'

'My name's always been Flora.'

'You know that's not what I meant. I wondered how you were coping without Malcolm.'

'Oh, you know,' I say, taken aback that Daniel has bothered to remember my husband's name.

'No, I don't know or I wouldn't have asked.'

Crikey. Daniel's conversational style is so different from Malcolm's that it keeps taking me by surprise. Malcolm is all bonhomie and jokes and schmoozing, while Daniel cuts through all that and is just... well, blunt.

I shake my head. 'I'm not sure. The shock of discovering Malcolm had been... you know. That's worn off a bit. I feel more numb about it now, as though it happened to someone else. It helps that I'm keeping busy in the shop and café, and getting involved in the Charter Day celebrations. Millicent, who belongs to our book club, knows S.R. Kinsley and is going to ask him to do a reading and talk in the shop on the day.'

'Wow, *the* S.R. Kinsley? That would be a real coup for Honeyford. I've read all of his books.' Daniel seems genuinely impressed and I mentally cross my fingers that Millicent will come up trumps.

'It's not confirmed, but I'm hopeful. Actually, I'm hopeful about the whole event. We're doing a bake-off in The Cosy Kettle, the café book club want to join the parade through the town, and I'm desperate for it all to be a great success.'

'Why?' asks Daniel, shifting round on the log so he's facing me. His knee is pressing against mine until I move my leg.

'To promote my business.'

Daniel tilts his head to one side and waits, as though he knows I'm not telling him the whole truth. Damn him and his loaded silences; I feel compelled to leap in and fill them.

'I want to be a part of the local community and I think contributing to Charter Day and making a success of things might help people think of me as being one of them. It gets a bit lonely when you don't feel a part of something.'

Daniel nods. 'Honeyford's a very close-knit place and it takes a while for people to really accept you. Luna can tell you all about that.' He picks up a stone and hurls it towards the pond. It plops into the water and green circles ripple away from the impact. 'So has your husband been very involved in the bookshop?'

'He's supportive,' I say, because that's what I always say about Malcolm, even when it's not entirely true.

'That's good.'

'It is good.'

We both stare across the water as white puffs of cloud bubble up behind the trees, and the truth bubbles up inside me.

'OK, I'll tell you,' I blurt out. 'The restaurant is Malcolm's thing. I took on the shop and invested in the café and he sees them as my hobby, really. I don't think he approves.'

'Hobby? Have you supported him with the restaurant?' asks Daniel, apparently unfazed by my torrent of truth.

'Of course.'

'Yet he hasn't supported you with your business venture? That sounds rather unfair.'

He's right. It is unfair. But Daniel criticising Malcolm – a man he doesn't know – doesn't seem fair either. My husband is more than a career-obsessed adulterer. He can be kind and caring and supportive or I'd never have stayed married to him for twenty years.

I take a deep breath. 'Malcolm does take an interest in my business. He's texted that he's coming into the shop tomorrow to talk to me.'

'How good of him,' murmurs Daniel.

'He's a very busy man,' I protest. *Though not too busy to have an affair with a member of his staff,* says the little voice in my head.

Maybe my face gives away what I'm thinking, but Daniel runs his hands through his thick hair and his shoulders slump. 'I'm sorry. Your life and your marriage are none of my business and I shouldn't be critical. I'm afraid my mouth runs away with me sometimes, even when I try not to be blunt.'

'Perhaps you should try harder?' When I raise an eyebrow at Daniel, he hesitates and then laughs. He looks completely different when he's laughing – less weighed down by the woes of the world.

'Do you know, I wasn't always like this.' He closes his eyes and lifts his face towards the sky that's fading from perfect azure to pale blue as the sun slips lower. 'I changed after Emma died. I shut down and, even though it's been years and Caleb and I are getting on with our lives, I sometimes think I haven't fully come back. What I'm trying to say is, I can be a bit of an ass at times.'

A muscle in his jaw is pulsing and, when he swallows hard as though it's taking every ounce of energy he possesses to keep himself together, my indignation fades away.

'It's all right. It must be hard, getting over what you've both been through.'

'It is. And I would imagine that the break-up of a marriage is also very difficult.' He clears his throat. 'By the way, do feel free to tell me any time that you can't believe I could ever be a bit of an ass.'

'I will… bear that in mind.'

When he grins at me, he suddenly seems more dangerous than ever.

I stand quickly and brush bits of bark from my trousers. 'Hadn't we better be getting back before it gets dark? Or Luna will send out a search party.'

Daniel slowly gets to his feet and stretches his arms above his head. 'I guess so, though Luna would just look in her crystal ball to find out where we are.'

Has Luna really got a crystal ball? I wonder as Daniel walks off. *Oh, come on, Flora. Of course she has.*

When I fall into step beside Daniel, he glances down at me and says gruffly, 'Thanks for telling me Caleb was upset. I'll have a word with him about it.' Then he heads back into the wood, with me following behind, along the narrow path that's edged with trailing ivy.

Our walk back to Starlight Cottage is mostly silent, apart from the occasional bit of small talk. I'm tempted to talk about *Day of Desire* – to tell him I've read it and loved it and deliver the critique that he requested. But that would only remind him of me snooping around in his bedroom, so I decide to save that conversation for another day.

Chapter Eleven

Becca is stressing out about the Honeyford Bake-Off. She was excited about it at first and I was relieved to hand the arrangements over to her. Callie is spending so many hours at the hotel coffee house now and most of my time is taken up in the bookshop. But Becca has started pacing today, which is a bad sign. She almost wore a groove in The Cosy Kettle's painted floor when her anxiety levels shot up just before the café opened. And now she's pacing in front of me in the shop – up and down, past the till and 'Fiction A-C'.

She's also gone for her anxious goth look today, which always hints at inner turmoil. She's dressed head-to-toe in black and has dyed her short hair navy blue overnight. It's harsh against her pale skin, making her look anaemic and unwell.

'Becca, what's the matter?' I ask, one eye on the door because I'm expecting Malcolm any second and my stomach is turning somersaults.

'Nothing, not really. Aren't you going to eat your snack?'

Becca says 'snack', I say mid-morning blowout. I stare at the tall vanilla latté and the huge slice of strawberry cake that Becca's plonked in front of me. The sponge is drenched in strawberry syrup, sandwiched together with fresh cream, and studded with plump red fruit. At this rate I'll regain every pound I've lost since my marriage imploded, and then some. Malcolm would not approve. He's packing a bit of extra weight himself but he always tuts if I so much as look at anything sweet.

'Would you rather have a profiterole instead or a cherry tart?' she stutters. 'Or you could have a cream scone, but I know you love strawberries and I thought you'd prefer this. I should have asked rather than just assuming you—'

'You assumed perfectly because this is exactly what I'd have chosen,' I say quickly, before Becca's anxiety can spiral even more. Normally a woman of few words, she becomes more loquacious when her stress levels soar.

I take a small bite of the cake to please her, and then another one because it's absolutely delicious. The rose-pink sponge is so light it almost dissolves on my tongue. I refused Luna's home-made bread this morning because I couldn't face breakfast, but I'm suddenly ravenous.

Becca gives me a shy smile but carries on pacing until I step out from behind the counter and stand in front of her, wiping cake crumbs from my chin.

'Are you feeling stressed about the bake-off?'

'How did you know?' asks Becca in amazement, as though I've just performed one of Luna's mind-reading tricks.

'Just a wild guess – plus, you're carrying a folder with *Bake-Off* in big letters across the front.'

'Oh, yeah. Bit of a giveaway.' Becca winces and thrusts the brown manila folder at me. 'Here. I've made a Honeyford Bake-Off plan.'

I open the folder and unfold the sheet of A3 paper inside. It's a spreadsheet with actions and deadline dates dotted across it: *Put up posters; Get coverage in local media; Find judges; Print entry forms; Sort out prizes.*

'This all looks fabulous.'

'My friend Zac helped me to lay it out. There are separate columns for what needs doing before the event and when, and what needs to happen on the actual day, with timings.'

'Looks like you've got it covered. So what's the problem?'

'The problem is I thought everything would be OK, at first. But then I realised I've never done anything like this before and I'm worried that I'll mess things up and let you down.' Becca swallows and screws up her forehead as though she's in pain. 'Why don't you or Callie take it over? You'll do a much better job than me.'

'I doubt that. Look what a great job you've done in The Cosy Kettle. We couldn't run it without you.'

'But this is part of Charter Day and it's a big deal and I'm not sure I'm up to it, really.' Becca stops and picks nervously at her nails as I try to decide what to do for the best. I'm hoping that the bake-off will help to bring me closer to the community in Honeyford and I can't risk it going wrong.

The easiest thing would be to take it away from Becca, which is what Malcolm would do in a heartbeat. He'd say her anxieties would hold her back and she wasn't the right person to take on the task – just like he told me I wasn't the right person to take on Honeyford Bookshop.

But I took a chance on the shop and Callie took a chance on Becca when she hired her to help out in the café. Becca's confidence has grown since I first saw her in the throes of a panic attack. She simply needs people to believe in her so she can start believing in herself.

'Just do your best, Becca,' I tell her, putting the spreadsheet into the folder and handing it back. 'That's all any of us can do. I've never run a bookshop or a café before and it's really scary.'

'You're not scared,' scoffs Becca, tucking the folder under her arm. 'Are you?'

'Don't tell anyone, especially not Millicent, but I'm absolutely terrified of getting it wrong and letting you and Callie down.'

'Gosh.' Becca's moss-green eyes open wide. 'I thought you were, like, confident about stuff to do with work.'

Oh, Becca. If only you knew. My state of mind can veer from fluttery excitement to abject fear within moments – and fear is starting to win when I think about Charter Day. I don't have an organisational spreadsheet, S.R. Kinsley could decline our invitation, and Stanley might do something crazy at the parade. No, Stanley will definitely do something crazy at the parade.

'So what do you want?' asks Becca, shifting from foot to foot.

What about my old, safe life back? murmurs a little voice in my head. But I plaster on a smile and point at the folder. 'I want you to do what it says on your spreadsheet, carry on organising the bake-off and I can help when you need me to. Does that sound all right?'

Becca pauses before giving a tight nod and a beaming smile. But the corners of her mouth drop when the shop door opens and Malcolm walks in, wearing the cream shirt I bought him a few weeks ago.

My heart sinks as he marches towards me and words stick in my throat. How am I supposed to greet him? 'How lovely to see you!' is far too friendly. 'How's Marina?', though understandable, is too provocative for an opening remark, and 'What the hell do you want?' is too aggressive.

I sigh and limit myself to a low-key 'Hi, Malcolm,' as he reaches me and grabs hold of my hand.

'Flora, we need to talk,' he announces, glancing at Becca. 'Not here where everyone can overhear us.'

'I can't drop everything to talk to you, Malcolm,' I say, pulling my hand away. 'I have a business to run and I'm busy.'

'I can see that.' Malcolm stares at the coffee and strawberry cake and raises an eyebrow. 'But this can't wait. I told you I was coming in and I have something urgent to tell you. It's something to your advantage.'

'The café's pretty quiet at the moment,' squeaks Becca, fiddling with the row of silver studs in her left ear. 'If you go in there, I can watch the shop for you.'

'The café it is, then. Better than nothing, I suppose,' says Malcolm, already heading for The Cosy Kettle. I trudge after him, before doubling back for my coffee and cake. No point in letting them go to waste.

The café is quiet for a change, apart from a couple of tourists huddled over a map in the corner. The gleaming coffee machine is silent.

'What do you want, Malcolm?' I ask, sitting opposite him, underneath a double row of colourful bunting that's looped across the ceiling. Phyllis is on a sewing splurge at the moment and we have strings of the stuff all over the place.

'I have good news,' he announces, staring at the shiny copper kettles lined up on their shelf.

The dents that Caleb inflicted are visible from here, but I don't mind. The flaws highlight the kettles' long history and make them more interesting.

'What sort of good news is that, then?' I pluck a strawberry off the top of the cake, drag it through the cream and take a bite, daring Malcolm to comment about calories.

His face twitches slightly but he sits back in his chair. 'I've left Marina. I've chosen you!' he declares, and then stops.

Um, is he waiting for me to thank him, to cry with relief, to throw my arms around him? I pick up my coffee with shaking hands.

'I was under the impression that you left Marina a while ago.'

Malcolm blinks rapidly. 'I did, as soon as you walked out and it fully hit home that I risked losing you. She's been badgering me ever since to get back together so, yesterday, I told her in no uncertain terms that I choose you because it's you that I truly love.' He reaches across the table and grips my arm. 'Please, pumpkin. I've been such a fool and I can't wait for you to come back to me and our proper life. I miss you so much and I know you miss me too.'

He gives me a soppy grin while I carry on sipping my lukewarm coffee. He's right, damn him. Even though Malcolm's behaved incredibly badly, I do miss having him around – and people get over their partners having affairs, don't they?

'We can move away from Oxford and start somewhere new, if that's what you want,' he says, gripping my arm tighter.

My coffee's almost cold but I keep on sipping as my brain goes into overdrive.

Having my old life back is tempting, especially when my new life makes me feel I've bitten off more than I can chew. I'm currently a lodger with no idea of where I'll end up. And who am I kidding that I'll ever be a real part of Honeyford? Luna's been here for years and still hasn't been properly accepted, according to Daniel. Maybe it *would* be easier to give up the bookshop and The Cosy Kettle, move somewhere new with Malcolm and start over – with no Charter Day to organise or anxious Becca to sort out, and no book club to placate or Daniel to avoid. Life could go back to normal.

I pull my arm out of Malcolm's grasp and put my coffee cup down. How could life ever be normal again? My trust in my husband has been eroded and my perception of 'normal' has shifted.

'I thought you'd be happy.' The corners of Malcolm's mouth turn down. 'It's you and me back together again, Flora. I've changed and given up Marina. For you.'

'You've said that already, but it isn't that simple.'

'Of course it is!' Malcolm looks so genuinely confused I want to slap him. 'I had a silly midlife crisis, Flora. That's all.'

'That's all?'

The tourists in the corner glance up when I scrape my chair across the floor, jump up and rush through the back door into the small walled garden. A warm wind is wafting across the potted petunias, and I can breathe out here. The garden's looking wonderful as summer beds in. But the beauty of our tree budding with apples and the purple-flowering clematis spreading along the pale stone wall is lost on me today. The children's windmills that Becca 'planted' in the soil are gently whirling in the breeze. And it strikes me that they mirror my life right now, as they go round and round, getting nowhere.

Ah, get over yourself, says a blunt voice in my head which, disturbingly, sounds a lot like Daniel.

'What's going on, Flora?' Malcolm is standing behind me. His familiar aftershave smell of woody musk drifts into the summer air. 'I thought you'd be happy that you've won.'

'Won?' I spin round and face him. There's a faint sheen of sweat on his upper lip. 'It doesn't feel like winning, Malcolm. Not after what you've done.'

'Do you want me to apologise? Is that what you need?' He wipes his mouth with the back of his hand. 'OK, I'm terribly sorry for what happened, Flora. I'm sorry that I was tempted by Marina, but I was lonely because you were so busy with this place. Come on, Flora. You can't prefer living at that weird woman's house to living with me.'

An image of me and Daniel sitting together in Luna's conservatory suddenly springs into my mind. What was it Daniel said about my husband? *'He sounds like a dick.'*

I pull myself up as tall as I can. It's time for me to really tell Malcolm how I feel. 'This place is my business, Malcolm.'

'The restaurant is our business.'

'No, the restaurant is *your* business. It was your dream to be a restaurateur and I went along with it, but it was never my dream. I know you find it hard to understand but running this bookshop and The Cosy Kettle are my dream. Whether they sink or swim is down to me. And I care what happens to Becca and Callie, and to people like Millicent and Phyllis and Stanley and Dick and Mary.'

Malcolm looks at me blankly, even though I've often talked about these people.

'They belong to the afternoon book club. Look, what I'm trying to say is that my business here gives me purpose and fulfilment, and it's definitely not a hobby.'

Malcolm pouts. 'Don't bear a grudge, Flora. That's most unbecoming. I only referred to this place as your hobby because I was so frightened of losing you.'

'Why would you lose me because of a bookshop and café?'

'I lost your attention. Of course I didn't mean your business was a hobby. You've done a fantastic job here and I'm hugely proud of you.' He swallows so hard his Adam's apple bobs up and down. 'I want the shop and The Cosy Kettle to succeed for your sake, Flora, and I'll support you all the way.'

'Do you mean that?'

'Cross my heart and hope to die.' Malcolm draws an imaginary cross over his chest. 'I will do everything I can to make your dreams come true too. So please pack your case and come home.'

He pulls me towards him and I let myself be held. Resting my cheek against his chest, listening to the beat of his heart, feels so familiar. This used to feel so right. So forever. I never thought my life would change. But it has.

'I'm not sure I can come home today.'

'Why not?' blusters Malcolm, colour flaring in his cheeks as he pushes me away. 'You can't like living with that witchy woman. We belong together, Flora. You and me, together forever. And it's not as if you've got anyone else.'

It's the laugh that does it. The incredulous little laugh that implies no other man would be interested in me and I'd only ever contemplate spending my life with him. I fold my arms and hunch my shoulders. 'You can't just breeze in and say everything's all right now and we can get back to normal. It doesn't work that way. You've hurt me, and I need to get my head around this.'

'Are you saying you won't ever come back home?'

'No, I'm saying I need time to work out how I'm feeling and to make sure that you're telling me the truth.'

'I always tell…' starts Malcolm, but he stops and bites his lip when I glare at him. 'OK, I admit it. I behaved badly but I've ended things with Marina because I love you. So how long is it until you'll come home?'

'I don't know. I need to be sure that we're going to be OK.'

'We will be,' says Malcolm soothingly. 'I've learned my lesson: you're the only woman for me and I'll back you and your plans all the way. Your business dream is now my business dream.'

'Things have changed, Malcolm. I've changed. Or at least, I'm changing. I don't know. Everything's so confusing.'

Malcolm leans forward and plants a soft kiss on my cheek. 'I was confused too, Flora, but now I'm thinking clearly. Will you please consider what I've said?'

When I nod, he holds my gaze as he backs out of the garden and into the café. Then he gives me a sad little wave before turning and walking away.

'Has he gone?' Becca pokes her head around the door and steps into the garden.

'I think so.' I self-consciously brush away a tear that's dribbling down my cheek.

'What are you going to do?'

'I beg your pardon?'

'About your husband. I know it's not my place but I wondered if you're going to go back to him. Only...' She gulps, panic flaring across her pale face. 'Perhaps you shouldn't.' Becca's eyes open wide, as though she can't quite believe what she just said. I can't believe it either. Becca never comments on personal stuff. Not with me anyway.

'You don't know anything about the situation,' I say, trying to keep my voice level. Becca's stressed and she's not behaving rationally at the moment; I know what that's like.

'No, but I know about men like Malc... um, your husband.' She clasps her hands and starts wringing her fingers together. 'Sorry. He reminds me of my dad, that's all.'

Becca rarely talks about her mother and has never mentioned her father before. My head's still reeling from my conversation with Malcolm, and all I want to do is sit in a dark corner and shove what's left of the strawberry cake into my mouth. But I can hardly just dismiss Becca if she's volunteering personal stuff.

'Tell me about your dad,' I say, taking her elbow and guiding her to one of the metal chairs on the tiny patio. She sits down and I sit opposite, looking at her across the table. Sunshine is warming my back but Becca's under the shade of the table's striped parasol.

She blinks and clasps her hands in her lap. 'My dad loves my mum in his own way, but he's not good for her. He's squashed her spirit, really. And I know that sounds stupid and you probably think I'm mad, but he chips away at her confidence and tells her that she can't do stuff. So she works in a job she doesn't really like and spends the rest of her time running round after him or ringing me in a panic to make sure I'm not dead.'

Becca gives a hollow laugh as I wonder if her spirit was squashed, too, along the way.

'And it just struck me that Dad reminds me of your husband. My dad's not a sleazeball. Oh!' She claps her hand to her mouth and starts shifting in her seat as though she's about to bolt. 'I'm not saying that your husband is a… I mean, that's not what—'

'It's OK, Becca.'

'Only I know I shouldn't be poking my nose in and you're probably going to fire me 'cos it's none of my business.' She starts twisting a strand of navy hair round her middle finger. 'I wasn't listening in deliberately but I couldn't help overhearing some of what he was saying and I've kind of gathered what's going on. I'm not stupid.' She stops abruptly and starts drumming her fingers on the tabletop.

'You're definitely not stupid. Don't forget that you are the supremo in charge of the grand Honeyford Bake-Off,' I say, leaning across the table and putting my hand on top of hers. Her fingernails are painted black and bitten to the quick.

She looks up and gives me a shy smile. 'Sorry. I tried to keep quiet but I couldn't because I wanted to help. I like working here and I like you.'

Becca's simple honesty hits me straight in the heart and makes my eyes water. 'I'm not always sure that you do. Like me, I mean.'

Becca thinks for a moment. 'I was scared of you at first, because you were so together and kind of perfect. But now you're just a mess like me, with a life that's a bit shit. Um, I don't mean—'

I cut across her before she can apologise again. 'So we're kindred spirits?'

'Yeah. Kind of. A bit. Sorry for being so blunt.'

'Don't worry, there's a lot of it about,' I say, moving my hand back into my lap and thinking of Daniel again, which makes me feel guilty. Shouldn't I be thinking of Malcolm right now, rather than a man I've only known for a couple of weeks? There's the sound of someone coming into the café and Becca jumps up in a flap. 'I left the shop unattended! I expect half our stock is gone.'

'Only if the shoplifter had a transit van waiting outside. Go and sort out our customer. Oh, and Becca,' I add as she gets to the door. 'Thank you for trusting me enough to talk about your dad.'

She shrugs. 'S'all right. I know I said all that stuff about my dad but I do still love him. You can still love people, even when they're prats.' And with those words of wisdom, she disappears indoors.

Becca could probably do with a hand. I expect we'll have an influx of locals soon for a lunchtime coffee. But I sit a little bit longer in the garden, soaking up the sunshine that feels like a warm hug.

Chapter Twelve

Sunday is a difficult day when you're on your own. It's a day for families and spending time with loved ones. But it's an absolute bugger if you don't have a proper home and your loved one has turned out to be not-so-loving after all. It's also a right pain if you have difficult decisions to make that you'd rather not face.

That's why I decide to go into the shop on Sunday afternoon. The café isn't open – Becca has Sundays and Mondays off, and Callie is enjoying a picnic with Noah. But I can man the shop for a few hours, sell a few books, and keep my brain occupied.

It turns out that Honeyford on a summer Sunday is bustling, and it was well worth opening, I decide, as I lock up the shop at five o'clock. It's been really busy, with locals and tourists wandering in to browse and buy. Though not proper restaurant-busy – Malcolm and I were always rushed off our feet on Sundays. I wonder how he's managing without me to help out, and without Marina too. I assume she's moved on to a different job, though Malcolm hasn't said so. And I didn't get around to asking.

Thinking about Malcolm and Marina makes me jittery so I take a walk through Honeyford before heading back to Starlight Cottage. Exercise might help to drown out the snatches of my last conversation with Malcolm, which keep replaying in my mind. And the town's beautiful buttery-yellow buildings are soothing, even though billowing white clouds keep blotting out the sun.

I wander past the market house, along Church Lane and over the ancient stone bridge that crosses the river. Two small children are paddling in the shallow water, whooping with delight as they splash in their wellies, and I watch them for a while. How wonderful to be young and full of joy, rather than middle-aged with hard decisions to make. Walking on, I pass the handsome manor house that's now the fancy boutique hotel, and reach the medieval church. It's a big church for such a small town, with stained glass in its oblong windows, stone tiles on its apex roof, and an arched opening into its weathered porch. A flag is fluttering from the top of its crenellated tower.

'Fancy seeing you here,' says a low, deep voice behind me as I'm staring at the church and imagining all the people who've been married and buried here over the centuries. The voice is familiar and I feel flustered, even before I turn around.

'Daniel, what are you doing here?'

'Just having a walk. I dropped Luna and Caleb at her shop. She's finishing off her stocktaking and paying him a few pounds to help her. Though I'm not sure how much help he'll be. He's got his head in the clouds half the time these days.'

'He does seem distracted.'

'Hmm.' Emotion flits across Daniel's face, then he nods at the church. 'It's a beautiful building, isn't it? Did you know it's made from wool?'

'I did not. It's amazing what you can do with a decent pattern.'

Daniel grins. 'The wool trade brought loads of dosh to the Cotswolds several hundred years ago and it was ploughed into posh houses and churches. Local sheep were big money-spinners, apparently.'

'Have you been reading Luna's local guide book again?'

'That obvious, is it?'

'Uh-huh.'

'Busted! Look, I was just going to the pub for a quick pint.' He pauses. 'Would you like to join me?'

Would I? It's such an innocuous question – 'would you like to join me?' But it's sparked a cascade of conflict in my brain. Say no and I'll seem unfriendly, but if I say yes and accompany him to the pub, I'll feel guilty because I'm not sure a married, albeit separated, woman should.

'It's not a date,' says Daniel, displaying his trademark bluntness, 'just a lemonade, if you're lucky.'

Oh, great! My cheeks start burning with embarrassment. Of course it's not a date. I never thought it was, but now he thinks that I thought…

'Yeah, that would be lovely,' I say, wishing I'd just gone straight back to Starlight Cottage after locking up the shop.

'Let's head for The Pheasant then. I'm parched.'

Daniel leads the way over the bridge and back along the still bustling High Street. He doesn't say a word while he marches along and I wonder if he's already regretting inviting me to join him. It did seem rather spontaneous. When we reach the pub, which is a bright burst of climbing plants and hanging baskets overflowing with flowers, he stands back so I can go inside first.

'After you, and mind your head.'

I duck under the low door of the old coaching inn and weave my way to the bar. It's warm in here, even though a gentle breeze is blowing through both front and back doors, which are flung wide open. There are a few people I recognise, chatting at the bar. And a large group of tourists are sitting at a corner table, poring over a local guidebook and sipping beer.

'Let me buy you a drink, Daniel,' I insist, delving into my purse. My hair brushes against his chin when I turn my head to speak to him. 'A pint, was it? Oh, look sharpish. There must be a table in the garden that's free.'

A tall, angular woman, who's come into the shop a couple of times, is standing in the doorway to the garden and beckoning me over. That's kind of her.

'I'm on it. A pint of bitter, please,' says Daniel over his shoulder as he starts walking towards her, past the huge stone fireplace which is blackened with soot. I watch him go, all long legs and broad shoulders, in grey chino shorts and a white T-shirt. His calves are dead muscly, I can't help but notice.

After a couple of minutes I catch the barman's attention and I'm soon heading outside to join Daniel, with a pint in one hand and a glass of rosé in the other. He's sitting at a table near the garden wall that's almost obscured by a huge curtain of soft-pink dog roses.

'Thanks. I could do with this. I nabbed the only free table – it's always busy out here in nice weather.' Daniel takes a few gulps of his beer and leans across the table towards me when I sit down. 'How was your afternoon at work?' he asks. 'Luna said you'd gone in for a few hours.'

'Good, thanks.'

'Great. Lots of customers?'

'A fair few. How was your afternoon *not* at work?'

'Very good. There's a lot to be said for doing absolutely nothing.'

'There really is.'

'Definitely. Especially when the sun's out.'

'Absolutely.'

If this *was* a date, I'd seriously need to improve the quality of my small talk. I'm so out of practice. Simply Red were number one in the UK charts the last time I went on a first date. Though *THIS IS NOT A DATE*, I keep telling myself. I'm still a married woman, and Daniel probably thinks I'm a bit of a prat.

He takes another sip of his drink and wipes froth from his upper lip, unaware of the monologue going on in my head.

There's Callie, Noah and Stanley! I wave at them, happy to see familiar, friendly faces, and Callie waves back from beneath their table's striped parasol.

'Who's that?' asks Daniel, twisting in his seat.

'That's Callie, who works with me sometimes, her boyfriend, Noah, and her granddad, Stanley. He doesn't look it but he's eighty years old.'

'What on earth is he wearing?' Daniel cranes his neck to get a better look at Stanley, who's rocking a shiny sky-blue shell suit, circa 1985, and a necklace of large wooden beads.

'Stanley's quite a character. He decided to live his best life on hitting eighty and that includes adopting his own unique fashion style. The shell suit's a new addition. He's usually in full camouflage gear or skinny jeans and ripped T-shirts.'

'Crikey. Good for him.'

'Indeed. He gets some strange looks but fashion should be an individual choice, don't you think? Look at your mum with her scarves and kaftans.'

'She does have her own distinct fashion flair. As do you. You always look really stylish.'

It's such an unexpected compliment, I don't quite know what to say. So I just gulp down more cold rosé and glance nervously around me. It's hard to shake the feeling that Malcolm's about to wander into the garden.

'Are you expecting someone?'

'No, no, not at all. No one. I don't really know many people so, no, I'm not expecting anyone. Nada.' Hell's bells, I think I made that clear enough. I sigh quietly and focus my attention back on Daniel.

'Did you ever find out what was bothering Caleb, the evening we went for a walk to the lake?'

'Afraid not. I did ask but he clammed up and claimed he was fine. He says everything's good and there's no reason to worry.'

'Did that make you feel better?'

'A bit. Though I've learned that becoming a parent means you never have peace of mind again.'

'I'm sure he's OK. He's such a lovely boy.'

'You're right. He is.' A broad smile lights up Daniel's face.

'And you've done a good job.'

'I try.' The smile fades and he starts tracing condensation on his pint glass. 'It's hard work being a single parent, and I don't always get it right.'

'Rest assured that you're doing a better job than I would.'

'It just takes practice, Flora. You might be a natural if you give it some time. So you and Malcolm never…?'

'Heavens, no. It never seemed to be the right time for children, and he wasn't that keen. Anyway, how could I possibly head up such a globally significant business as Honeyford Bookshop and The Cosy Kettle with kids in tow?'

'The world is very grateful.'

'That's good to know.' I take a long swig of wine to hide the rush of emotion that's come to the surface. Not having children was a joint decision but, every now and then, I can't help wondering *what if?*

'So how are you doing these days?' asks Daniel, suddenly.

'I'm OK.'

'Really?' Daniel puts his beer down and his eyes meet mine across the sticky wooden table.

Oops, here we go – zero to one hundred in the blink of an eye. Daniel's flashes of brooding intensity are still disconcerting, even though I'm starting to get used to them. I give a nervous, brittle laugh. 'What can I say? I'm still living apart from Malcolm and figuring out what to do long-term, but I'm scraping by and earning a crust, thanks to my little hobby.' Does that sound too bitter? 'I'm managing OK,' I add, firmly.

'I'm not always sure that you are,' says Daniel, leaning further across the table towards me.

'What do you mean?'

'What I mean is you look stressed half the time and sad the rest.'

Is that code for 'You look awful'? It seems I've got the clothes right but the face, maybe not so much.

'I'm managing the best I can in the circumstances,' I say, wearily. 'But I feel rather lost without my old life and it's weird without Malcolm, even though he let me down. This is the first time he's ever had an affair.'

It seems important to get that fact out there, though memories of Malcolm are surfacing in my mind – him, flirting with my friends in Yorkshire, insisting on always kissing female acquaintances on the cheek, standing very close to the female chef who preceded Pierre. I never did properly find out why she left in such a hurry.

'What did Malcolm want when he called in the other day, by the way?'

'He wanted to let me know that he's ditched Marina. He wants me to come home,' I tell Daniel, surprised by just how much I'm sharing with a man I only met a couple of weeks ago. I think it helps that he doesn't really know me or Malcolm.

Daniel sits back in his chair, until his hair is brushing against the dog roses, and stretches out his long legs. 'I see. And will you go home?'

'I don't know. I miss lots of my old life and it would be easy, in many ways, to just go back to it. Starting over is pretty scary. But, on the other hand, there are bits of my new life that I wouldn't want to give up.' I add, quickly, 'Like the shop and the café, and getting involved with the local community on Charter Day,' just in case he thinks I'm referring to him.

'Well, I think it's great that you're taking a chance and doing something you really want to do in Honeyford. Trust me, it's better than being shoe-horned into someone else's life.' Daniel clamps his lips shut as though he's finally said too much.

I can't resist asking, 'Do you feel shoe-horned then?'

'Sometimes,' he says, a muscle twitching in his jaw. 'Working as an accountant, living with my mother and bringing up my son alone wasn't exactly my dream.'

I should shut up now because our conversation has veered far enough into challenging territory. But tall, slightly scary Daniel suddenly looks so vulnerable, I can't help myself. 'What are your dreams, then, Daniel? What do you want out of life?'

He gazes into the distance and gives a sad smile. 'A different career would be rather nice.'

'You're not a dyed-in-the-wool accountant then?'

'Ha, hardly! Let's just say it's not my ideal job, but it brings in a good salary for me and Caleb so I can't complain.'

'So you'd like a different career. What else? Riches, fame, being signed up by Manchester City?' I'm assuming that Caleb supports the same team as his father.

Daniel laughs. 'That would be marvellous, plus a private jet, a villa in Antibes, and a relationship, maybe, with a woman who loves me and my son.'

'Have you…? I mean, since Emma, have you, um…?' I wish I hadn't started this question.

Daniel raises an eyebrow. 'Have I had sex with a woman since my wife died in a car accident?'

That, honestly, was not going to be my question. Or, at least, not in those exact words, seeing as my relationship with bluntness is not as advanced as Daniel's.

He smiles at my obvious discomfort. 'Yes, I've been on dates and I got close to one woman in particular, but it didn't work out. She and Caleb didn't gel, and my son has to be my first priority. Talking of which…' He nods towards the pub, where Luna's standing in the garden doorway, hand in hand with Caleb. Spotting his dad, Caleb gives one of those enthusiastic waves that starts at the shoulder. 'I'd better take them home for tea,' says Daniel, downing what's left of his pint in one. 'Are you coming with us?'

'No, I think I'll have a quick word with Callie before I head back.'

'Well then, thanks for the drink. And the company.' Daniel stands up and shakes out his long legs. He hesitates as though he's going to say something else but then turns and walks towards his family.

'Oh, by the way, I really enjoyed that book you lent me,' I call out, but a sudden burst of laughter from the people on the next table drowns out my words.

After Daniel, Luna and Caleb have disappeared into the pub, I slip my feet out of my sandals and sit, for a moment, with my bare feet on the cool grass. It's gorgeous out here, drinking wine in the sunshine. Birds are twittering in a nearby tree that's casting shadows across the grass and a Dalmatian is lapping water from a bowl near the door. All around me are couples, groups of friends and families, laughing and relaxing on a late Sunday afternoon.

A wave of heartbreaking loneliness suddenly sweeps over me. I get up quickly, push my feet back into my shoes and hurry over to Callie before I'm engulfed.

'Hey, Flora. Did you open the shop today?' Callie gives me a beaming smile and pushes her wavy blonde hair over her shoulder. 'If you'd let me know, I'd have come in to give you a hand when I finished at the coffee shop. I only went for a picnic with Noah afterwards.'

'No, I didn't want to intrude on your time together.' I smile at her handsome, square-jawed boyfriend, who grins back. 'When do you start your new job in Oxford, Noah?'

'Tomorrow. This is my last day of freedom.'

'Ah, good luck. And what about you, Stanley? How are you?'

'I'm sick,' says Stanley, pulling at the beads around his neck.

'Oh, I'm sorry to hear that.'

Callie rests her hand on my arm. 'He's absolutely fine. He means sick as in "great". It's his favourite slang word at the moment.'

'Only one of my favourites,' insists Stanley, rustling about in his shell suit. 'Along with "wicked", "salty" and "goat".'

'Goat?'

Stanley shakes his head. 'Short for "greatest of all time". Honestly, Flora, I'd have thought you'd know that, what with you being such a young 'un.'

'Talking of young,' butts in Noah, his pale blue eyes twinkling, 'did you know that Stanley has decided that dance is his latest passion

and a good way of staying young and supple? He's looking into doing
ballet classes.'

'Um, I didn't realise that. No.' A vision of Stanley wearing a pink
tutu and doing pliés floats into my mind, as Callie groans quietly.

'I have a bad case of elderly FOMO,' declares Stanley. 'Fear of
missing out,' he adds, helpfully. 'So, before the Grim Reaper calls, I'm
trying my hand at all sorts of things. What do you think about me
being the next dance sensation?'

'I think it's wonderful,' I tell him, and I mean it. Stanley isn't opting
for a life that's familiar or safe. He's breaking away from the norm, and
I'd love just a little of his courage and chutzpah.

'By the way, when are we going to meet to discuss the book club
taking part in the Charter Parade?' he asks. 'I've got loads of ideas to
help us stand out from the crowd, though I'm not sure Millie will go
for them.'

'We can have a chat about it at book club next week and maybe
get a planning meeting organised?'

Stanley nods. 'Better had. There's a lot to sort out in a short amount
of time.'

Tell me about it. Customers keep mentioning our part in the
Charter celebrations when they come into the shop and it's making
me nervous. I so want it all to be a great success.

'Talking of book club' – Callie leans forward across the table, eyes
shining – 'I've just finished *Day of Desire* and it's brilliant! Who the
hell is this April Devlin woman and why haven't I heard of her before?
She really gets women, and her writing is amazing.'

'Isn't it? I've been recommending her book to everyone, and there's
a real word-of-mouth thing going on in the town. I've had to order in
more copies to keep up with demand.'

'It's a shame the cover isn't more appropriate for the book. That lets it down but, once you get past it, wow! Gramp is reading it at the moment.'

'What do you think of the book, Stanley?'

He sniffs. 'Personally, I think it's a bit over-emotional and, going by the cover, I was expecting a bit more hanky-panky. But it's easy enough to read, I suppose.'

Day of Desire was never going to find favour with Stanley, who prefers the sort of thrillers that he refers to as 'blokey'.

'By the way, who was that you were having a drink with?' asks Callie.

'Oh, that was Luna's son. We bumped into each other in town and he invited me to have a drink and I didn't have anything else to do so I said I would, rather than head straight back to Starlight Cottage and…' I tail off, aware that I'm saying far more than I need to, and my cheeks are starting to burn. It's ridiculous but I feel caught out. As though I've been doing something I shouldn't.

'He looked nice.' Callie slides her hand onto Noah's and laces her fingers through his.

'He is, kind of. Bit grumpy at times. He's got a nine-year-old son, Caleb, and he's living with Luna at the moment because they both needed a fresh start. His wife died tragically in a car crash a few years ago.'

I'm doing it again. Oversharing for no good reason. And when Callie and Noah share a quick glance, my paranoia goes into overdrive. What did that look between them mean? Do they think I'm cheating on my husband by having a drink with a man in a pub? Does it count as cheating if your husband is already a cheat, and the man you're having a drink with is far too blunt and complicated for romance anyway?

'Must go. I promised Luna I'd help her with the cooking this evening,' I lie. 'It's lovely to see you all, and best of luck with the new job tomorrow, Noah.'

'Thanks, Flora. I appreciate that.' Noah's pale stubble grazes my skin when he kisses my cheek.

I wave when I get to the pub door, but Callie and Noah aren't looking at me. As I watch, he puts his arm around her shoulder, pulls her close and gazes at her with such adoration it takes my breath away.

A sharp spear of envy stabs at my heart. That's what I want. One hundred per cent unconditional love from a man I can trust. Is that too much to ask?

Chapter Thirteen

'It's all sorted,' announces Millicent, storming into the shop and standing in front of me.

I'm on my knees slotting some newly arrived paperbacks onto a bottom shelf and I stand up slowly, brushing my hands down my skirt. 'What's sorted?' I ask, my mind still partly on Malcolm and the text he sent this morning: *Are you coming home today, Flora? You've made your point x*

Millicent sighs loudly. 'Why, Sebastian, of course. He's agreed to come and speak at the bookshop's Charter Day celebration. Keep up!'

'He'll come and speak here?' I gasp, Malcolm's text forgotten.

'That's what I said. Honestly, Flora, reading trash is addling your brain. You need to stick to the classics. Maybe a blast of Hemingway or Nabokov will do the trick.'

She frowns at me while I contemplate throwing my arms around her. She won't like it but what the hell. When I pull her into a hug, Millicent stiffens but goes with it while I whisper in her ear, 'That's fantastic. Thank you so much.'

'You really need to check out some Proust or Mark Twain as soon as possible,' she sniffs, disentangling herself from me and patting her hair back into place. 'Why is everyone so over the top these days?'

'Sorry. I'm just delighted that S.R. Kinsley has agreed to be our star speaker, and I don't have to try and get someone else at short notice for our high-profile event. It's wonderful to have some good news for a change.'

'Hmmm.' Millicent glances around us to make sure we're alone. 'You don't have to tell me anything if you'd rather not but what's going on? I'm not blind. I can see that you're sad and distracted, and a friend of a friend saw you in the local pub a few days ago with a man who didn't sound like your husband. Are you having an affair?'

When I blink, taken aback by Millicent's in-your-face attitude, she pulls her lips into a thin line. 'It's none of my business, but' – she pauses – 'think of the other woman.'

'Oh, I am,' I tell her, pulling her into a corner of the shop. 'I'm thinking pretty much non-stop about the other woman who's been sleeping with my husband.'

Millicent's mouth falls open and I'm horrified to see tears sparkling in her eyes. 'Don't get upset,' I tell her. 'It's fine. Honestly.' That's weird. I seem to be comforting Millicent because *my* husband was sleeping with someone else.

'Of course it's not fine,' she whispers. 'I'm so sorry, darling.' She pats my arm while I reel from the term of endearment that's so not Millicent at all. After a moment, she gulps. 'Actually, my husband is rather friendly with his young PA. He says there's nothing in it and I'm being overdramatic, but I'm not stupid. So I know how you feel.'

Millicent has hinted at this before but I've never felt brave enough to ask her outright about it. We're such different people. Although… maybe not so much, now.

Good grief, I've morphed into Millicent! We both have cheating husbands and don't have children – Millicent, temporarily while her children are working abroad, and me, permanently because Malcolm and I never got around to making babies.

'I'm sorry, Millicent. About the PA, and everything.'

'Ah well, it is what it is.' She shrugs. 'Anyway, what have you done about it?'

'I've left him. For now.'

'So where are you living?'

'I'm staying for a while with Luna who runs the magical emporium further along the High Street. And her son and grandson live with her too. It was her son who I was having a drink with in the pub.'

'I see. I've heard that Luna is rather strange but if it doesn't work out with her, you could always move in with me until you get yourself sorted. We have lots of room and I wouldn't mind some company. It can get a bit lonely now the children have moved out and are getting on with their lives.' Millicent swallows and stares at her sensible flat shoes while I fight the urge to give her another hug.

'That's so kind of you,' I say, gently, 'but I'm happy enough with Luna, and I rather think that I might get under your feet.' This is a huge understatement. Much as Millicent and I have developed a tentative friendship, we'd likely kill each other if we lived under the same roof. She knows it too, but I'm incredibly touched by her offer.

Millicent lifts her eyes and gives me a sad smile. 'You're probably right but let me know if I can help in any other way.'

'Have you ever thought about leaving your husband?' I ask, softly, as a mum and two whooping children bundle through the shop door.

'Oh, I'm not as brave as you,' she whispers.

'Brave? I'm certainly not that. I'm absolutely bricking it at the thought of being without Malcolm for good.'

I'm not sure Millicent will approve of the phrase 'bricking it', but she doesn't bat an eyelid.

'I think it's very brave to try and make a new life on your own. It's not easy to turn your back on years of marriage and security, especially when you're hardly in the first flush of youth. You risk sliding through your middle years, alone and uncared for. I couldn't do it.'

Hmm, thanks Millicent. I suddenly feel like a very nervous ancient runaway.

She snaps back into usual Millicent mode and raises her voice. 'I couldn't possibly leave Jonathan, anyway. How would I cope without my gold credit card, my top-of-the-range kitchen and foreign holidays twice a year? Right, let's get back to business, Flora. As I say, Sebastian will make an appearance on Charter Day and talk about his wonderful writing career.'

'What about payment? I can't afford much.'

'He's very generously waived a fee. He says he loves the Cotswolds and is glad to get out of London for the day. He just asks that you cover his travel expenses and collect him from Oxford station. He'd also like to sell a few of his books, obviously.'

'Of course.'

I can already picture a fabulous array of Kinsley bestsellers in the window and a display of his books at the front of the shop. Getting him here is a real coup that will put the town on the literary map and encourage new people into my shop and The Cosy Kettle. I'll feel a real part of the local community.

Millicent heads off for her fortnightly facial and I keep busy in the shop. It's Saturday, always our busiest day of the week, and we're buzzing with customers. Just wait until S.R. Kinsley is in!

Not all of today's visitors are buying books, sadly – some have just nipped in for a browse – but a fair few are drawn by the rich smell of coffee that's wafting from The Cosy Kettle. Not for the first time, I thank my lucky stars that I ran with Callie's suggestion to open the café, back when the shop was new to me and I didn't have a clue what I was doing.

Stepping into the café, I can't help but smile. It's always warm and inviting in here, and today Becca has put small vases of flowers from the garden on every table. She's busy steaming milk near our display of mouthwatering cakes – they make me feel hungry just looking at them. The local bakery that supplies us has excelled itself today. Long eclairs oozing with cream are vying for space with huge slabs of sugared fruit cake, slices of frosted sponge, fruit-studded flapjack and iced cupcakes.

Some of the people seated at tables are tourists taking a break from wandering around picturesque Honeyford. But I recognise a couple of locals – the sweetshop owner, Amy, who's sinking her teeth into a chocolate brownie, and Ivor, who's run the newsagent's shop for the last thirty years.

A tall man with a very straight back twists in his seat and my stomach does a weird flip when I realise it's Daniel. What's he doing in here? I've hardly seen him since our chat in the pub because he's been getting home from work late – something to do with a major client having a nervous breakdown over his tax bill.

He spots me and half-raises his hand but stops as two arms snake around my waist from behind and I feel Malcolm's hot breath on my cheek. He smells faintly of onions. When I move away, Malcolm smiles sadly and his shoulders slump. 'Can't I give the woman I love a hug?'

His hangdog expression wrongfoots me. I've spent years trying to make Malcolm happy and now his whole demeanour screams that I'm not doing a very good job. There's a very good reason for that but, irrationally, I still feel guilty.

'Why are you here?' I ask, rather more sharply than I meant to.

'I just wanted to call in to give you some moral support with the business. That's allowed, isn't it, seeing as you've stopped replying to my texts.'

'That's because your texts say the same thing over and over again, and I don't know how to reply. Nothing's changed since the last time we spoke.'

Malcolm brushes away my words with a wave of his hand. 'I wanted to see you because, as I told you, we're in this together now and your dreams are my dreams. Plus, I wanted to bring you these.' He picks up a large bunch of flowers he must have dropped on the floor before giving me a hug. 'Here you go. I know you've got a thing about lilies.'

When he thrusts them into my arms, a familiar tickle starts at the top of my nose. I've got a thing about lilies all right. I never buy them because the pollen irritates my nose and makes my eyes stream.

'That's kind of you, Malcolm, but now's not a good time. I'm too busy to talk at the moment.'

'As usual,' says Malcolm, petulantly. He's looking less groomed today than usual. His pale grey shirt is creased as though it's been badly ironed. He breathes out slowly and smiles. 'Anyway, let's not argue. It's good to see the shop and café so busy for a change. And I wondered if you'd had the time – although I know you're very busy – to consider when you'll be coming home.'

Not *if* I'll be coming home, but 'when'. Out of the corner of my eye, I notice that Daniel is watching us as he sips his coffee.

'Not yet, Malcolm.'

'Then when?' he demands, assuming that I'm talking about coming home, rather than merely considering the issue.

'I'm sorry but I don't know.'

Malcolm frowns at a man who walks past us towards the cake display and lowers his voice. 'Is this delay to punish me, Flora? I've already apologised and don't know what else I can do. I'm human, I was tempted in difficult circumstances, and I made a mistake. But that's behind us now and your home and your life is with me. What else are you going to do? Live with strangers forever?'

'Maybe I'll get my own place and make a new life for myself,' I retort, stung into standing up for myself.

Malcolm's mouth drops open. 'You've never been on your own before, Flora, and who else will you spend the rest of your life with, if not me? I'm only being cruel to be kind but neither of us are getting any younger. You and I belong together and the only person stopping that happening right now is you. We're soulmates, Flora. You know we are. And soulmates like us can weather the occasional spot of rain.'

More a full-on monsoon than an April shower, I think, but I keep quiet. A busy café on a Saturday afternoon isn't the time or place to discuss the future of my marriage.

'Anyway,' says Malcolm, as I sneeze loudly and start ferreting in my trouser pocket for a tissue. 'I'm going to have a drink in your dinky little Cosy Kettle and think about how proud I am of you for building this up. All I ask is that you think about what *we've* built up together and achieved over the years.'

Daniel has pushed back his chair and is walking towards me as Malcolm wanders off. The two men pass each other without a glance. I prop the damn lilies up against the wall and stand back so Daniel has room to get through the café doorway. But he stops.

'That's the husband, I presume,' he murmurs. He's so different from Malcolm – a head taller with sharper cheekbones and wearing jeans and a T-shirt. He's definitely more broodingly handsome than

Malcolm, who was handsome when we first met, but years of working in a restaurant have left their mark – he's still a good-looking man, but his belly is more rounded and his cheekbones have all but disappeared.

'Yes, that's him,' I sniffle, blinking my stinging eyes.

'Are you crying? What did he say to you?' asks Daniel, peering at my face. Concern flares in his deep brown eyes and he pulls a tissue from his jeans pocket. 'Here, have this. It's clean.'

'Thank you. I'm fine, really. I'm just reacting to the flowers that Malcolm brought me. Lily pollen always has this effect.' I nod at the bunch of tall white blooms and dab at my eyes with the tissue.

'Does he always buy you flowers you're allergic to?'

'No, he's never bought me lilies before.'

To be honest, it's been ages since Malcolm bought me any flowers at all. Our lovely bright flat in Oxford was always filled with flowers but I bought them myself. *Marina had flowers in the cold store, the first time I saw her and Malcolm together*; the memory passes across my mind but I bat it away for the moment. The suspicion that Malcolm bought flowers for her will be back to haunt me tonight.

'Anyway, what are you doing in The Cosy Kettle?' I ask Daniel.

'I was in town picking up a few things and I thought I'd call in to support your business, preferably without knocking any china over this time. You were busy with a customer when I came in or I'd have said hello.'

'That's kind of you. What do you think of the place?'

'It's all looking very jolly and it's busy today. There's a real buzz about Charter Day and the baking competition. Everyone's talking about it.'

They are, thanks to Becca's poster plastered around the town inviting people to DUST OFF DELIA AND TAKE PART IN THE FIRST EVER HONEYFORD BAKE-OFF. It's poster number six – she dismissed the five earlier versions she produced as 'not quite right'. No one could ever accuse Becca of not putting her heart and soul into a project.

'Lots of people have entered the bake-off already, and I've just heard that S.R. Kinsley has agreed to be guest of honour at our writing event.'

'That's brilliant, Flora. I know how much it means to you.' When Daniel smiles, his eyes twinkle. I've never noticed that before.

'Thank you. I really need the day to go well so I'm a bit nervous, but S.R. Kinsley is a huge boost.'

'I'm sure he'll be very popular.' Daniel glances at Malcolm who, as luck would have it, is sitting in the chair that Daniel's just vacated and watching us intently. 'So what does your husband want?'

I sigh. 'He's still asking me to come back to him.'

'Do you still love him?'

Daniel's straight question doesn't faze me at all. I'm definitely getting used to him. 'Maybe. I don't know. But he's sure I'll come back eventually because who else is going to be interested in me now I'm getting on a bit?'

'Did he actually say that?'

'More or less. Things usually go Malcolm's way so he kind of takes it for granted that I will go back to him once I've made my point.'

'And will you?' asks Daniel, staring at his feet.

'Maybe. Maybe not. But it would be nice if he wasn't so convinced that he's my only option.'

Daniel bites his bottom lip and leans close. 'What about if you challenged that perception?'

'How?'

Without another word, he dips his head and leans closer. He's staring at my mouth, but he wouldn't... *surely* he wouldn't.

His mouth is getting closer and I should step back, or turn my head, or make a run for it. But I feel rooted to the spot, as though I'm hypnotised. There's no way he'd kiss me in the middle of my shop on a busy Saturday afternoon, not even to flick a metaphorical V-sign at a cheating husband. He doesn't even like me over-much.

Daniel's mouth is now so close, I can make out the faintest shadow of dark stubble above his upper lip.

Move, Flora, move! But my feet are like lead weights and I close my eyes as his lips brush… my cheek. It's the briefest of kisses – the kind that would be fine between friends or on the back of a great-aunt's hand. It's perfectly, totally appropriate between acquaintances in a busy shop, and I can't help a twinge of disappointment. Does that make me a bad person?

When I open my eyes, Daniel has moved back and is looking at me with an unreadable expression on his face. 'That should do the trick,' he murmurs, swallowing and pressing his lips together. He glances at Malcolm, who's staring at us, completely frozen, his fresh cup of steaming coffee halfway between the table and his mouth.

'Uh-huh,' I grunt, not trusting myself to speak.

'I'll see you later then, I guess.' Daniel pauses and opens his mouth as though he's about to say something else. But then he gives his head a slight shake and strides off into the shop.

Without thinking, I pick up the bunch of toxic flowers and hug them to my chest.

'Who the hell was that?' demands Malcolm, who's abandoned his coffee and scooted across the café.

'What, him?' I ask, watching Daniel's trim backside disappear into the distance. 'Just a man I know.'

'I gathered that much. What sort of "know"?' he blusters, pulling at the neck of his creased shirt. 'He seemed rather overfamiliar with you.'

'He only kissed me on the cheek, Malcolm. Daniel's like that with everyone,' I tell him, though I truly doubt he's much of a cheek-kisser.

'Daniel, is it? He looks like a Daniel.'

I have no idea what that means and I don't reckon Malcolm does either. It's the first time ever that I've experienced Malcolm being jealous, and I quite like it.

When I don't proffer any more information, Malcolm bites the inside of his cheek. 'So what does this "Daniel" do?'

He puts 'Daniel' in air quotes for some strange reason, as though he's a figment of my imagination.

'Daniel works in finance.'

'Sounds boring.'

'It probably is.'

Malcolm starts shifting from foot to foot. 'And where does Daniel live?'

I shouldn't. I really shouldn't. But I can't resist it. 'He lives just outside Honeyford, with Luna,' I say, sweetly.

It takes a moment for the penny to drop, but when it does, Malcolm's face clouds over.

'Luna? That witchy woman, Luna, with the auras and freaky weirdo stuff? Don't *you* live with Luna?'

'Yes, Malcolm, I do,' I say, turning on my heel. 'If you'll excuse me, I have work to do and I'd better get these flowers in water before they wilt.' And with that, I walk away, leaving my cheating husband opening and closing his mouth like a goldfish out of water.

After Malcolm has swept out of the shop in a sulk, I start sorting out a more prominent *Day of Desire* display, while sneezing every few seconds.

Those lilies are a menace. Sniffling pathetically, I pile the extra copies of the book that I've ordered onto a table with a printed notice above them: *Who is April Devlin? Read this poignant tale of love, longing and regret by a mystery author. Highly recommended.*

I feel like a proper bookseller, promoting a little-known book that I feel passionately about. And it's having an effect. I overheard two women in the post office the other day talking about the book after seeing it in my shop and deliberating over who April Devlin might be.

A middle-aged lady who's been into the shop a few times comes to stand beside me and picks up a copy of the book. 'What's this all about, then?' she asks, waving it under my nose.

'It's a poignant love story with real insight into how women feel. I've read it and I absolutely love it.'

The woman squints at the cover and wrinkles her nose.

'Honestly, it's worth considering if you're looking for something a little different that hits the spot. Don't be put off by the cover. It's not as raunchy as it might appear.'

'Shame.' The woman laughs as she scans the first page and peers at me over the top of her gold-rimmed glasses. 'And you don't know who the author is?'

'That's right. The book's self-published and there's nothing about the author April Devlin online.'

'That's intriguing.' She smiles. 'I only came in to find some books to keep my grandchildren quiet.' She tilts her head towards two blonde-haired girls who are sitting on the floor cross-legged, leafing through picture books. 'But maybe I'll treat myself as well. We all need a bit of mystery in our lives.'

In the end, she buys *Day of Desire,* as well as books for her grand-daughters, and I sell another two copies before the shop closes.

Chapter Fourteen

'This place gives me the creeps,' declares Becca, helping Phyllis into the wheelchair I've just taken out of my car boot. She glances up at the blank windows of Luna's cottage and shivers. 'What do you think, Phyllis?'

'I'm just looking forward to a night out for a change, love,' says Phyllis, settling into her chair. 'Quite frankly, I don't care if the house is crammed to the rafters with spirits of the undead intent on dragging us down into the depths of hell.'

'You're not helping, Phyllis,' mutters Becca, tucking a thin shawl around the older woman's legs. We're going through a week of traditional British cool and cloudy summer weather and there's a nip in the air once evening sets in.

'I didn't take you for someone who's scared of ghosts, Becca,' I laugh, waving at Millicent, who's just driven up, with Knackered Mary, in her black Audi. Her gleaming car has personalised number plates and, not for the first time, I wonder just how wealthy Millicent is.

'I'm scared of just about everything, Phyllis,' Becca explains, 'spiders, mice, loud people, dead people, crowded public transport, the colour orange—'

'Orange?' I glance down at my thin cashmere jumper, which is a deep shade of tangerine.

Becca shrugs. 'I reckon it's an unlucky colour and I'm a bit superstitious.'

'You'll get on fine with Luna, then.'

'I'm not as bad as my mum, though,' continues Becca. 'She'll cross a busy road rather than walk under a ladder and she's always chucking salt over her shoulder. You don't want to stand behind her when she's cooking. Salt in the eye really stings.'

Becca hasn't mentioned her family to me since she told me about her dad. She opens up more to Callie and the nervousness she used to show when I was around is still there sometimes.

'My mum claimed not to have a superstitious bone in her body but she'd never open an umbrella indoors,' I say, keen to keep our conversation going.

But all conversation comes to an abrupt halt as Dick arrives at speed. We move Phyllis back, just in time, as his ancient sports car screeches to a halt and Stanley clambers inelegantly out of the passenger seat.

'Drives like a complete madman! It's a miracle we got here at all,' he moans, before waving at us. 'Hello, everyone. Callie and Noah send their love.'

'Aren't they coming?' calls Phyllis.

'Nope. They're loved-up and in their own little bubble. They'll enjoy having the house to themselves for a while – though I hope they don't get amorous on the kitchen table. I did once with my Moira and my back's never been the same since.'

That's far too much information and Dick looks rather sick but Stanley, bless him, doesn't bat an eyelid.

'Is this Luna's place, then?' he asks, taking in Starlight Cottage. 'I've lived in Honeyford most of my life but I've never been here. And having seen Luna's shop, I wonder what delights her house will have in store. I hope I won't be disappointed.'

'It's very good of your landlady to have us round,' says Millicent, before pursing her mouth into a moue of distaste as a squawking chicken runs down the path, being chased by Caleb.

'Ariadne's escaped again,' he puffs, picking up the bird. 'Gran says the fox will have her if she's not back in the coop tonight.' He glances up at us through his blonde fringe.

'Caleb, these are some friends of mine from the café who are here for our book club meeting. Everybody, this is Luna's grandson.'

'Hello,' says Caleb, shyly, holding the bird under his arm. 'Gran's all ready for you and she says to go through to the front parlour.'

Oh dear. I was hoping the book club could meet in Luna's warm and cosy kitchen because that room's fairly normal, apart from the cauldron bubbling over the fire. The parlour is kept for special guests and it's been decorated in Luna's more eccentric style. But it's sweet of her to pull out all the stops for us. All I did was mention that Phyllis rarely went out of Honeyford these days and Luna insisted on hosting a night out for the book club. So we postponed our club meeting this afternoon and we're holding it at Starlight Cottage instead.

'Shall we go in?' barks Millicent, wincing as she steps in a dollop of mess made by escaping Ariadne. 'I'm told that this Luna woman is a little… um, unusual. I've never been into her shop. It's not really for me.'

'Luna's lovely,' I assure her, 'and really incredibly normal.'

Millicent doesn't know that my fingers are firmly crossed behind my back. It doesn't really matter what people think of Luna – I don't suppose she cares. But she's been kind to me and I'd like everyone to see the warm, generous woman I know, rather than be blindsided by the weird stuff.

'Watch your head, Dick,' warns Stanley when we troop through the front door. 'There's some of them dream-catchy dangly things that'll have your eye out if you're not careful.'

Dick dutifully bends his tall frame and steps into the hall. 'Which way now?'

'Follow me,' I say, a little too brightly. 'The parlour's this way.'

I'm on edge now I know we're in the parlour because heaven knows what Luna's been up to. She banished me to my bedroom half an hour ago so she could 'get the place ready' and refused my offer of help. Daniel offered to help too but she insisted she could manage and the last I saw of him, he was lying on his bed, scrolling through his iPad.

'This place is mega-creepy and weird,' whispers Becca, holding on to the back of my jumper, like a child clinging to its mother.

'Honestly, you've no need to worry,' I whisper back. 'There's nothing spooky or weird about Starlight Cottage or Luna. Nothing at all.'

'You've arrived. Welcome, one and all!' booms Luna, stepping out of the parlour.

Good grief. She's gone full-on mystic for the occasion. Her long hair is wrapped in a silver silk scarf, and she's wearing a shimmery gold kaftan shot through with flecks of metallic thread that catch the light. Around her neck is a yellow crystal so huge that I'm surprised she can stand upright. Her eyelids are shining with thick slicks of silver shadow, and golden stars are stuck to her cheeks, like astral freckles. She looks totally amazing – and absolutely barking mad.

'A huge welcome to Starlight Cottage and may the goddesses grant you peace during your visit,' says Luna, throwing her arms out wide. 'Follow me and settle yourselves in the circle.'

'Circle?' squeaks Becca, behind me.

'The Circle of Creativity that will enhance the flow of your energies.'

'Lead on, matey!' chortles Stanley. 'This is going to be good.'

We follow Luna into the parlour, and gasp. *Oh, my!* Luna has upgraded the parlour from its usual New Age weirdness to full-on fairy grotto. There's only one small window and the room is always gloomy, whatever the weather. But this evening it's aglow with the flickering light of candles – dozens of them. Luna must have sparked a candle shortage in the local area.

The air is thick with the smell of herbs. Bunches of dried flowers have been pinned to the dark ceiling beams and fairy lights are scattered around the painted flowerpots on the wide stone mantelpiece. A fire is flickering in the grate, and, on the wall above it, there's a huge painting that I've never seen before. The painting, of a woman in flowing robes, is gorgeously colourful and the woman is smiling munificently – but the third eye in the middle of her forehead is, frankly, disturbing.

'Gosh, you've been busy in here, Luna.' I take her hand and give it a squeeze.

'What a gorgeous smell,' breathes Mary, who's already giddy at the thought of escaping Callum's bedtime routine.

'I mixed my own special blend of herbs to promote creativity. I'm so glad you like it,' says Luna. She points at a circle of large sequinned cushions on the floor. 'Why don't you all take a seat and I'll sort out drinks for everyone.'

'On the floor? I don't think so,' murmurs Millicent, who's standing just inside the low doorway, with her back to the wall.

Luna glides across to her and holds her palms to the sides of Millicent's head.

'What's she doing?' Millicent glances at me with alarm.

'I'm reading your energies, darling,' says Luna, closing her eyes and swaying slightly. Crikey, she's brave. I doubt even Millicent's husband would call her 'darling' without permission. Luna tilts her head to one side and opens her eyes. 'You're a woman of many strengths. Your energies are strong and vital. But they're blocked. I sense that you're chronically underappreciated and overlooked by the people around you who should recognise your talents.'

'You can say that again,' huffs Millicent. 'Do you... sense anything else?'

When Luna glances over at me, I swear she gives a slight wink. 'I'm sensing a strong streak of morality and sensibility that makes you a role model for those around you, although this can be a heavy burden in today's uncertain world. But you bear it well. The book club is lucky to have you as a member.'

'Hmm,' says Millicent, but she moves away from the wall and sinks with a loud *oof* onto one of the enormous cushions.

Stanley, who's been gazing around the room with childlike glee, prods at a cushion with his foot. 'It's kind of you to have us here, Luna, and I love the hippy cushions idea. They take me right back to the 1960s. But sadly, I'm not in my twenties any more, and I'll never get up if I spend an hour down there.'

Luna laughs. 'Of course. Anyone who doesn't want to sit on the cushions is welcome to sit on the furniture, as long as you pull the chairs into the Circle of Creativity.'

'Now she tells us,' mutters Millicent, but she stays where she is, with her legs tucked under her. She even unzips her beige gilet and smiles at Mary, who's propped up against her cushion and nodding off before we even get started.

'Let me get you all a drink before you start talking about books,' says Luna, pushing her long trailing headscarf away from candle flames. 'I have a range of herbal teas, organic vegetable juice from my own garden or there's some sloe gin. Home-made.'

Really? I'd assumed herbal-tea-drinking Luna was teetotal. For some reason, I got the impression alcohol might be frowned upon. But here she is, brewing up the hard stuff on the quiet.

Mary's eyelids flicker open at the mention of gin and everyone who's not driving plumps for the alcoholic option. Luna's going to so much trouble. I give her a grateful smile and offer to help, but she insists she can manage and I should get the book club started.

The book we're discussing tonight is *Cider with Rosie*, which Mary chose for its Cotswolds connection, but she admits she hasn't finished it.

'Don't worry,' I tell her. 'I don't suppose young mums ever get much time to read. Not without falling asleep.'

'It's not that.' Mary pushes her long brown hair away from her face. 'I manage to read in the bath a bit, though I keep nodding off and dropping books in the water. But I didn't finish *Cider with Rosie* because I got sidetracked by the next book we'll all be reading – the one you recommended.'

As Mary finishes speaking, I'm aware of heavy footsteps coming down the stairs and I glance through the open door. Daniel is sitting on the bottom step and putting on his shoes. His shadow is a dark shape on the wall next to him.

'Good grief, not that *Day of Desire* thing,' scoffs Millicent. 'Heaven knows why you suggested that one, Flora. You know it's the sort of book I'd never have in my house and—'

'Well, let's get back to *Cider with Rosie*,' I butt in, aware that Daniel can probably hear every word. But Millicent isn't easily deterred.

'You know the kind of book I mean,' she continues, very loudly, 'breathless prose, no plot to speak of, paper-thin characters. What sort of moron would read a book like that? I can only conclude that you've included it in our repertoire as light relief, Flora. As a bit of a joke.' She laughs, while I contemplate whacking her with one of Luna's cushions for being such a literary snob – and for having such a piercing voice.

'You might be pleasantly surprised, Millicent, if you actually give it a try,' I say, quickly, but Daniel has already grabbed his jacket and the front door bangs as he heads into the garden.

It's hard to concentrate after that. If Daniel heard what Millicent said about the book, will he think I included it as a joke? We've been getting on better since our chat in the pub and I don't need a new black mark against me.

The conversation about *Cider with Rosie* continues but I'm distracted and I don't really register what's going on around me. Not until Phyllis starts singing Boyzone songs at the top of her voice and declaring her undying admiration for 'that lovely lad Ronan Keating'. She's had far too many of Luna's nuclear-strength gins.

Stanley's been knocking them back too and, by the time the book club winds up, he's claiming he can't feel his extremities. Callie will kill me for getting her granddad wasted and I don't envy Dick as he folds a giggling Stanley into his tiny car for the journey home.

I'm no puritan. If I could have glugged back a few alcoholic drinks, I would have. They might have blotted out all my cares and worries. But having to drive Becca and Phyllis home saved my liver from Luna's gin on a work night.

Luna has been pretty scarce all evening, although we invited her to join us. I spot her through the kitchen window after I've returned from Honeyford and parked my car at the back of the cottage. Light is spilling onto the dark garden and she's silhouetted against the glass.

I let myself into the warm kitchen and slide the bolt across the top of the heavy wooden door. A pile of freshly washed glasses are standing on the drainer so I grab a tea towel and start drying.

'Thank you, Luna. It was so kind of you to have us here. Phyllis in particular had a wonderful evening out, and she loved your gin.'

'I thought she might. She could do with some fun in her life,' says Luna, wiping a cloth across the worktop. She's changed out of her fabulous kaftan and is in a long fleecy dressing gown. But, with her hair still wrapped in the silver scarf, she's rocking her nightwear.

'What did you think of my book club members?' I ask her. 'You must know some of them?'

'I know Stanley and Dick to nod to in the street and I've seen Mary pushing her pram past my shop. The poor mite always looks dead on her feet. Millicent's new to me, and I think I rather frightened Becca.'

'I frighten her sometimes too.'

'Such a shame. She has a radiant soul but it's shackled. Maybe one day she'll break free. It's a terrible thing to be reined in by fear, or' – she glances at me across the top of her dishcloth – 'lack of confidence in one's own abilities.'

'Do you think I lack confidence?'

Luna laughs, as though surprised I should even ask the question. 'You're confident on the surface, but I can see beneath the façade. Your confidence has been stifled, but you're starting to break free. Your energies are rising, Flora.'

'Are you sure?' I rub at my tired eyes and stifle a yawn. It's been a long day.

Luna stops cleaning and stares past my shoulder as though she's aware of things I can't see. She does this regularly, and it freaks the life out of me every time.

'This is a period of great upheaval for you, my dear. You're standing at a crossroads and I'm lighting a candle for you every evening to help you choose the right path. I light one for Daniel too.' She sucks her lower lip between her teeth. 'Do you still love your husband, Flora?'

I can see where Daniel gets his intensity from. I kneel down to push the last dry glass into its cupboard and close the door. 'I don't know. Probably. I know he's behaved badly but he's been a part of my life for so long, he's almost shaped the person I am, if that doesn't sound too ridiculous. What I mean is, I'm not sure who I am without him. And when he begs me to give him a second chance, I keep thinking that maybe I should.' I get to my feet and breathe out loudly. 'What if I'm not capable of living a different life, Luna? We're not all as brave as you are.'

Luna's still staring into the distance. 'Reinvention takes courage, and that is something you definitely don't lack, Flora.'

'Are you sure? I feel like a right old scaredy-cat at the moment.'

She stops gazing at nothing in particular and looks at me. 'It took courage to take on the bookshop and open the café, and to invest in the coffee shop. Especially if your husband wasn't keen on you doing so.'

'It just felt like something I had to do.'

'And is it going well?'

'In some ways. I'm definitely getting more confident about my choices for the shop and the café.' I shrug. 'I think some people see me as confident all the time, but it's mostly an act, especially since everything imploded with Malcolm.'

'Of course.'

'And if I don't go back to Malcolm, it's really important that I feel at home and accepted in Honeyford. But I still feel…' I pause, lost for words.

'Like a square peg in a round hole?'

'Yes! That's it exactly.'

'It takes time to be properly accepted in a small town like this. But it'll happen if you don't try to force it.'

'But you've been here for years and…' I stop before I say something that might sound unkind, but Luna throws back her head and laughs.

'And the locals still think I'm an oddity? That's because I seem so different from them, but you're normal so you'll fit right in. Eventually.'

'I'm not saying you're not normal.'

'I know that, Flora. But who the hell wants to be normal anyway? Whatever normal is. Stanley's finding that out, rather late in life, and he's doing a damn fine job of it.'

'I rather admire him.'

'Me too,' says Luna, walking over to me and putting her hand on my shoulder. The flecks in her silver nail varnish glint in the light. 'Honestly, Flora, you'll be absolutely fine if you truly follow your heart. Now, let's get ourselves off up to bed.' She waits for me to walk into the hall before switching off the kitchen light behind me.

'Did you reinvent yourself after your husband died?' I ask when we get to the bottom of the stairs. Well, she was the one who started asking personal questions.

Luna pauses with her hand on the banister and gives the ghost of a smile. 'I suppose you could say that I did, yes.'

'So who were you before?'

'Before I became Luna who runs a magical emporium in a tiny Cotswold town? Before this life, I was Kenneth's wife and Daniel's mother and, more recently, Caleb's grandmother. I'm still all of those things but now I'm at one with Gaia.'

'Gaia?'

'The goddess Gaia,' says Luna, cheerily, as though being at one with an ancient Greek deity is an everyday occurrence.

'So what was your name before you became Luna?' I plough on, feeling bolder.

'Does it matter?'

'No, I don't suppose it does. I was just curious.'

'Curiosity is a gift that adults often lose.' Luna narrows her amazing amber eyes. 'My name was Mabel, Mabel Purfoot, and I lived a very ordinary life in a 1960s semi, and I was happy enough. And then my husband died and I made some changes. I followed a path that was always beckoning but I thought was closed off to me. And now I'm happy in a different way.'

'Mabel isn't an exotic enough name for you. I can't imagine you as a Mabel.'

Luna giggles. 'I must admit I wasn't a very good Mabel. There was always a Luna underneath, bursting to get out.'

'What would your husband think of your new life?'

'Oh, he'd hate it!' Luna suddenly claps a hand to her mouth. 'Oops, I've forgotten to blow out the Circle of Creativity candles, and I don't want another fire.'

Another fire? I follow Luna into the parlour, which is still aglow and a total fire hazard. While I'm helping to blow the candles out, I ask as nonchalantly as possible, 'Did Daniel mind his home being invaded this evening?'

'I don't think so. He's a good man. Though he seemed a little distracted. A little down and out of balance, which is a shame because he's had enough to cope with. Do you know why he was out of sorts?'

'No, why would I?'

Luna looks up, her face golden in the flickering light of the last candle. 'No reason.' She pinches the wick with her thumb and forefinger, and her face disappears into the darkness.

Back at the bottom of the stairs, she briefly strokes my cheek with the back of her hand. 'Sleep well, Flora, and may the goddess visit you in your dreams.'

I'm not sure I want any weird visitations in the night but I bid Luna a good night too and switch off the hall light while she heads upstairs. Before following her, I stand for a moment and listen to the cottage creak and groan as it settles. Becca's scared of this old building, with its nooks and crannies, gloomy corners and cobwebs. But I've grown accustomed to the place, with its smell of candle smoke and herbs and the faint caustic odour of damp.

Luna has made a go of things, I tell myself as I climb the creaking stairs. And I can too, even if I don't get back together with Malcolm and throw myself into the shop and café and Honeyford instead. Maybe the new path I'm treading isn't quite so scary after all.

Chapter Fifteen

By the time I've brushed my teeth and got into bed, I've decided that treading a new path is actually pretty terrifying. Mabel always felt there was a Luna ready to burst out, but I've never felt like bursting. I've always been Flora – daughter, wife, restaurant helper, round peg in a round hole.

I lie in bed, worrying, as the seconds tick past on the alarm clock next to me. First, I worry that my business will fail and I'll be run out of Honeyford as a big, fat failure. Then my worries become more scattergun, as worries often do. *Will the Charter Day celebrations in the shop and The Cosy Kettle be a success? How long can I live at Luna's without overstaying my welcome? What do the book club really think of me?* After a while, my thoughts turn to Daniel, and I start worrying that he overheard Millicent and now thinks I'm making fun of him for reading *Day of Desire. And why did he kiss my cheek in the shop?* I wonder.

My sigh sounds especially loud in the quiet room as I snuggle down under the duvet. The kiss obviously meant nothing to him because he hasn't mentioned it since. But I can't seem to stop thinking about it.

Malcolm sometimes kissed me on the cheek when I got home from work. But Daniel's kiss was different. He smelled of citrus and unfamiliar spices, and he had to lean down further to reach me. His lips seemed warmer and softer – and, I'm ashamed to admit it, they sent shivers down my spine in a way Malcolm's quick pecks haven't for years.

Ten minutes later, after abandoning any hope of sleep, I switch on the lamp and blink as light floods the small room. I'll nip to the loo and then read for a while, until the words dance across the page and I'm woken with a start as the book thwacks into my face.

Daniel's bedroom door is closed when I pass by in my dressing gown on the way back from the bathroom. But a sliver of light is spilling from underneath the door onto the landing's dark, polished floorboards.

Would it be unwise to speak to Daniel now and make sure he didn't overhear Millicent? It certainly wouldn't be the sensible thing to do. Though I might sleep easier if I know I haven't horribly offended him.

Before I can change my mind, I creep back to his door, give a tentative knock, and immediately regret it. There's no answer. Phew!

I'm about to scuttle back to my room when I hear Daniel's deep voice. 'Yes? Come in.'

Damn! Opening the door a crack, I peer inside. 'Only me!'

I cringe. What kind of moron announces themselves like that at almost midnight?

'Yes, I can see it's only you.'

Daniel puts down the book he's reading and stares at me. He's propped up against the pillows in his double bed with the cover pulled across his legs. The waistband of his pyjama trousers is just visible above the cover, but his top half is naked. His chest is almost hairless and slightly tanned and his abdominal muscles are rippled under his skin. I didn't expect an accountant to have a six-pack. Crikey, I think I'm staring.

'Is there a problem?' asks Daniel in a monotone. He looks tired and decidedly unfriendly.

'Nope. No problem. I just wanted to thank you for putting up with my book club this evening.'

'That's all right.' He glances down and pulls the cover higher. 'You could have thanked me tomorrow.'

'Indeed. Sorry to bother you. I'll head for bed. Sleep well and may you be visited in the night by a goddess.'

What the hell? I can't believe I said that and neither can Daniel from the look he's giving me. His bare chest is definitely discombobulating me.

'Um, you too?' he says, slowly.

When he picks up his book, I should close the door, go to my room and sink into a deep, goddess-free sleep. That's what anyone who wasn't a total idiot would do. I push the door open a little wider. 'Did you hear us talking about *Day of Desire?*'

Daniel sighs and lays his book down again, on top of the midnight-blue cover. 'I heard the posh woman in a gilet making fun of my reading material, if that's what you mean.'

Oh dear. That's not only exactly what I meant, it's exactly what I feared.

'Look, I'm sorry, but it's not what it sounded like.' When there's a creak from Luna's bedroom, I step into Daniel's room and push the door closed behind me. I'll have the whole household involved in this conversation if I'm not careful. 'All that happened was I suggested club members should read the book you lent me.'

'Why? As a foil to the usual highbrow literature you read? Something to have a giggle about.' He huffs, but there's a glimmer of hurt in his eyes.

'No, not at all,' I insist, walking towards the bed. 'I thought it would do them good to read something different, to challenge their preconceptions and see that a book can surprise them.'

'Did it surprise you?'

'It did. I loved it. The writing is fabulous and the relationship between the two main protagonists is heartfelt and beautiful. I liked it so much, I ordered in some copies for the shop and they've been selling well. It's a real hit with the locals.'

'You thought it was well-written?'

'I did, and I'm sure Millicent will too once she gets over being a literature snob and actually reads it.'

'You really liked it,' he repeats, slowly.

'I honestly did. I've never read anything else by the author. What's her name? April Devlin? Do you know much about her?'

'Not really,' says Daniel, but, when the corner of his mouth lifts, I don't believe him. There's nothing about the author online and the book's self-published so… Oh! The answer to the mystery hits me like a sledgehammer. The author was his wife. That's why he's being weird about it.

'Are you sure you don't know who April Devlin is? I mean I just thought… I wondered if…' *Oh, just go for it, Flora.* I take a deep breath. 'I wondered if it might actually be Emma?'

'*My* Emma?' Daniel shakes his head. 'What makes you think that?'

'It doesn't seem the sort of book you'd normally read, I guess.' I sneak a peek at the abandoned book resting on his legs. It's a thriller set in Scandinavia, packed full of snow, artfully decluttered houses and dead bodies.

'You should know, more than most, that people's reading tastes can be eclectic,' says Daniel. 'No, *Day of Desire* wasn't written by Emma. She loved reading and, who knows, she might have written a book one day, but she never had the time.'

So much for my brilliant brainwave! Though I'm not completely convinced because Daniel definitely looks shifty.

He clears his throat. 'How do you think Caleb's doing these days? I'd be interested in your opinion.'

I know a deliberate change of subject when I hear one, but I'm so ridiculously pleased to be asked about Caleb that I don't care. No one's ever asked my opinion about a child before.

'He seems quiet but maybe he's always like that?'

'Not really.' Daniel frowns. 'He does worry me.'

Without thinking, I perch on the edge of the bed. 'I'm sure Caleb will be fine. It can be hard being a kid, especially with what's happened to him, but he has you and Luna. He's surrounded by people who love him and that's the most important thing.'

'I hope so. I saw you reading to him yesterday. Did you bring the book home specially?'

'Yeah, it was new in, all about dragons and wizards. He looked like he needed a bit of downtime and he enjoyed it.'

To be honest, I enjoyed it just as much. Especially when Caleb snuggled up to me on the sofa to look at the illustrations. The rush of protectiveness I felt for a child I hardly know quite took me by surprise. Maybe that's what motherhood feels like. I suddenly feel very weary and I rub a hand across my eyes. It's time for bed and I think I might sleep now. But when I go to stand up, Daniel lays his hand on my arm.

'We haven't had a chance to talk for a couple of days. How are things going with your husband?' He lets go of my arm and leans back against his pillows.

'I don't know. I'm still confused about what I want to do. He'd still like me to come home, and he's been even more attentive, sending me loads of complimentary texts, since… well, since…' I stop talking and wrap my thin dressing gown more tightly around me.

'Since I kissed you on the cheek in front of him? I thought that might do the trick.'

'It did. He's very uptight about it, especially as he knows we're living under the same roof.'

'How does he know that?'

I wrinkle my nose. 'I might have let it slip. Accidentally, of course.'

'Of course.' Daniel grins and shifts his long legs under the covers. 'He'd have self-combusted if I'd properly kissed you. Can you imagine?'

I can imagine. In fact, that's what I'm imagining right now: Daniel in the shop, giving the toxic lilies a hefty kick before sweeping me into his strong arms and pressing his mouth against mine. Up yours, Malcolm!

'He would have hated it,' I squeak, swallowing loudly.

'I wish I'd done it, then. Right there, in the shop.'

Outside the window, an owl is hooting in the distance and moths are flapping their wings against the glass. But inside the bedroom everything is still, quiet – and hot. Very hot. In fact, so damn hot, I feel as if I'm the one about to self-combust as Daniel leans towards me.

I stop breathing as our mouths gets closer. He's actually going to kiss me. A man who isn't Malcolm is going to kiss me, and I'm going to like it.

Daniel's head suddenly turns as there's a scrabbling noise at the door and he slumps back against his pillow when the door swings open to reveal Caleb rubbing his eyes. I jump up off the bed and pull my dressing gown even more tightly around me.

'What's happening, Dad?' Caleb slurs, his voice heavy with sleep. 'What are you and Flora talking about in the middle of the night?'

'Nothing, champ. Flora and I were just saying good night to each other. Come here.' Daniel opens his arms wide and Caleb stumbles towards him and snuggles into the bed beside him.

'Sorry, Caleb. Your dad and I didn't mean to wake you,' I gabble. 'I was passing and thought I'd say good night because I couldn't sleep. I was on my way back from the loo and heading for bed so I'll go now and get back under the covers or I'll be totally knackered tomorrow.'

Too. Much. Information. And am I allowed to say 'knackered' in front of a nine-year-old? I bite down hard on my lip to stop more words tumbling out.

'Night, Flora,' mumbles Caleb, as Daniel bends his head and kisses his son's nose.

'Night. Sleep tight,' I manage, before rushing out of the room and closing the door behind me.

I stand on the landing with my forehead pressed against the bumpy wall and my head spinning. Basically, I – sensible, married-for-ever Flora Morgan – just barged into Daniel's bedroom in my old M&S pyjamas, sat on his bed and almost kissed him. It didn't get that far, thanks to Caleb, but Daniel knew what I was thinking. That's why he leaned in towards me.

If life was confusing before, it's now a maelstrom of conflicting emotions. Embarrassment and guilt – which is annoying because Malcolm has behaved appallingly – plus excitement that I actually wanted to kiss a man who wasn't Malcolm, and disappointment that it didn't happen.

Though that's just as well, I tell myself as I slip off my dressing gown and climb back into my narrow single bed. I need a clear head to choose the right path ahead.

*

Breakfast at Starlight Cottage is always a rushed affair, with no time to chat before we all head off in different directions. But it's more rushed and awkward than ever this morning.

Daniel hasn't caught my eye once since he came into the kitchen to grab a quick bowl of home-made muesli. And I was careful not to brush against him when I reached into the cupboard for a plate for my toast. We dance around each other, hardly acknowledging one another's presence, as Caleb slurps down a yoghurt with berry compote and Luna wraps his lunchtime sandwiches in greaseproof paper.

It's probably for the best if we forget what happened last night. I'm the sensible one. That's what Malcolm says. And kissing a man who's not my husband – a man who doesn't always seem to like me very much – is definitely not sensible. That was the last thing I thought of as I finally drifted off to sleep, and the first thing I thought of when I woke up every hour on the hour.

'Are you all right, Flora, love?' asks Luna, flicking her silver hair away from the sandwiches. 'You're very quiet this morning and you've left half your toast. It's my best home-made brown nutty loaf.'

'I'm fine, thank you, and the bread's lovely. I'm just tired because I didn't sleep well.'

Daniel glances up from his bowl of cereal, but looks down again before our eyes can meet and spoons in another mouthful of muesli.

Well, this is awkward. I take another bite of buttered toast and try to stop wondering what would have happened if Caleb hadn't walked in when he did. Would I still have woken up this morning in my lumpy single bed, or would all sense have deserted me?

A vision of the two of us in Daniel's big double bed floats into my mind. I shovel in the rest of the soggy bread as I try to push the image away, then I grab my car keys and bid everyone a hasty goodbye.

Chapter Sixteen

It's ridiculous having a sort-of crush at my age. That's what I can't stop thinking as I open up the shop, sort out deliveries and contact customers to let them know their books have arrived. I blamed Malcolm for having a midlife crisis and now I appear to be doing something similar.

My life's been rather sheltered, so maybe my crisis isn't completely unexpected. But fixating on a tall, dark, handsome man who's presented a glimpse of excitement to a wronged and lonely wife: *h*ow stereotypical can a middle-aged woman be?

I consider packing up my things and kipping on Callie's sofa. Or turning up at Millicent's with my suitcase. She did offer, after all. But there's no need to over-react, I tell myself – and I like living at Luna's, mostly. The peace of Starlight Cottage and the surrounding countryside is soothing. And I'd miss Luna's comfortingly bonkers presence, and Caleb, whose infectious laughter and enthusiasm for life brightens my day. I ignore the fleeting thought that I'd miss Daniel too.

'Come on, Flora. Concentrate!' chides Millicent, frowning at me. 'He'll be here any minute and we need to be prepared.'

Alan, chairman of the Honeyford Heritage Society, is visiting the shop to check out our plans for the charter celebrations – and the Queen herself calling in to pick up a romcom could not have caused more of a kerfuffle. Millicent has roped in Phyllis to help 'sort out' the shop and café. And she's even ditched her ubiquitous gilet and is wearing a dress and a double strand of iridescent pearls.

'Alan is a very important man, don't you know.' Millicent pauses from her task of arranging a huge bunch of chrysanthemums in a massive grey vase. She brought the flowers and vase with her. 'I know you do your best, Flora, but you're busy and rather distracted, what with Callie being enamoured with Noah and away on holiday at the moment, and your marriage... difficulties.' Her frown softens into sympathy. 'Anyway, we thought you could do with some help.'

'*She* thought you could do with some help,' grumbles Phyllis, who's dusting low bookshelves from her wheelchair. 'Personally, I think it's a lot of fuss over nothing. He's just an ordinary, very noisy, bloke.'

'Far from it,' harrumphs Millicent. 'Alan has reinvigorated the Honeyford area since he moved here a few years ago after a successful acting career in London. He's a master of the arts and he was in a well-received play close to the West End in the 1990s.'

'Really? Has he been in anything I'll have heard of?' I ask, tidying up the already tidy area around the till.

Millicent pauses from her flower arranging and sniffs. 'It was all rather highbrow stuff, so I doubt it.'

Charming! Before I can think of a suitably withering response, the shop door tings open and Alan steps inside. He's as rotund as I remembered and his fleshy face is even more flushed – he looks like a heart attack waiting to happen. Following behind him is the skinny woman who was sitting next to him at the community meeting. She's wearing a navy blue jumpsuit that accentuates her slim frame.

'Good morning, all!' shouts Alan. His booming voice echoes through the shop and Becca pokes her head out of The Cosy Kettle in alarm. He looks around him and places a paw-like hand on the *Day of Desire* display. 'Must admit, I've not been in for a while because the place isn't the same without old Ruben. We're all missing him like mad. But it looks as if you've been doing your best.'

Damned with faint praise and he's only been in the shop for thirty seconds. I take a deep breath and plaster a smile on my face.

'I'm Flora. Welcome to Honeyford Bookshop.'

'Thank you.' He clasps my hand and shakes it. 'And this is?' Alan nods at Millicent, who dips a slight curtsey, and ignores Phyllis, who's giggling behind her.

'I'm Millicent. We have met before actually. You came to a dinner party at my home in Little Besbridge and we discussed the works of Samuel Beckett over prawn canapés. It was a marvellous evening. Do you remember?'

'Of course,' booms Alan, vigorously shaking her hand. He obviously doesn't have a clue who she is. He strides over to Phyllis and shakes her hand too, the one holding the yellow duster. When the woman he came in with coughs, Alan turns and waves his arm at her. 'This is my very own trouble and strife, my wife Katrina, who dabbles in the heritage society.'

'I'm actually the very busy secretary of the society,' says Katrina, giving her husband a well-practised eye-roll.

'And she fulfils the role very well. We'd be lost without her efforts,' says her husband with a patronising pout, as her eye-rolling goes into overdrive. 'Anyway,' he announces, rubbing his hands together, 'we're here to discuss your plans for the charter celebrations and I, for one, can't wait to hear what you've got in store. We're expecting great things.'

'Are you? That's great. Would you and your wife like to sit and have a drink in The Cosy Kettle while we talk about what we've got in mind?'

'The Cosy what?' Alan looks enquiringly at his wife.

Katrina sighs. 'The café that Flora's opened at the back of the shop. I've already told you about it.'

'You have a café, too? How clever!' He turns to me with an expression of amazement and delight, as though I've just discovered a cure for the common cold. 'Though, to be honest, I'm not sure Ruben would have approved.' He puts his bear-like paw on the small of my back. 'Lead the way. I could absolutely murder a macchiato.'

'Would you like our support, Flora?' calls Millicent. 'Any help with outlining your schedule or bullet-pointing your business and community goals?'

What business and community goals? Phyllis clamps the duster to her mouth to stifle her giggles.

'That's very kind of you, Millicent, but I'm sure I can manage. Of course, you're welcome to stay and have a coffee, as a thank you for your help.'

'No, that's fine. If we're no longer needed, I'll take Phyllis home,' grumps Millicent. She gives the flowers a quick tweak, grabs the duster – which she also supplied – and shoves it into her tote bag.

Oh dear, I think I've upset her but I can't cope with her fawning over Alan and bullet-pointing for the next ten minutes. I'm already thrown by Alan being a one-man Ruben fan club.

Becca is ready and waiting for us in the café; it's never looked so gorgeous. Sunshine is pouring through the garden window, bouncing off the burnished copper kettles and pooling on the floor. The gleaming chrome coffee machine is hissing in the corner and an enticing array of confectionery is displayed under glass nearby – tarts filled with creamy custard, sticky ginger sponge, plump choux buns slicked with shiny chocolate and my favourite, strawberry cake. Half of the tables are already taken by people eating and drinking, and the air is filled with a buzz of conversation and the rich aroma of coffee beans.

'Well, I say,' declares Alan, salivating at the cake display. 'This is splendid. Did you manage all of this by yourself or are you helping your husband out?'

'It was all little old me, with help from my staff and a few local people,' I reply, with a strained smile. 'Why don't you take a seat and I'll get us a drink.'

Katrina follows me to the counter where Becca is waiting for our order.

'Just an Americano with skimmed milk for me, thank you,' she says, delving into her designer handbag for her purse.

'Don't worry. It's on the house.' I call over to her husband, 'What would you like, Alan? Was it a macchiato?'

'I'll change my mind and have a hot chocolate, if there's one going, plus one of those rather wonderful cakes. You choose one for me,' shouts Alan, licking his lips.

'Which would he prefer?' I ask Katrina, who's scanning the list of coffees we offer.

'Just give him the biggest one.' Her mouth rises in one corner as I go behind the counter and place a large choux bun on a plate, and a tiny cake fork next to it. 'And a splodge of extra cream, if you've got it.'

Warding off a spousal heart attack doesn't appear to be high on Katrina's priority list.

Alan attacks the pastry with gusto while Becca makes herself a cappuccino and joins us. She sits silently, with her hands in her lap, until Katrina gives her a nudge with her elbow.

'Becca, is it? I absolutely love the colour of your hair. Have you used permanent dye?'

'No, just a cheap one that last for a few washes. It's scarlet now, but it was blue before. And I've been green and purple in the past.'

'A rainbow of hair colours. How lovely.'

Becca nods and lapses back into silence but I smile at Katrina for taking the trouble to try and draw Becca out. I don't think Alan's even noticed Becca's dazzling hair colour. He's too busy with his cake.

'So what have you got planned?' he asks, wiping a thick blob of cream from his upper lip. 'I'm sure you'll do your best but we need to make sure that all events on Charter Day are in keeping with the general timbre of the occasion.' He rolls the 'r' so much on 'timbre' that tiny flakes of pastry spray in all directions. 'We certainly don't want any more tarot readings,' he adds, raising a bushy eyebrow.

'I'm rather looking forward to Luna's evaluation of my future,' I tell him.

Truth be told, I have no intention of letting Luna anywhere near me with her spooky deck of cards. But, having lived in her house for a while now, she feels a bit like family – which means I can moan about her weird ways 'til the cows come home but no one outside the 'family' is allowed to do the same.

'Hmm, well I dare say her fortune telling will be popular. Though it seems a little... tacky,' huffs Alan. 'Her shop sticks out like a sore thumb on the High Street in my opinion. But enough of my views on Honeyford's retail sector. Tell me what you have planned for Charter Day. I'm all ears, darling.'

I let the inappropriate endearment go because I get the feeling it's a term that luvvie Alan uses regularly. 'Becca is organising the Honeyford Bake-Off with a prize for the best cakes, which will then be sold in the café in aid of the community centre roof,' I tell him.

'That sounds acceptable. And I will, of course, be available to oversee judging of the entries.'

'Um,' squeaks Becca, sinking into her chair. I know for a fact she's already asked the owner of the local bakery that supplies our cakes to be Head Judge. 'I'm… um, I'm afraid…'

'We can finalise the judges another time,' I say quickly. 'We might have a semi-final round, depending on the number of entries, so your services might well be required to judge that.'

'The *semi*-final,' repeats Alan, with a pained look. 'I'm not sure a man of my standing—'

'And what about the bookshop?' interrupts Katrina. 'What have you got planned there?'

'We'll have a few events on the day – such as a book-themed lucky dip and a Book Surgery to recommend novels people might not have previously considered – with all profits from related sales going to the community centre fund. And the highlight of our day will be a talk from our special guest, S.R. Kinsley.'

'The bestselling author?' asks Katrina. 'I've read all of his books and think he's marvellous. So he's coming to little old Honeyford, is he? Well done. I doubt Ruben could have pulled off such a coup.' When her mouth twitches and she gives me a wink, I decide that I like Katrina very much.

'Well, that's rather impressive,' says Alan. 'One of his books was made into a film and I very nearly got a part. The actor they chose in my place was abysmal, more fool them, but that's by the by. We can certainly promote Mr Kinsley's visit as a highlight, if not *the* highlight, of Charter Day.'

'That would be wonderful. Actually, our VIP speaker is all thanks to Millicent, because she knows him.'

'Millicent?' asks Alan, wiping his finger around his creamy cake plate.

'The woman you met when you came into the shop.'

Alan frowns.

'The one in pearls who said she'd met you before.'

'Ah, yes.' Alan pops his finger into mouth and smacks his lips. 'Top-notch confectionery, Flora, and I do believe that concludes our business this morning.'

He stays to finish his hot chocolate, declaring it 'the best I've ever tasted', and buys himself a slice of strawberry cake 'for later'. Then he sweeps out of the shop, booming greetings to customers as he goes. Apparently he has 'people to see and places to go, darling'.

Katrina stands in the doorway as her husband marches off along the High Street, swinging his cake in a paper bag.

'You mentioned a Book Surgery. What would you recommend for someone like me? I usually read thrillers and autobiographies but I'm open to a change.'

I run my eye over her. Not a hair is out of place, her navy court shoes match her pristine jumpsuit, and her make-up is a flawless mask. Being married to Alan can't be easy. She seems like a woman who would benefit from some tender escapist romance in her life.

'What about this?' I point at the *Day of Desire* display, which has been causing rather a stir. Three young mums came in yesterday, specifically to buy a copy of the book, presumably after hearing Knackered Mary rave about it. I felt rather proud as I rang up the sales, as though I'd 'discovered' a new literary sensation.

'Heavens!' Katrina picks up a copy, stares at the cover and puffs out her cheeks. 'I'd enjoy some light and entertaining literature but I'm not sure this kind of book is really me.'

'I thought exactly the same when I first started reading it, but I think you might be surprised. I certainly was. It's a beautifully written study of female awakening and the story's pretty good too. It's very romantic. Why don't you give it a go?'

When Katrina hesitates, I pull out my copy of the book from under the till counter. 'Here you go, why don't you borrow mine and bring it back when you're done?'

'I couldn't possibly. I don't want to do you out of a sale.'

'No, it's fine. My only request is that you let me know what you think of the book when you've finished with it and, if you like it, you encourage people to come in and buy a copy.'

'Done,' says Katrina, giving me a broad smile before shoving the book into her handbag and zipping it closed. She reads the notice I've balanced on top of the display. 'What's all this about the author being incognito?'

'I'd love to know more about her and her writing, but there doesn't seem to be any information out there.'

'How curious,' says Katrina. 'And how clever of you to make a feature of the mystery. Oh dear!' Alan has appeared outside the shop window and is gesticulating for her to follow him. When he calls her name, his voice penetrates the glass and echoes around the shop. 'Duty calls,' she sighs. 'Thank you so much, Flora, for the coffee and the book. And congratulations on securing S.R. Kinsley for Charter Day. Very impressive.'

When she's gone, I stand at the window, watching the two of them walking along the High Street. What first brought such disparate people together? Maybe they were more alike when they first knew one another – more in tune with each other; more in love? Have they grown apart over the years, like Malcolm and me?

I breathe a sigh of relief as the odd couple turn the corner into Weavers Lane and I slip off my sandals which are rubbing my toes. We seem to have survived our VIP inspection intact and news that S.R. Kinsley's visit will likely be the highlight of Charter Day is exciting, though scary too. It really is more important than ever that our plans for the day go well.

That reminds me, Becca needs more card to print bake-off posters. I've just grabbed my bag for a trip to the newsagent when I spot a group of children, in purple sweatshirts from the local primary school, spilling out of the market house. The youngsters are hard to miss because they're all wearing luminous yellow tabards, which are stark splashes of neon colour against the weathered stone.

A young man and woman shepherd the children into a straggly line and they all start walking towards my shop, their excited high-pitched chatter piercing the mid-morning air. The snaking crocodile is on the other side of the road but I suddenly spot Caleb, bringing up the rear. He's slightly apart from the other children and so deep in thought that he doesn't see me when I go to the shop door and wave.

I could call his name, but I remember from early experiences with my mother that this would be classed as 'embarrassing behaviour'. I used to beg my mum not to show me up in front of my friends, which basically meant no calling, no hugging and absolutely no kissing. Poor woman.

The children come to a halt at the bus stop and start jumping around, laughing and shouting. Coaches often pull up here and disgorge tourists, but there's no transport waiting to take the youngsters back to school.

Caleb is standing quietly, staring at the pavement. He's still the new boy, I guess, and no one is paying him any attention. As I stand watching, he draws up his little shoulders and tucks his chin into the neckline of his sweatshirt, as though he's trying to disappear. Poor lad. I know what it feels like to be the out of place newbie who doesn't quite belong.

The young female teacher is looking at her watch and talking into a mobile phone now, presumably chivvying up the absent coach driver. She and her colleague seem distracted and neither of them are paying attention to what's happening at the back of the sprawling line of children.

A tall boy with short brown hair suddenly approaches Caleb and cuffs him across the top of his head. Wow! I flinch on Caleb's behalf and watch, feeling helpless, as a couple of the boy's friends circle the smaller child like wolves. Without a word, Caleb reaches into his rucksack and pulls out a small package wrapped in greaseproof paper. The tall boy looms close and snatches it. The package holds the sandwiches that Luna shoved into Caleb's hands this morning as he and Daniel were heading out of the cottage. Those bullies have made him hand over his lunch.

Without stopping to put on my shoes, I run out of the shop and over the road towards the huddle of children. A flicker of relief in Caleb's sad eyes when he spots me approaching is swiftly replaced by alarm as I get closer.

'All right, Caleb? I thought it was you,' I say, giving the bullies a hard stare. The taller boy sneers at me but backs off sharpish, sandwiches still in his hand, as the male teacher wanders over.

'The coach will be here in a few minutes, children.' He turns to me and glances at my bare feet. 'Can I help you?'

'I know Caleb and I had to come over when I saw…' Caleb gives a slight shake of his head and swallows hard. He clasps his hands together as though he's praying and opens his eyes wide at me.

'What did you see?' asks the teacher, sighing with relief when he spots a coach turning slowly into the narrow High Street.

'I saw…'

Caleb looks as though he's about to cry. His lips are pressed so tightly together they've gone white. He flicks his eyes towards the bullies and gives another almost imperceptible shake of the head.

'I saw that Caleb was here and I remembered that he'd forgotten his lunch. I was going to bring it into school later but he may as well have it now. Here you go.' Delving into my bag, I pull out the chickpea and avocado sandwich I made for myself on Luna's home-made bread, and I thrust it into Caleb's hands.

'Are you Caleb's mum?' asks the teacher, before realisation dawns. 'Oh no, we were told that his mum… well… that she—'

'I'm a friend of Caleb's family,' I interrupt, before the teacher ties himself up in knots. 'I offered to drive to the school later and deliver his lunch.'

'It's lucky that you saw us, then,' says the teacher, shepherding the children away from the pavement edge as the coach pulls up beside us. 'They'll all be starving after a morning outside the classroom. We've been doing a history tour of the town as an end-of-term treat.'

'Excellent! This place positively reeks of historical significance.' Reeks of historical significance? That makes Honeyford sound slightly dirty.

The teacher gives me a sideways glance as he pulls one child back from the coach wheels. But I wasn't concentrating on my words – I was far too busy wondering if it's sensible to keep a bullied child's secret.

Caleb clasps the sandwiches to his chest and sticks to the teacher like glue as the children troop onto the coach and take their seats. Then he presses his forehead to the window and watches me until the coach pulls away. My heart suddenly aches for the poor child, who seems to have the weight of the world on his small shoulders.

Should I have told the teacher what I'd seen? I'm so busy deliberating over whether I did the right thing that I don't notice Malcolm standing outside the bookshop until I almost fall over him.

'Who was that?' he asks, pushing another bunch of flowers into my arms. This bunch is lily-free, thank goodness, and looks as though it's been hastily bought in a local garage. The sticky residue of a badly removed price sticker is visible on the gerberas' cellophane wrapping. 'And why are you barefoot? You're not turning into a hippy like that Luna woman, are you?'

He stares at my feet with thinly disguised distaste. Malcolm likes to be well dressed on all occasions and has always expected the same of me. Bare feet, in his book, are the start of a slippery slide into drug-fuelled psychedelia.

'I was hot,' I say, pushing open the door and letting Malcolm go in ahead of me.

Actually, again today he's looking rather less well dressed than usual. His shirt has a few creases down the arms and there's stubble across his usually clean-shaven jaw. In spite of myself, my stomach clenches at the thought he might not be looking after himself properly.

'Who was that child you were giving something to?' he asks, nodding hello absent-mindedly at Becca, who's standing by the shop window.

'Was Caleb all right?' asks Becca. 'I saw him getting on the coach and he looked a bit upset. I thought—'

'Who the hell is Caleb?' butts in Malcolm.

He's the son of the man I almost kissed last night and now I keep thinking of Daniel and me, a tangle of arms and legs, under the trees at

Honeyheaven Lake. For one weird Luna moment, I worry that Malcolm can read my mind. But he leans against the counter, looking puzzled rather than horrified.

'Well?' he demands.

'He's Daniel's son,' says Becca. She spots a flicker of alarm pass across my face and blushes deep pink. 'Um, I'd better go and clean the coffee machine.'

She scoots off while Malcolm narrows his eyes and smiles. 'So this Daniel's got a son, has he? Daniel's married, then. I thought as much.'

I should leave it there. Let Malcolm think what he wants to think and carry on with my life – perhaps with our life. But it's the smug smile that gets under my skin. It's the smile of a man who's confident that his betrayed wife couldn't possibly be getting up to any hanky-panky because she's far too 'sensible'.

'He *was* married,' I say, slowly, 'but, sadly, his wife died a few years ago.'

'She died,' splutters Malcolm.

'That's right, so Daniel's on his own with Caleb.'

I know it's wrong but I suddenly want to inflict just a little of the same upset on Malcolm that he's inflicted on me. Does that make me a bad person? Right now, I don't much care.

Malcolm does a double take at Millicent's magnificent chrysanthemums and scowls. 'And I suppose he bought you those.'

I shake my head because I can't take this too far. Malcolm's likely to turn up at Luna's after having a few too many and challenge Daniel to a duel, or something equally ridiculous. He sometimes turns into a bit of an arse when he's been drinking.

'Millicent brought me the flowers,' I tell him.

'Millicent?'

'A woman who belongs to The Cosy Kettle's afternoon book club. I'm sure you've seen her – tallish, tends to wear gilets, looks like she owns a horse, though she doesn't. At least, I don't think she does.'

'It doesn't really matter who she is, but why is she buying you flowers?'

'They're to impress Alan, who runs the Honeyford Heritage Society. He paid us a visit this morning to discuss the Charter Day celebrations.' When Malcolm looks blank, I point at one of Becca's bake-off posters on the wall near the biographies section. 'We're a part of the community in Honeyford, so we're a part of the celebrations.'

'Have you worked out what you'll be doing on the day?' He runs his hand along the reading glasses for sale and starts leafing through the book-cover postcards we stock.

'More or less. We're finalising the programme at the moment but the day culminates with a talk by S.R. Kinsley.'

Malcolm's head flicks up. 'You've got *the* S.R. Kinsley coming to your shop?'

'I have. He lives in London but he's promised to be here that afternoon if we cover the cost of his train fare. He knows Millicent, apparently, and loves the Cotswolds.'

Malcolm thinks for a moment and smiles. 'That's quite a coup, Flora, and he'll be a great draw for your shop and café. Well done for bagging such a big name.'

My shoulders soften at Malcolm's encouragement. 'I know. It's a big deal for me, the shop and for Honeyford, and I'm desperate for it all to go well. It'll kind of prove that I do belong here.'

'I want it to go well too and for your shop and café to be a great success. You know you have my one hundred per cent support, don't you? I admit that I haven't always supported you as much as I should have, and I hadn't realised quite how much being a part of Honeyford meant to you. But that all changes from now on.'

When I don't reply, he pushes his hands through his hair. 'How can I prove to you how much I value what you've done here and how much I want you to succeed? I shouldn't have tried to tie you to the restaurant and what I want. You need to be your own woman, Flora. So you can decide what's best for you – which I hope is coming home so our life can go back to normal.'

Malcolm is saying all the right things and I so want to believe that he means them.

'Please, Flora. You can't keep me on a string with all this wavering. Are you trying to be cruel?'

'Have you ever known me to be cruel?'

'No. But I need to know one way or the other what's happening. Are you coming back?'

As Malcolm waits for my answer, I notice a dull throbbing just beyond my hairline and realise I'll have a cracking headache before long. Bombastic society chairmen, children with secrets and needy husbands are just too much to cope with in one go.

'Look, Malcolm. I'm not trying to be difficult but I honestly don't know what to do. I'm confused about the whole situation and there's so much going on here with Charter Day, I can't think straight at the moment.'

'OK, I get that you see Charter Day as a watershed moment for you and your business, and you've got a lot on your mind. But once the celebrations are over, surely you can decide one way or the other if you're coming home?'

'Yes, that seems only fair.'

'That's sorted then. You'll give me an answer on' – he peers at the Bake-Off poster – 'the third of August.'

'And if I promise to give you an answer then, you won't keep on badgering me about my decision?'

Some breathing space, without Malcolm's constant texts and unannounced visits with garage-bought flowers, seems inviting.

'I hardly think it's badgering,' pouts Malcolm, but then he smiles. 'Of course I'll give you all the space you need, Flora, and to show you how much I want you to succeed on your own terms, why don't I help you out by providing hospitality for Mr Kinsley? I can pick him up from Oxford Station, give him a lovely lunch at The Briar Patch and then drive him over afterwards.'

'I don't know. There's no need. I was going to arrange for someone else to collect him.'

'Someone else like Daniel?'

'I doubt it.'

'Just let me do this for you, Flora.' Malcolm grabs hold of my hands. 'Let me help your day to be a great success so I can prove how proud I am of you. And then you can give me your answer.'

'All right. Thank you. It would be helpful if you could meet Mr Kinsley and bring him to the bookshop fed and watered.'

'It's the least I can do,' says Malcolm, and he looks so concerned and contrite, I feel rather guilty about last night's kiss that never was.

Malcolm seems happier after his offer of help has been accepted and he busies himself pushing his flowers into Millicent's arrangement, even though the browning roses and wilting carnations look horribly out of place.

He doesn't hang around because he has to pick up supplies for the restaurant. But as he's leaving, he twists his mouth like he always does when he's considering a problem, and asks, 'Does that man have any more children?'

'Who, Daniel?'

He nods.

'No, he just has Caleb.'

'But I imagine even one's too many as far as you're concerned. You never did want children, did you.'

'It wasn't that I didn't want them. It just never happened. Being childless wasn't a definite choice.'

We were always too busy with Malcolm's latest restaurant venture and it never seemed the right time to have a family. He always said we were happy, just the two of us.

'No, of course not. I wasn't implying that it was,' blusters Malcolm, one foot inside the shop and the other on the pavement outside. 'I just know that you don't like children much.'

'I don't feel particularly comfortable around children. But I'm very fond of Caleb and he's had a lot to cope with in his short life.'

An image of the tall boy laughing in Caleb's face flashes into my mind and I wonder again if I've done the right thing.

'I'm sure. But think about how lovely and peaceful it'll be back in our flat, without children yelling and running about. You can concentrate on building up your business, with my help, obviously. You will always have my support. I promise.'

I watch him stroll back to his car, which is parked on double-yellow lines outside the town pharmacy. *You need to be your own woman, Flora.* Malcolm hasn't sounded so heartfelt or looked so vulnerable since… I don't know when. As he revs his car and screeches off along the High Street, I vow that I'll get myself sorted out and give him an answer on Charter Day.

Chapter Seventeen

Caleb is in his bedroom when I knock on his door before tea.

'Yeah?' He opens the door a crack and pokes his pale face through. There's a trace of surliness in his expression that hints at the teenage years to come. Good luck, Daniel!

'Can I have a quick word with you?' I ask, smiling broadly to show I come in peace.

'What about?'

'About what happened this morning.'

'Oh.' His face falls and he suddenly looks sad, as though he was expecting this conversation but not looking forward to it. He opens the door wide without another word.

'I just want to make sure you're OK. That's all.'

Stepping over the plastic action figures scattered across his floorboards, I walk into the centre of the room and go to sit on his single bed, with its X-Men duvet cover. But it reminds me of sitting on his father's bed – what was I thinking? – and I veer off towards the window. Outside, thick grey splodges of cloud are nestling on top of the hill and spots of rain are splattering the glass.

'The weather's too rubbish for you to play outside this evening. That's a shame.'

Caleb shrugs and sticks out his bottom lip. 'It's all right. There's no one to play with,' he says, without a trace of self-pity.

'Couldn't you invite someone round for tea one night? I'm sure Luna wouldn't mind. She could cook one of her lentil stews or her fabulous apple pies. They're even better than the apple pies we sell in The Cosy Kettle.'

'No, you're all right. I don't mind being on my own. It's better really.'

Caleb picks up a *Horrible Histories* paperback off his bed and starts leafing through it.

'Can we talk about what I saw this morning, outside my shop?' I ask him, gently.

He carries on leafing and mumbles, without looking up from the pages, 'I just forgot my lunch, that's all.'

'Are you sure that's all that happened?'

'Yes.'

'Caleb, I saw that tall boy hit you and then his friends surrounded you and were saying things. What were they saying?'

'Nothing. And it wasn't a hit. Not really. It didn't hurt anyway.' He sniffs, still with his head buried in his book.

Gently taking the book from him, I kneel down on his fluffy cream rug so we're face-to-face. 'Is it happening a lot at school?'

Caleb bites his lip and shakes his head.

'But it's happening sometimes?'

'It's only 'cos I'm new,' he whispers.

'It doesn't matter if you're new, it shouldn't be happening at all, and we need to speak to your dad about it.'

'No,' shouts Caleb, snatching the book back in a panic and hugging it into his chest. 'You can't tell my dad anything.'

'Why not? He'd want to help.'

'But he wouldn't help. He'd tell them at school and it would just make things worse when the teachers weren't looking. And it would make Dad sad again. He's more happy now we're here with Granny and you.'

Well, with Granny, maybe. I sit back on my heels and run my hands through my hair. 'Your dad would still want to know, Caleb. He loves you.'

'I know but kids have rights and I want to do this my way. Whatever you say to my dad, I won't tell him anything. Not a thing. And I'll run away where no one can find me.'

A single tear is tracking down Caleb's cheek and I wipe it away with my thumb. I can cope with broken coffee machines and stroppy customers and even difficult husbands, up to a point. But distressed nine-year-olds are a different thing entirely. He seems so alone without a mum to confide in.

'Will you at least tell *me* what's going on if I don't say anything to your dad at the moment?'

Caleb eyes me warily. 'You have to promise on my life not to tell my dad or anyone else.'

'I'm not going to promise anything on your life. That's far too serious.'

'You have to or I won't tell you anything.' He folds his arms across his skinny chest and we stare at each other as the summer storm outside grows more fierce. Wind moans around the weathered eaves of the cottage and the room gets darker.

I'm the first to blink. 'OK. I won't say anything but you have to tell me what's going on. You shouldn't have to deal with this stuff on your own.'

Caleb sits down on the floor, crosses his legs and tucks his ankles under his thighs – just like I used to in school assemblies, thirty-odd years ago.

'It's just Rupert and his friends,' he says, so quietly I have to lean forward to hear him. 'They don't let me play with the other children and they're mean to me sometimes because they think I'm not cool like them.'

'I'm not sure any nine-year-old boys are cool.'

Caleb gives me a withering look. '*They* are, and they're ten.'

'Who says they're cool? Them? Do you think they're being cool when they're saying mean things to you? Or stealing your lunch?'

When he shakes his head, I take his sticky hands in mine – there's an open packet of chocolate buttons on the floor.

'Those boys are definitely not cool, Caleb. They're bullies. Have they taken your lunch before?'

'Only a couple of times,' he murmurs, screwing up his face. 'And they say that Gran is a witch and Starlight Cottage is haunted. But she isn't and I haven't seen any ghosts. There aren't ghosts in here, are there?'

When his bottom lip starts to quiver, I pull him onto my lap and wrap my arms around him. The book he's holding digs painfully into my ribs, but when I don't let go, he starts to soften against me.

'This is definitely not a haunted house and, between you and me, I don't think ghosts exist anyway. All you'll find at Starlight Cottage are your gran's candles and crystals, and lots of love. Oh, and chickens.'

Caleb half giggles and half sobs into my shoulder. 'Sorry,' he sniffles. 'Rupert says big boys don't cry.'

'Rupert knows nothing,' I tell him, squeezing him tight. 'Some of the strongest men in the world cry and that's perfectly fine.'

Caleb's reply is so muffled, I can hardly hear it and I bend my head towards him. 'What did you say?'

'I said my dad cries sometimes, when he thinks I'm not looking.' Caleb stares up at me with his big blue eyes. 'I think being a grown-up is quite hard work, actually.'

'It can be,' I laugh, ruffling his blonde hair. 'But being a kid isn't all fun, is it?' He stays sitting on my lap when I loosen my hug.

'So what are we going to do about Rupert and his friends being mean to you?'

'They'll get bored and start picking on someone else soon,' says Caleb, displaying wisdom beyond his years. 'But you promised you wouldn't tell my dad or anyone else. And you keep your promises, don't you, because you're a grown-up?'

He glares up at me fiercely through wet eyelashes.

'I'll only keep your secret if you promise that you'll talk to me about what's happening at school, so that you're not coping with it on your own. Is that a deal?'

I hold out my hand and Caleb regards it coolly for a moment before putting his small sticky hand in mine. He gives my hand an exaggerated shake; his face is a picture of concentration. 'Deal!'

When he gives me a toothy smile, my broken heart breaks a little bit more.

'Do you cry? he asks, suddenly. 'Even though you're a grown-up?'

'Gosh, yes. Loads.'

'That's probably because you've had a fight with your husband. Was he mean to you?'

I go to say no – but Malcolm had sex with someone else in our bed. If that's not mean, I don't know what is. 'He was a bit mean, but it's complicated.'

Caleb nods as though that makes sense and jumps when a deep thrumming sound echoes through the cottage. Luna picked up an old dinner gong a few days ago in an antiques shop and has been whacking the hell out of it ever since.

'Grub's up,' I tell him, setting him on his feet and getting up off the floor. 'I'll tell your gran you're on your way down so you've got time to go and wash your face.'

I've reached the landing before Caleb calls me back.

'Yep?' I ask, poking my head back through the doorway.

'Thanks, Flora. I feel much better now.'

He scampers into the bathroom to wash away his tears while I head down for tea, feeling like the best in-loco-parentis person ever. Caleb opened up to me and what I said made him feel better.

Yay, Flora. Maybe you're not so rubbish with kids after all.

But my heart sinks when I push open the kitchen door and see Luna and Daniel sitting at the table. Basically, I've just promised to keep a really big secret from Caleb's gran and dad. Is that the sensible thing to do? Probably not. The In-Loco-Parentis Person of the Year Award remains a long way out of reach.

When I pull out a chair and sit down, Daniel gives me a tight smile and I give a wobbly smile back. Luna glances at the two of us and starts piling chopped red peppers and lamb's lettuce onto our plates.

'Still tired?' she asks me.

'I beg your pardon?'

'You said you didn't sleep well last night. Any particular reason?'

'No, not really,' I reply, shovelling down a mouthful of Luna's home-made nut roast and avoiding catching Daniel's eye.

Starlight Cottage suddenly feels full of secrets.

Chapter Eighteen

'Hey, Flora!'

Someone's waving at me madly outside Amy's sweet shop but the sun is in my eyes and they're nothing more than a blur. I fish my sunglasses from the bottom of my bag and shove them on. It's Katrina, dressed all in black even though the temperature is nudging twenty-eight degrees Celsius. I wave back and wander over.

'I was just about to come into your shop to find you,' she says, stepping to one side so she's not blocking Amy's customers. There's a large paper bag in her hand and she frowns when she spots me looking at it. 'It's not for me, though this shop is always tempting. It's chocolate limes and liquorice dip dabs for Alan, who's getting into character for his role as King Henry on Charter Day.'

'Did King Henry have a thing for confectionery?'

'Heaven knows. He probably didn't have a sweet tooth at all, but Alan has decided to play him very much in the vein of his descendant, Henry the Eighth. And he reckons he's far too method to wear padding.'

'O-K,' I say, slowly, thinking that Alan probably wouldn't need much padding anyway. 'Is he trying to put on weight for the role? That is true suffering for his art.'

'Hardly suffering when he loves stuffing his face with sugar. His doctor's already told him he's borderline diabetic.'

'Should he be eating sweets at all, then?'

'*Meh*, probably not. But who am I to keep a master of the arts from his craft?'

She raises her eyebrows at me while I try to work out whether she's devoted to her husband, or doing her best to bump him off.

'Anyway, Flora, the reason I yelled at you across the street is because I wanted to give you this back and say thank you very much.' She delves into her huge handbag, pulls out *Day of Desire*, which is looking rather battered, and starts stroking the cover.

'Have you finished it already? You've only had it a few days.'

'I know but I started it and I just couldn't put it down. I was reading until one thirty this morning to get it finished and, oh, that ending!' Tears fill her eyes and she delves into her bag again for a clean tissue.

'I'm so glad you enjoyed it, Katrina. I wasn't sure if it would be your thing but I wasn't sure it would be mine either and I loved it.'

'I didn't just *enjoy* this book, Flora. I thought it was absolutely beautiful. The writing was sublime, the way the love affair was described was so touching, and April Devlin – whoever she is – truly understands women and relationships. Plus' – Katrina gives me a conspiratorial grin – 'Alan saw me reading it in bed, glanced at the cover and thought I was reading hot porn. It gave him quite a shock.' She smirks. 'He thought he had a lot to live up to.'

Visions of Katrina and Alan making out have filled my head. Rather disturbingly, Alan is in full Henry VIII regalia with a jousting pole in his hand.

'Flora? You're miles away,' laughs Katrina, pushing her face closer to mine. 'I was asking if you've managed to solve the mystery of April Devlin?'

'Not really.' I still can't shake the feeling that the author might be Emma, but Daniel told me it wasn't and he'd have no reason to lie. Would he?

'Not really, as in not yet but you're getting closer to her identity?'

'Afraid not. She doesn't have an online presence and she doesn't seem to have published anything else, unless she's written other books under a different name.'

'Well, we need to track her down and insist that she writes more books, if she hasn't already. I'm spreading the word about her like mad and encouraging everyone I know to call into your shop and buy a copy of *Day of Desire.* How did you discover her?'

'Oh, you know. Working in a bookshop I come across all sorts of brilliant novels.' I don't want to say I discovered her beside the bed of the man I'm sharing a house with. The man I almost kissed while he was topless in that bed, and who is now being ultra-polite whenever we're in the same room together. As though he's embarrassed that the near-kiss ever happened. The very same man who is unaware that his son is being bullied at school because I made a rash promise not to tell him. What a mess!

'If you do find out any more about our elusive author, please let me know. You're very clever to have discovered her, and I think you're doing a brilliant job in the bookshop, whatever people say.'

'Why, what do people say?' I ask, feeling slightly sick as hot sunshine beats down on my head.

'No, I didn't mean it like that. You're always going to get people in a close-knit place like this who take a while to get used to change.' Cool-as-a-cucumber Katrina is looking flustered, and a single bead of perspiration starts rolling slowly down the side of her cheek. She dabs it away with her tissue. 'Ruben was an old dinosaur and a dreadful old sexist, to boot, but he'd run the bookshop for years.'

'And I've only been there a short while and I'm already making big changes.'

'Changes for the better, but it takes a while to be properly accepted around here.'

'You and Alan seem to have managed it.'

'We've been here a lot longer than you, and Alan didn't really give anyone any choice in the matter. He can be rather forceful.'

'I hadn't noticed.'

Katrina throws back her head and laughs. 'You'll be fine, especially with all you've got planned for Charter Day. S.R. Kinsley will knock everyone's socks off and your standing in the town will skyrocket.'

'I hope so. Fingers crossed lots of people enter the bake-off, too.'

'And I hear that you're taking part in the parade, dressed as punks, or something?' Katrina scrunches up her button nose. 'You'll make a fabulous Johnny Rotten.'

'Punks! Really?' I swallow hard, wondering who Stanley's been talking to. That kind of rumour has Stanley written all over it. 'It's The Cosy Kettle's afternoon book club who are taking part in the parade. We've got a meeting about it tomorrow, actually.'

'Well, have fun.'

'Oh, we will,' I tell Katrina, already slightly dreading tomorrow's get-together. Millicent will totally go off on one if Stanley insists that she parade through Honeyford in ripped trousers with her hair teased into spikes. It's going to be a tricky couple of hours.

So far, Stanley hasn't mentioned anything about transforming his book club companions into punks. He's far too busy staring open-mouthed at Millicent's sunny sitting room, which is absolutely gorgeous.

We all jumped at the chance when Millicent suggested the book club meet at hers to discuss the parade. And now here we are, sitting drinking Earl Grey tea from bone china in her house, which is even more impressive than I'd imagined.

It's set back behind a screen of trees, so all you see as you go past is a gravel drive and a glimpse of butter-yellow stone. But, as I turned into the curving drive and saw the beautiful building in front of me, I was hit by a severe case of house envy.

Millicent's home is nearly new, yet built to look like it's been a part of picturesque Little Besbridge for centuries. It has gables and a stone-tiled roof, a double garage with dove-grey doors, and a riot of deep pink roses climbing around the front door.

Inside, the walls of her bright, square hall are lined with watercolours of Cotswolds countryside, and her sitting room is terribly tasteful, with a modern vibe.

Pristine paperbacks are lined up in the black modular bookcase that's dotted with huge chunks of coloured glass, sculpted into waves. Hardback travel books, which also look untouched, are scattered across the low coffee table, and the sofas – the room is large enough for two – are covered in immaculate cream fabric.

I carefully place my fragile cup in its saucer. Millicent probably wouldn't much like her sofa being splashed with tea.

'This is a bit posh, innit? Old Millie's not short of a few bob,' says Stanley, stretching out in his big squashy armchair. 'Have you seen the garden, Flora? You could fit my house and your shop in it and still have room for a quick game of squash. Did I tell you I've taken up squash?'

'You did, Stanley.' I stand up and wander over to the French windows. 'Are you enjoying it?'

'I am, though Callie's sure I'm about to croak on court.'

'Maybe you should take it a bit easy. Wow!' The exclamation is out of my mouth before I can help it. Millicent's garden is amazing! There's decking, and patio circles with garden furniture, huge stone pots bursting with flowers, ornamental trees in vibrant shades of red and orange, and a bridge. A bona-fide wooden humpbacked bridge over a small stream that runs along the end of her land.

Millie's absolutely rolling in it. And yet, for all her wealth, she never seems particularly happy. I glance at the silver-edged photo standing on the black baby grand piano in the corner. Millicent, her children and her husband are staring out from the picture. The children, at a guess in their late teens, are smiling at the camera – glossy-haired, in logoed clothing. Millicent is standing, ramrod-straight, next to her husband, who looks ill at ease in jeans, as though he'd rather be wearing a suit. And they're not touching. There's a formality to the picture that goes beyond the awkwardness of posing for the camera.

'Would you like one of these, Flora?' asks Phyllis, dropping crumbs on Millicent's oatmeal carpet as she passes me a plate piled high with a selection of biscuits. 'They're dead posh, from some overpriced shop in London. Millicent has them specially delivered.'

'More money than sense,' mumbles Dick, who's already powered his way through three foil-wrapped chocolate biscuits and is attack-ing his fourth. Mary's snoozing on the sofa but wakes with a start when Millicent comes into the room with Luna, Daniel and Caleb following behind her. Caleb gives me a shy smile and a wave, and I wave back.

'Right, we're all here now,' says Millicent. She frowns at Dick, whose foil wrappers have fluttered to the floor, and picks them up with a sigh. 'Luna and Daniel, grab yourselves a seat while I bring in your drinks, and then we can start planning the Charter Day parade.'

We're not arranging the whole parade, thank goodness. Heaven knows how that would turn out. Stanley would probably hire a tight-rope walker, a stunt driver, and a Harry Houdini tribute act. But the idea of the book club taking part has snowballed to also include Luna's Magical Emporium. She reckons that being visible in Honeyford's biggest event for several years can only be good for business and she's keen to support the local community.

Luna sits cross-legged on the carpet, with Caleb beside her, while Daniel sits down on the distressed-leather armchair that looks as if it's been battered with a rolling pin, but probably cost a fortune. He looks good in the high-winged chair – like a devilishly handsome aristocrat with a penchant for vintage port and serving wenches. He nods at me and I smile back because we're still being ever so polite to each other. Our paths haven't crossed recently because I'm busy with Charter Day stuff and he's been working overtime. It's just as well, seeing as memories of our late night 'moment' are driving me nuts. Mostly, I'm shocked that I almost kissed a man who isn't my husband and while my ongoing marital situation is far from clear that's really not sensible. But – so deep down I hardly admit it, even to myself – I'm disappointed that I didn't.

All in all, it's best that we don't spend too much time together until I've made up my mind about Malcolm and, if our split is going to be permanent, have found myself somewhere else to live.

'Here you go,' trills Millicent, coming back into the room with a china teapot, two floral teacups and a glass of orange juice on a tray. Her forehead creases into a frown when she spots Luna on the floor. 'Wouldn't you prefer to sit on a chair?'

Luna serenely folds her hands together in her lap. 'No, thank you. I feel more earthed when I'm in contact with the ground. Do ley lines converge on your property, Millicent? I'm sensing some strong energies hereabouts.'

'I have absolutely no idea.' Millicent pours a cup of tea for Luna and Daniel, and hands the juice to Caleb, before taking a seat at her desk in the corner. The curved wooden desk holds only a large computer screen and a white keyboard.

She opens a blank Word document and places her fingers, ready, on the keys. 'I'll make notes as the discussion progresses.'

Everyone starts talking at once until I hold up my hand.

'One at a time, people. Why don't we go around the room and see what ideas we have for the parade.'

Some of the ideas put forward are great, some are a bit *meh* and a couple are downright bonkers. I don't think Alan will go for Dick appointing himself King of Honeyford and walking through the town in fur-lined robes and a crown – not while he's channelling King Henry. And Stanley's punk suggestion is quickly shouted down. But the discussion is moving along nicely until the doorbell rings.

'Who's that?' barks Millicent. 'We're not expecting anyone else, are we?'

I shake my head. 'Becca's keeping an eye on the shop for an hour and Callie said she was going out to a beauty spot for a picnic with Noah.'

'They're going up Crawford's Tump so they can canoodle in the woods,' says Stanley, fiddling with his new diamanté nose stud. 'They can't keep their hands off each other. It's like me and my Moira – we were at it like rabbits at their age.'

'Good grief. There are children present,' murmurs Millicent, heading for the door. A few moments later, she's back and shoots me an anxious glance. 'Look who I found on my doorstep. He's here for the meeting, apparently.'

When she steps aside, my heart sinks because the person she found was Malcolm. He strides into the room, looking rather red in the face.

'There you are, Flora. I thought I'd better come and join you, seeing as I'm involved in Charter Day. I'm surprised you didn't tell me about this meeting.'

'I didn't think you'd be interested because we're only talking about the Charter Day parade. Do you want to take part in that?'

'Good Lord, no,' laughs Malcolm. 'I'll be far too busy organising hospitality for your VIP guest.' He scans the room and his gaze hardens when he spots Daniel. 'Aren't you going to introduce me to everyone, Flora?'

I'd really rather not. But there's no getting out of it.

'This is Malcolm, my... um... my husband. And Malcolm, these are the members of The Cosy Kettle's afternoon book club: Millicent, Phyllis, Stanley, Dick and Mary. You've already met Luna, who runs a shop near mine. This is Caleb, her grandson, and Daniel, her son.'

'It's good to meet you,' says Daniel, leaning forward with his hand outstretched. With only the slightest of hesitations, Malcolm walks over and gives his hand a brief shake before settling into an empty chair nearby.

'So how did you know I'd be here?' I ask him.

'That scared girl told me when I went into the shop. She said she'd text you. Anyway, carry on. Don't let me interrupt you.'

Millicent goes back to her desk and starts tapping on her keyboard, and the discussion about the parade begins again. But the atmosphere in the room has changed. Malcolm and Daniel keep eyeing each other up, Luna is frowning as though she has a headache, and I feel queasy.

I delve into my handbag and pull out my mobile. Damn, I switched it to silent last night when I was reading a bedtime story to Caleb, and forgot to switch it back. He started dozing halfway through the chapter and I sat stroking his forehead until I was sure he was fast asleep. Yep, Becca did contact me. I tilt my phone, so there's no chance of Malcolm seeing the screen, and open her text: *Problem! Malcolm came in shop. Wouldn't leave till I said where you were. Think he might be on his way? Sorry x*

A kiss! Becca must be really sorry. But it's not her fault. Malcolm can be very persuasive when he wants to be. Though I'm still not really sure why he's here. Is it to keep an eye on me, or on Daniel? Phyllis looks at the two men eyeballing each other across the room and gives me a thumbs up. What on earth will people think is going on?

With a sigh, I turn my attention back to the discussion. Stanley appears to be proposing that the book club dress in swimwear to walk through the town – I have no idea why – and Millicent is saying she'd rather die than get her legs out 'for the masses'. Malcolm and Daniel sit in wary silence as the discussion continues, back and forth. And I'm so distracted I stay quiet too – until Dick and Stanley start bickering and I decide to take charge and bring things to a close.

'Why don't you all agree to do what Mary suggested and dress up as literary characters? That gives everyone a lot of scope, and it will link back to the book club.'

'Can I be Elizabeth Bennet, in a bonnet?' asks Phyllis.

'Great idea! And Caleb, you could dress as Harry Potter or as a superhero. I can just imagine you as Superman.'

Caleb gives a gappy grin – he lost another tooth yesterday. 'Can I be Spider-Man?'

'Absolutely. You'll look brilliant.'

Malcolm clears his throat. 'Point of order – I'm not sure Spider-Man counts as a literary character. He's mainly in films.'

'And comics,' says Daniel, leaning down to ruffle his son's hair. 'Flora's right. You'll make a fantastic Spider-Man.'

Malcolm glowers and folds his arms.

'If films and comics are allowed, can I come as one of the Living Dead?' yawns Mary. 'With the bags under my eyes, I won't need any make-up. What about you, Millicent? Who do you fancy being?'

Millicent thinks for a moment. 'Possibly Jo March from *Little Women* or a classic Shakespearean character. Maybe Juliet, Rosalind or Viola.'

'Or Lady Macbeth,' murmurs Stanley, with a wink in my direction.

'We'll need a sign or a placard to walk behind, to say we're from the book club and Luna's place,' chips in Dick, before Stanley can say any more.

Daniel raises his hand. 'Dressing up's not really my thing but I can make the sign, if you'd like. It'll be good to do something practical for a change.'

'You're not normally a practical man, then, Daniel?' says Malcolm. 'That's a shame. I'm very practical, particularly in the kitchen.'

Daniel sucks his bottom lip between his teeth and nods slowly. 'Is that right?'

'Absolutely. I could have been a professional chef but I was too busy being the boss.'

'Shall we agree on the literary characters theme then?' I squeak, sliding forward and perching on the edge of my seat. Even without Luna's special gifts, I can sense when a storm is brewing.

But Malcolm ignores me. 'Do you have experience of running a business, Daniel?'

'I'm a manager at the accountancy company where I work but I'm not in charge.'

'Accountancy?' Malcolm pulls a face. 'That sounds *really* boring.'

'It can be, at times,' replies Daniel, in a calm, low voice. 'But it pays the bills.'

Malcolm tuts sympathetically. 'It must be awful to hate your job. But not everyone has the creativity and vision that's needed to run a business. Leadership requires confidence and the courage to take risks, rather than just number crunching.'

OK, I've had enough of Malcolm's willy-waving, or whatever he thinks he's doing. I jump up and clap my hands together. Everyone turns to me, except Phyllis, who's still staring at Malcolm and Daniel, with her mouth open.

'We'd better not outstay our welcome now we've decided on a theme. Everyone decide which literary character you'd like to be, start working out your costumes, and we can finalise things at the next book club meeting. Daniel, if you could make us a sign that would be great. And I'll speak to Alan and let him know what's happening. Thank you so much, Millicent, for having us in your fabulous home.'

And with that, much to her surprise, I grab Millicent's hand and give it a hearty shake. I hardly know what I'm doing, to be honest. I'm that flustered. Malcolm and Daniel in the same room totally messes with my mind and I can't wait to escape.

A few hours later, I'm leaning on the fence at the bottom of Luna's garden, watching the sun slide behind the hill, when I hear footsteps behind me. I know, without checking, that it's Daniel.

'It's beautiful, isn't it?' he says.

'Absolutely glorious.'

We stand side by side, necks cricked towards the sky which is on fire. Slashes of orange and gold are painted across the heavens, and it's a comforting sight. Whatever happens to me, whatever I decide to do, the sun will come up and the sun will go down. And Starlight Cottage will bear witness to these fabulous displays of nature's awesomeness. Luna must be rubbing off on me – I'm not usually so philosophical.

When I glance at Daniel, he tilts the glass of red wine in his hand towards me. 'Do you fancy a sip?'

It feels like a peace offering after the awkwardness of the kiss that never was.

'No, thanks. Is Caleb in bed?'

'Yeah, Luna's reading him a story. He said you read to him last night when he couldn't sleep and you stroked his head, like his mum used to.'

'I didn't realise she did that.'

'Every night. It was the only way Caleb would settle down. He's a good lad now but he was a tiny terror back then.'

'I find that hard to believe.'

'No, really. I've had tantrums in Tesco, meltdowns at the zoo and a particularly embarrassing wetting-himself incident on a friend's brand-new sofa.'

'Oops.'

'Oops, indeed. Our invitation to "call round any time" was swiftly rescinded.'

'Bit harsh if he was only a little kid.'

'That's what I thought, but my friend was terribly house-proud at the time and childless. He's got three kids under six now which I feel is divine retribution.' He grins. 'How do you think Caleb is now? He seems a bit happier to me.'

'I think he is,' I say, feeling awful that I can't tell him any more. But I don't want to break my promise to Caleb, who's started nabbing me for a little chat about the boys at school. Though they've backed off a bit, they're still making him miserable at times but he says that talking to me really helps. I hope it does.

'I'll bring him in at the weekend to choose some more bedtime books. Talking of which, how is *Day of Desire* selling?'

'Like proverbial hotcakes.'

'Really?'

'People love it and the mystery surrounding April Devlin is just fuelling their interest. I'd really love to know who April really is. Or was,' I say hopefully, just in case Daniel wants to leap in and tell me that it was Emma, after all. But if that's the case, I don't know why he'd want to keep it a secret. Unless it's just too painful to talk about? Daniel's expression gives nothing away and I don't pursue the matter.

He takes another sip of wine and stares at the sky, which is already dimming. The sun has slipped behind the hill and the heavenly colours are fading to pastels.

'Did Malcolm get off from Millicent's all right?' he asks, suddenly.

'Yes, though I'm not quite sure why he bothered coming along in the first place. It was hardly worth him turning up.'

'He wanted to see you.'

'I guess so.'

'And he's helping you out on Charter Day, isn't he?'

'A little bit, but we could have discussed that on the phone. I didn't think he'd be calling by unannounced, not now we've come to an arrangement.'

'What sort of arrangement?'

'He's agreed to give me some breathing space in return for me making a definitive decision about what I'm going to do with the rest of my life by Charter Day.'

'Ah, you're on a countdown.'

Daniel swirls the ruby-red wine around his glass and takes a large swig.

'So, what did you think of Malcolm when you met him this afternoon?'

It shouldn't matter to me what Daniel thinks of my husband, but it does.

'He was exactly as I imagined him to be.'

'Which is?'

Daniel stares at me, as though weighing up whether I really want to know or not. Then, he shrugs. 'Confident, successful, used to getting his own way…' He scuffs his feet through the grass. 'It was hard to tell, really, on such a short meeting. Hey, you're shivering. Are you cold? Do you want to go in?'

I'm trying not to shiver but the temperature is dropping as the fields around us fade into gloom and night creeps in.

'It's suddenly got chilly but I'd like to stay out here a bit longer. I'll grab my jacket in a minute.'

'Here, have this.' Daniel pulls his blue V-necked jumper over his head in one swift movement and holds it out to me. 'I'm going in to give Caleb his good-night kiss so I don't need it. And I don't like to think of you being cold.'

The jumper's soft, and I hug it to me as Daniel walks up the garden and disappears through the open kitchen door. The thin cashmere smells faintly of lemons and spices and the scent envelops me when I slip it over my head. Hugging my arms around my chest, I lean on the fence and watch as the hill fades to a black mound, then a dark shadow, and then to nothing at all.

Chapter Nineteen

Honeyford has gone Charter Day crazy. Bunting and fairy lights are strung up across the town, and people in the shop and café are talking about little else as plans for the celebrations become ever more elaborate.

At first, the parade was a simple march by locals along the High Street. But now it's grown to include an array of floats and a samba band has been formed specially for the occasion. The evening barbecue has turned into a hog roast, and 'a few fireworks' in the Memorial Park has grown into a full-scale pyrotechnic display.

It's going to be a fabulous day that does Honeyford proud – and S.R. Kinsley's visit is the jewel in the crown, according to the posters that Alan's plastered across the town. This is brilliant, but also terrifying. I've emailed Mr Kinsley to organise everything, and Becca's had loads of entries for the bake-off, but I still feel wracked with nerves as Charter Day approaches.

It doesn't help that the clock is ticking on my decision about Malcolm and I'm still not sure what to do. My mind changes depending on my rollercoaster confidence levels – when they're high, I can imagine a life without him, but when they plummet, I crave the security and safety of what's familiar. Even if 'familiar' isn't perfect.

So I distract myself by keeping busy and getting the shop and café ready. This includes ordering in a huge pile of S.R. Kinsley's bestsellers, causing quite a buzz with customers, along with April's book, which is more popular with every passing day.

'I keep hearing good things about this,' says a woman with long blonde hair a few days before the celebrations. She places a copy of *Day of Desire* on the counter in front of me, as I try to remember why I recognise her. Ah, she was one of the teachers with the children from Caleb's school.

'I'm sure you'll enjoy it,' I reply, ringing up the sale and placing the book in a paper bag. 'Excuse me for asking but are you a teacher at Honeyford Vale Primary?'

'I am. Was it the purple paint under my nails that gave me away? The children have been expressing themselves through art as part of our end-of-term celebrations and it got a bit messy. I'm Jemima, by the way.'

Jemima can't be a day over twenty-one. Her poker-straight hair is secured on one side by a sparkly pink clip, and she has the wide, beaming smile and golden tan of a Californian beach babe. She looks like a presenter on children's TV.

'I'm Flora. It's lovely to meet you.'

'So you're the woman who's taken over from Ruben. I must say, you've got a fabulous array of children's books in now. Ruben had a small selection but I'm not sure he wholly approved of youngsters being in his shop.'

'I think Ruben was quite' – I try to think of a diplomatic way of saying that Ruben was a curmudgeonly old dinosaur – 'set in his ways. But I'm really keen to encourage children to read and enjoy the world of books. Actually, I know one of your pupils – Caleb Purfoot.'

Jemima tilts her head and blinks her bright blue eyes. Her teeth are perfectly, fabulously white. I can just picture her on telly, showing children what they can make with two cereal boxes, an old pair of trainers and an egg whisk.

'Caleb's in my class and he's an absolutely lovely boy,' she gushes. 'How do you know him?'

'I live with his father.'

Oops, that doesn't sound quite right.

Jemima instantly leaps to the wrong conclusion. 'It's lovely that Caleb has a mother figure in his life. It's terribly sad that he lost his mum so early.'

'It's very sad, but I wouldn't describe myself as a mother figure. His dad and I aren't really together. We live together, but his mother owns the house and I'm a lodger. So, even though we are technically living together, we're not really "living together" living together, if you know what I mean.' I peter off, feeling like a prat. *We're not having sex.* That's the shortcut I'm looking for but couldn't possibly say out loud. *Even though you sometimes imagine what it would be like,* whispers a voice in my head.

Jemima's smile falters a little but she quickly recovers. 'Well, I'm sure it's good for Caleb to have you around. Is he looking forward to the holidays?'

'I imagine so. He's finding school a bit challenging so a break will probably do him good.'

'Challenging in what way?'

Jemima pushes her new book into her handbag while a silent debate goes on in my head. How can I answer her question when I faithfully promised a small child that I wouldn't say anything? I promised on Caleb's life and, while I'm not superstitious like Luna, if I broke that promise and something bad happened to him, I'd never shake the feeling that I was somehow responsible. Luna would definitely blame me. She'd probably get herself a voodoo doll and stick pins in it.

'It's always difficult starting a new school,' I say, wondering if proper parents ignore these kinds of promises when a child's happiness is involved. Or is 'never ever renege on your promise to a child' rule number one in the parenting handbook?

Jemima gives me a reassuring grin. 'Absolutely. But children are very adaptable.'

'It can take a while for other children to accept a newcomer though.'

'Indeed, but all the children at Honeyford Vale Primary are lovely.'

Jemima seems oblivious to the fact that at least a few of her 'lovely' children are lunch-stealing bullies.

'Surely not every single child can be lovely?'

'Yes, they are. We're very lucky.'

Oh, come on, Jemima. I'm telling you in code but you're not picking up the signals. I try again. 'I dare say a few of the existing pupils might take advantage of a new boy.'

Smiley Jemima finally cottons on that all might not be perfect in her primary school paradise. 'Is there something in particular you wanted to raise about Caleb?'

Caleb's ghostly white face as he pleaded with me to stay silent suddenly swims into my mind. 'I get the impression that some of the other boys are being a little unkind to him sometimes,' I say, choosing my words carefully.

Jemima frowns. 'Do you know who?'

'Not really but maybe you could keep an eye on Caleb to make sure he's settling in OK?'

'Of course. I'll give Mr Purfoot a ring about it.'

'There's no need because I'll be seeing him later,' I gabble, panicky at the very thought. 'And I'd be grateful if you didn't mention any of this to Caleb. He doesn't like me interfering.'

'If you think that's for the best.'

I have no idea if it's for the best, Jemima. Not a freaking clue. But I nod and cross my fingers that she'll be able to nip any bullying in the bud, very quietly. Hopefully, she won't let on to Caleb that I said anything because his trust has been hard-earned and I'd hate it to slip away. But mostly I hope she won't let on to Daniel that I'm keeping such a big secret about his son from him.

'Who was that?' asks Millicent, who passes Jemima leaving the shop as she comes in.

'It's Caleb's teacher. She was buying *Day of Desire,* which makes three copies I've sold just this morning. They've been flying off the shelves ever since I ordered them in.'

'Ah.' Millicent gives me a sideways glance before inspecting her fingernails. She definitely looks shifty. I come out from behind the counter and stand in front of her.

'Is everything all right? Is there a problem with the parade?' Crikey, I hope not. A lot of my time's being taken up with reassuring Becca about her bake-off arrangements and I'm kind of relying on Millicent to chivvy up the book club.

'It's all fine,' she says, fiddling with the mother-of-pearl buttons on the cuffs of her blouse. 'So *Day of Desire* is proving popular and selling well, is it?'

'Yes, why?'

Millicent takes a deep breath. 'I may have been a tad hasty in my judgement of that book. I assumed it would be awful and you said I should give it a try and I thought you were being ridiculous but I did read it' – she runs out of air and takes another breath – 'and you were right. It is a wonderful book. A *really* wonderful book, actually.'

My face breaks into a huge grin as I resist the urge to say 'I told you so'.

'Anyway,' continues Millicent, 'I wanted to tell you now, rather than in front of everyone at book club. I'd rather not admit publicly that I was...' she whispers, 'wrong.'

'Don't worry, Millicent. You're not the only person in town who judged the book by its cover and has since found out they were a tad hasty.'

'I know! Everywhere I go people are talking about it. It's become a local sensation and everyone wants to know who April Devlin is. You've certainly done well in championing it, Flora.'

'That's my job,' I say, simply, feeling like a proper bookseller who's discovered the Next Big Thing. Well, in Honeyford, anyway.

I pick up a sheet of paper from the counter and wave it at Millicent. 'Have you heard about the Best Book I've Read survey that we're running, with the winner to be announced on Charter Day? Why don't you vote for *Day of Desire*?'

Millicent sniffs as if there's a bad smell under her nose. 'I wouldn't go that far, Flora. It's not exactly Brontë or Dostoevsky, is it.'

'You're not voting for the best book you've *ever* read. It's for the best book you've read in the last three months.'

'Oh, in that case...'

Millicent takes the pen I offer and fills in the survey form in small, neat writing before slipping it into the collection box next to the till. There's quite a pile of completed forms in there already.

'Now you've expanded your reading horizons, Millicent, maybe you'd like to try out some of the other books in the shop that you might not have considered before? Who knows what surprising gems are waiting to be discovered?'

'I'll think about it. Oh, by the way, I got an email from Sebastian Kinsley, saying that he'll be arriving at Oxford Station at quarter to twelve on Saturday. Did he email you too, and is your husband still able to pick him up?'

'Yes and yes. I spoke to Malcolm on the phone and he's going to give Mr Kinsley lunch. He's being very helpful, actually.'

Since turning up at Millicent's house, Malcolm has been falling over himself to help with Charter Day and I'm beginning to think I might have misjudged him. Maybe he really is keen to make amends and help me build up my business?

'Talking of Charter Day,' says Millicent, grimacing, 'did you know that Stanley is threatening to dress as Spartacus in the parade? Or should I say undress. Can you imagine? Honeyford does not need eighty-year-old men in loincloths parading through its streets and heaven knows what a man of discernment like Mr Kinsley will make of the whole thing.'

'Does Callie know?'

Poor Callie. Whenever Stanley is planning one of his more madcap schemes, the first thing anyone asks is 'does Callie know?' But I'm feeling rather worried at the thought of a near-naked Stanley marching behind a Cosy Kettle placard. Coffee, cake… and senior-citizen nudity. That's not the homely image we're going for.

Millicent snorts. 'I shouldn't think she knows. I doubt she'd allow her grandfather to display his wares to all and sundry.'

'Probably not, though I'm not sure she could stop him because Stanley is a force of nature. I quite admire him, actually.'

'He is one of a kind and I suppose he can do what he wants. But I'm not walking anywhere near him if he's got his wrinkly backside hanging out. I know we're friends, but there is a limit.'

'Of course – and he's very fond of you.'

'He's got a funny way of showing it, embarrassing me in front of people.'

'I'm sure that's the last thing he wants to do,' I assure her, though I'm not so sure.

By the time Millicent leaves she's calmed down about the parade and the prospect of seeing Stanley's bits. I, on the other hand, am feeling more anxious by the minute about Charter Day in general, and talking to Caleb's teacher in particular. Have I done the right thing?

In the end, I'm so jittery I raid the box of herbal teabags that Luna insisted on giving me for work and I give chamomile a try. It's horrible. But I carry on drinking until I've drained the cup. Right now, I can do with all the help I can get.

Chapter Twenty

Charter Day has finally arrived, The Cosy Kettle has never been so busy and I am incredibly relieved. I was convinced that hardly anyone would turn up but all the chairs are taken and people are standing and chatting in little huddles.

In front of them, laid out on a long trestle table covered in gold paper tablecloths, is a fabulous display of Honeyford home baking – and my mouth is watering. Plump Victoria sandwiches, oozing jam and buttercream, are jostling for space next to rich fruit cakes, crumbly apple strudels, deep treacle tarts and cheesecakes dripping with fruit.

'Has that judge made his mind up yet?' asks Stanley, pointing at John, who's been running his own bakery for years and enjoys sampling his own products, if his very baggy shirt is anything to go by.

'Not yet. It must be hard choosing the best one. Which cake is yours, then?'

I'm joking, but Stanley jabs his finger at a large foil plate that has a round, iced cake sitting on it. White icing has pooled in a dip in the middle of the cake, and doesn't quite reach the edges, which are slightly charred.

'It's pound cake,' Stanley declares, proudly, 'and I made it all myself from scratch.'

'That's very impressive. I didn't know you were a home baker.'

'I'm not. This is the first cake I've ever made. My Moira was a magnificent cook and Callie's taken over the cooking since her gran died. But I thought it was about time I had a go. It was all going so well until the smoke alarm went off. And then I dropped it when I was getting it out of the oven, but I gave it a good wipe-over with the tea towel.' I make a mental note to avoid the pound cake as Stanley squints at the groaning trestle table. 'Which of these is Dick's then? He reckons he's a bit of a Jamie Oliver on the quiet.'

When I point out a coffee sponge layered with walnuts, Stanley walks over to it and gives it a sniff.

'Not bad,' is his considered opinion. 'Though I saw him loitering near the cake mixes in Tesco and he walked off sharpish after spotting me. Just sayin'. Anyway, what's the prize for winning?'

'Free coffee in The Cosy Kettle for a month, plus a fabulous trophy. What do you reckon? It's right at the back, there.'

Stanley stares at the trophy and whistles through his false teeth. 'My Moira would have loved that. It's a real beauty.'

He's right. Becca has excelled herself with the inaugural Honeyford Bake-Off trophy which she's sculpted out of copper wire. When she first suggested making the trophy, I was worried it would be a bit *meh*. But Becca proved me wrong in spectacular fashion. She turned up a week later with dozens of wires intricately twisted and wound around each other to form the shape of a kettle.

'I like making stuff,' was Becca's only comment when I heaped praise on her for such an amazing creation. It made me wonder how many other talents are hidden beneath her anxious and unassuming exterior.

Today her trophy has pride of place in The Cosy Kettle, next to Moira's beloved copper kettles that gave the café its name.

'Good day to you, Mistress Flora!' booms suddenly in my ear and I jump, spilling the coffee I'm holding.

Alan has come into the café and he's already parade-ready, in full costume – mustard tights, a knee-length bronze tunic caught in at the waist with a wide yellow sash, a long, yellow fur-edged jacket with puffball sleeves and a feathered hat.

'Gosh, Alan, you look magnificent,' I splutter.

'Though I don't fancy your wife's chances much,' sniggers Stanley.

'Pray tell, fellow, what dost thou mean with thy most strange remark?' asks Alan, taking off his hat and giving Stanley a sweeping bow. He gets full marks for being in character, if not for the historical accuracy of his costume.

'You're Henry the Eighth, aren't you? That bloke who kept chopping his wives' heads off?'

'I'm Henry the First,' hisses Alan, his round red face clouding over. 'The king who granted Honeyford its charter nine hundred years ago.'

'Oops, my bad,' says Stanley, giving me an eye-roll. 'I could have sworn you were the other fella, but at least I got the Henry bit right.'

'Huh,' grunts Alan, wandering off and wedging himself, as best as he can with his huge puffball sleeves, into a corner.

'That bloke's totally barking, don't you think?' says Stanley, rather more loudly than I'd like. 'And his put-on actory voice is so—'

'Oh, look, John's made his mind up!' I grab Stanley's arm and lead him closer to the trestle table where John is clearing his throat and preparing to speak.

'Thank you to everyone who's entered the town's first ever bake-off,' says John, to a cheer from the crowd. 'And thank you to Flora and Becca for inviting me to be Honeyford's answer to Paul Hollywood.'

Alan gives an even louder grunt.

'The standard has been incredibly high, your cakes taste wonderful and some of you could definitely give my bakery a run for its money. Right, on to business. First, I'll announce the bakers who were highly placed, then the winner, and then, most importantly, we can all tuck into these fabulous creations.'

There's another cheer from the crowd as John starts reading from a sheet of paper. 'Three bakers were highly placed – Melanie Milton for her sticky choc-chip sponge, Dick Pomfrey for his coffee and walnut cake, and Patricia Benn for her citrus chiffon gateau. But the winner of the Honeyford Bake-Off is…'

He pauses, and we all lean forward, but John is in no mood to tell us quickly. He's watched the *Strictly Come Dancing* results show and he wants to ramp up the tension by making us wait.

'Come on, mate,' shouts Stanley. 'I'm eighty, you know, and I need to find out who the winner is before I pop my clogs.'

'It's Shelley Holloway,' declares John, 'for her amazing organic carrot cake with courgette and beetroot frosting.'

'Less a cake and more a vegetable patch,' grumbles Stanley beside me, but the café erupts into applause when Shelley steps forward to accept Becca's wonderful work of art. Stanley's still muttering beside me. 'I can't believe Dick was highly placed for a cake mix. I was robbed.'

'Never mind.' I pat his skinny arm. 'Are you going to carry on baking?'

'Doubt it. It's much less faff to nip to Sainsbury's for a Battenberg. Oops, looks like it's your turn.'

John is beckoning me forwards. 'Excuse me, everyone!' he shouts above the chattering of the crowd. 'It's time for a few words from our bookshop and café owner. Flora, over to you!'

'Thanks, John,' I say, feeling a bit wobbly as all eyes turn to me. 'Thank you for being such a brilliant judge and a special thank you to Becca for not only organising this competition, but also for making the magnificent trophy.'

There's an 'ooh!' from the crowd and Becca dips her head in embarrassment.

'Slices of bake-off cakes are now on sale and profits will go to the community centre, so please start buying. And don't forget that there's lots going on in the bookshop this afternoon – a raffle and Book Surgery, and we'll be revealing the best book that's been read in Honeyford in the last three months. There will also be a talk from our VIP guest, the bestselling author S.R. Kinsley.' I pause for another 'ooh' from the crowd. 'So I really hope you'll stay for a while now and come back later.'

I've hardly finished speaking before people descend on the cake table like vultures. Fingers crossed we're going to raise loads for the community centre. Things have gone really well and, for the first time today, I relax and my shoulders drop. Becca has played a blinder and I'm so glad I put my faith in her. I made the right decision and that gives my confidence a real boost.

'Congratulations, Flora,' says a deep voice behind me. When I turn around, Daniel is standing there in a white shirt with his hands in the pockets of his black cord trousers. 'It all seems to be going well. I'm really pleased because I know how much it means to you.'

'Thanks. It really does. Is Caleb with you?'

'He's with Luna, helping to marshal her tarot card customers into an orderly queue. Her mystical skills are in demand.' When he smiles, I feel wobbly again. 'No Malcolm, then?'

'Not yet. He's feeding S.R. Kinsley and bringing him over later.'

'I expect your husband's keen to get here, what with it being decision day.'

Daniel's brown eyes meet mine and I don't know what to say. Just like I still don't know what I'm going to say to Malcolm later. It makes sense, I suppose, to go back to him and see how it goes, especially as he's trying so hard to be supportive. But, on the other hand…

Fortunately, I'm saved from saying anything at all by Katrina, who sidles up with a huge slice of oozing chocolate cake on a paper plate.

'Hi, there. What a lovely spread. Alan's already had a large piece of the chocolate ganache gateau and he sent me up for seconds.' She notices Daniel and does a double take. 'Who's this?' she asks, flicking her hair over her shoulder with her spare hand.

'This is Daniel, whose mother runs Luna's Magical Emporium.'

'Really?' Katrina laughs as Daniel smiles and shakes her hand. 'Your mother's shop is driving my husband mad so tell her to keep it up. A little gentle outrage keeps him occupied and out of my hair.' She lowers her voice. 'By the way, Flora, any chance of a sneak preview of the Best Book You've Read result?'

'I shouldn't, but' – I lean in close – 'it's *Day of Desire.*'

'Yes!' shouts Katrina, punching the air and sending chocolate crumbs flying. 'All my friends voted for it so I'm not surprised. Most of the women in town seem to be totally in love with that book. I'll see you later when you unveil the survey result. Lovely to meet you, Daniel.'

'What book did you say?' asks Daniel as Katrina makes a beeline for her husband.

'No one's supposed to know until this afternoon, but the winner is *Day of Desire,* which is brilliant news. I'm so chuffed and I'd never have discovered the book without you. Aren't you pleased?'

Daniel doesn't look like a man who's pleased. His face is pale against his dark hair and he's no longer smiling.

'Are you all right? I thought you'd be chuffed too seeing as—'

'Come with me,' he murmurs, grabbing my arm. He steers me past the crowds, out of the café and into a corner of the bookshop.

'What's going on, Daniel?'

'I need to have a word with you in private.' Daniel glances around us and bends his head until his hair brushes against mine. He smells of citrus and vanilla, like laundered sheets on a Provençal washing line. A sudden image of Daniel in swimwear under a hot French sun drifts into my mind, and I take a step backwards.

Nearby, people burst into peals of laughter and he frowns. 'This isn't private enough. Follow me.'

Why would Daniel want to speak to me in private? Unless he's about to confess that *Day of Desire was* written by Emma, and my nagging suspicion was right all along?

He weaves his way through the book browsers into our tiny shop kitchen, with me trotting behind. *Oh, I wish he hadn't come in here.* The kitchen's a tip, with dirty cups piled up in the sink that's still stained in spite of industrial quantities of bleach. I scrape scattered toast crumbs off the tiny worktop into my hand and dump them in the bin.

'Sorry about the mess. We've been so busy getting the shop and café ready, this room has been rather neglected.'

Daniel waves his hand, dismissively. 'It doesn't matter. I just needed a word. The truth is…' He lurches forwards as the kitchen door slams into his back.

'There you are, Flora,' says Becca, stepping into the room. Her jaw drops when she spots Daniel. 'Sorry, I didn't mean to bang into you and I'm sorry for interrupting, but Mr Morgan – Malcolm – just rang to say he's picked up Mr Kinsley and will be here at three.'

'OK, thanks, Becca.'

I lean back against the sink and take a deep breath. It's great that Mr Kinsley has arrived in Oxford, but I'm still nervous about hosting a renowned author who sells shedloads of books worldwide.

Becca swallows. 'Mr… Malcolm also said to tell you that he's expecting an answer, but I didn't understand what he was talking about. Sorry.'

'Don't worry. I know what he means.'

'Oh, and someone called Jemima was looking for you. She said she wanted to speak to you about Caleb. Something to do with stuff happening at school?'

Daniel's head shoots up. 'Do you mean Caleb's teacher, Jemima? Why does she want to speak to you, Flora, about my son?'

'I met her in the shop and mentioned that I know Caleb, so she probably just wants to say hello.' I'm such a hopeless liar. My over-bright tone of voice gives me away every time.

Daniel narrows his eyes at me, before peering through the open kitchen door.

'I can see her over there. Let's ask her, shall we?'

Becca spots the panic that must be written all over my face and starts shaking her head. 'I might have got the message wrong. I do get messages wrong sometimes. My friend Zac says I don't concentrate properly and I get things muddled. It's a curse.'

'Jemima!' shouts Daniel. He waves his arm above his head, and I catch a flash of white teeth as Jemima spots him and starts making her way through the crowd. My heart sinks into my sandals.

'Hello there, Mr Purfoot, I didn't realise you were here. And hi, Flora, I've been looking for you.' Beaming, Jemima steps into our tiddly kitchen, which is now totally rammed with four people. She wedges herself into a gap next to the ancient fridge and smooths down her shiny blonde hair. 'I must say, Flora, that I'm very impressed with the bake-off and what you've got planned this afternoon.'

'Thank you. That's really kind of you to say, especially when I'm sure you've got loads of other people to chat to. I think I saw some of your pupils browsing in our children's section.'

I start shuffling towards the door but Jemima stays wedged between the fridge and the crockery cupboard.

'Actually, while you're both here, I was hoping to have a quick word about Caleb if… um.'

She glances at Becca.

No, Becca! Please don't leave me alone with Daniel and Jemima. That's clearly what my eyes are saying. I can't open them any wider or stare any more beadily. But Becca is in a bit of a panic and oblivious to my silent cry for help. She apologises profusely – I'm not sure what for – and beats a hasty retreat. The kitchen door bangs shut behind her.

'Is everything all right with Caleb?' asks Daniel, looking worried.

'Yes, I think so,' says ever-smiley Jemima, who's showing lots of tanned leg in a short blue skirt. 'I've been keeping an eye on him and you were right, Flora, that there have been a few friendship problems and some low-level bullying which needed to be tackled. So I just wanted to let you know that I'm very glad you said something and there's nothing to worry about when Caleb comes back to school next term.'

'That's good to hear,' I squeak, as Daniel stands silently beside me.

'Anyway, I'm glad that's all sorted.' Jemima grins so hard, huge dimples appear in her cheeks. 'Now, I'm going to have some of the amazing cake that's on offer. Honestly, choosing which one to try is a nightmare. I'll see you both later.' She waggles her fingers at us and heads back into the bookshop, leaving me and Daniel alone.

For a moment, neither of us speak and then Daniel swings round towards me.

'What did she mean?' His voice is low and calm but a tiny muscle is fluttering beneath his left eye.

'I mentioned that I knew Caleb when Jemima came in to buy a book.'

'She talked about bullying.'

'Well, friendship problems, really.'

'Nope. She definitely used the word "bullying", which came as rather a shock to me, seeing as I've heard nothing about it. Are you going to tell me what's been going on?'

'It wasn't really…' My shoulders slump with the realisation that there's no getting out of it. I need to fully break my promise to Caleb, as I probably should have done from the start. Here goes… 'A couple of weeks ago, I saw some boys take Caleb's lunch when they were on a school trip in Honeyford.' I ignore Daniel's sharp intake of breath and plough on. 'So, I spoke to Caleb about it and he said some of the boys were being mean to him. He didn't want to speak about it and he only told me when I promised not to tell anyone else.'

'By anyone else, do you mean his father?' Daniel's voice is still ominously low and calm.

'Yes,' I say, miserably. 'He was desperate not to make you sad again, Daniel.'

'So you kept it from me? Good grief, Flora!' Daniel starts pacing up and down the kitchen – with his long legs, it's no more than five steps each way. 'How could you keep something so important from me? He's my son. He was in trouble and you didn't tell me. That's unbelievable.'

'I wanted to tell you but he made me promise on his life that I wouldn't tell anyone.'

'And you made that promise? He's nine years old, Flora. Whatever was agreed, you should have told me.'

'Yes, I expect you're right but he was adamant and I didn't want him to stop talking to me and be miserable on his own.'

'So you said nothing to me or to his grandmother.' Daniel's handsome face is a picture of incomprehension. 'I was beginning to think you were good for Caleb, but now I find out I can't trust you with him.'

'Of course you can trust me. I care a great deal about Caleb and I wanted to help him but didn't know how. So I hinted at what was wrong to Jemima and it sounds as though she's sorting things out.'

'You hinted? Jemima seems a good teacher in many ways but she's not the sharpest knife in the block. What if she hadn't cottoned on to your hints? You may as well have been sending up smoke signals while thugs were beating up my son.'

'The boys weren't beating up Caleb. You're being over the top.'

'Really? I've just found out you knew that my son was being bullied and you didn't tell me, and you went behind my back to his teacher.'

'Yeah. Put like that, it doesn't sound great. Look, I'm really sorry if I screwed up. I was trying to keep my promise and do what was best for Caleb, and it seemed the most sensible thing to do, in the circumstances.'

'But it wasn't the right thing to do, Flora.' Daniel presses the heels of his hands against his forehead and breathes out slowly. 'I'm sure you were doing your best but it's not how I choose to parent and protect my son.'

'You can't protect him from everything.'

Daniel shakes his head. 'How would you know, Flora, when you never got around to having children?'

That's a low blow and Daniel knows it. He frowns and steps towards me. 'I didn't mean that the way it sounded. I'm just upset about… urgh! Really?' He grits his teeth as the door bashes into his back again.

'Sorry, sorry,' says Becca, poking her head around the door and grimacing at Daniel. 'I wouldn't have bothered you, Flora, but it's kicking off in the café. Alan's arguing with John that he got his judging wrong. He just banged his fist on the trestle table and sent Melanie's choc-chip sponge flying. It looks like there's been a chocolate massacre in The Cosy Kettle.'

Oh, Lord.

Daniel shrugs. 'You'd better go and sort it out.'

'Will you be all right?'

'Of course. Caleb and I are always all right.'

He flattens himself against the counter but I can't help brushing against him as I rush out of the kitchen to act as peacemaker in a cake war. It seems I peaked too soon with my positive feelings after the bake-off.

In so many ways, Charter Day isn't turning out quite the way I'd hoped.

Becca wasn't exaggerating when she said it was kicking off in The Cosy Kettle. Melanie is standing in the remains of her smashed cake, shouting at Alan, who's waving what looks like a sponge finger in John's face.

'This is better entertainment than *It's A Knockout*,' chortles Stanley. He takes a mobile phone from the pocket of his jeans and starts snapping pictures.

'Pack it in,' I yell, wading into the fray and almost slipping on spilled cream. 'Stanley, please stop taking photos and go and keep an eye on the shop for me. Now, what on earth is going on?'

'There has been a major travesty of justice,' booms Alan, waggling the sponge finger at me. Channelling an autocratic monarch has obviously gone to his head. 'I've been tasting the cakes—'

'He's been taking a spoonful out of each, even though I asked him not to,' confirms Becca.

'… and Mrs Holloway has baked a perfectly sound cake. It's light with a very pleasant taste, but it is not the winning bake in my opinion. That honour should go to this one here, the coffee and walnut creation by' – he squints at the little flag on a cocktail stick that's rammed into his cake of choice – 'a Mr Dick Pomfrey.'

Fabulous! I can only imagine the to-do if Stanley finds out about this and starts flinging cake-mix accusations all over the place. This conflagration will look like a minor skirmish, in comparison.

'The judge's verdict is final,' I tell Alan, pushing the sponge finger away from my nose. 'In John's opinion, Mrs Holloway deserved to win and that judgement can't be rescinded.' When Alan scowls, his jowls start to wobble. 'The bake-off is over but I was rather hoping, Alan, that you'd speak to some of my customers in the shop. They're very impressed with the brilliance of your costume and, um, general characterisation of King Henry the First. I overheard someone saying that you had a look of' – I dredge my brain for an actor of suitable repute – 'Damian Lewis about you.'

'Golden Globe winner, Damian Lewis? Really?'

No, not really, Alan. But he swallows it, thank goodness, and, with a final withering glare at our poor judge, he bustles out of the café.

By the time I've apologised profusely to John and herded everyone out of the café, Becca has started clearing up the mess.

'I'll do it,' I tell her, putting on my apron and taking the dustpan and brush from her. 'If you go and relieve Stanley, who's keeping an eye on the shop, I'll clean this up and then we can let people back in to finish off the cakes.'

Becca gets to her feet and wipes smudged chocolate cake from her knees. 'Are you sure?'

'Absolutely. Just let me know if Alan starts punching customers.'

Becca grins. 'It's OK. Katrina's in there and she kind of keeps him under control.'

'Kind of.'

Once Becca's gone, and the café is blessedly quiet, I kneel down and start scraping smashed cake into the bin. Crumbs have scattered everywhere. Alan is a right pain and should be cleaning this up himself, but I'm enjoying a few moments of peace and quiet. I knew Charter Day was going to be full on, but I wasn't expecting to sort out a cake war and be outed by Jemima to Daniel before – I check my watch – midday. And just when Daniel and I were settling into a slightly less awkward relationship.

I sigh and dip my fingers into the only pile of cake that hasn't been trodden into the concrete. Then I push my fingers into my mouth and suck off the sickly sweet concoction. Chocolate, and lots of it, is the only thing that will do the trick for me right now. The café door creaks open as I'm mid-suck and Caleb comes in. He walks purposefully towards me, his little face deadly serious, and stands with his hands on his hips.

'You told my teacher about the boys taking my lunch. I trusted you and you promised, but you told her, and now my dad knows, too, and he's upset and it's all my fault.' He pushes out his bottom lip and starts blinking really fast. He's breaking my heart.

'Your dad's upset because of me, not you.'

I wipe my fingers on my apron, sit back on the floor and open my arms wide, in case he needs a hug. I'm expecting some resistance but he immediately wraps his arms around my neck and cuddles into me. I hug him tightly for a few moments before pulling him onto my lap.

'I'm sorry, Caleb. I promised I wouldn't tell anyone but I should never have made you a promise like that. The truth is I was worried about you so I told Jemima, your teacher, that life was a bit tricky for you at school. I honestly didn't say anything about the boys taking your lunch.' I sigh. 'Maybe I shouldn't have said anything at all to your teacher. I only did because I care about you so much. But I definitely should have told your dad what was happening, Caleb – promise, or not – because he loves you and he wants to look after you. I made a big mistake in not telling him and now he's angry with me, not with you.'

Caleb snuggles further into me and, when I stroke his soft fair hair, he pushes his thumb into his mouth. I tighten my arms around him and lay my cheek on the top of his head. This feels so right.

'Do you want some cake?' I ask, my head still resting on his.

'Deffo.'

As I'm scooping up a handful of untrodden cake and giving it to Caleb, I glance across the café and spot Daniel standing by the door. His eyes meet mine across the top of Caleb's head and then, without a word, he turns and slips out again.

Chapter Twenty-One

King Henry himself could not have chosen better weather for Charter Day. The sun is high in a china-blue sky and the town is filled with excited voices and children's laughter, but I can't relax. I keep reliving the kitchen scene with Daniel and wishing I'd told him from the outset about the bullies targeting Caleb.

Did I really make it worse? I was only trying to do the right thing. A small girl, her hair in bunches, walks past hand in hand with her mum, and my stomach clenches. I bet her mum wouldn't make such an almighty cock-up of things if she found out her daughter was being bullied at school.

'Are you all right, Flora?' asks Becca, who's been an absolute star all morning. She nudges me gently. 'I'm sorry if I got in the way a bit in the kitchen when you were talking to Mr Purfoot.'

'Daniel.'

'Yeah, when you were talking to Daniel.' She starts hopping from foot to foot. 'I hope you don't mind me asking, and I'm not trying to interfere, but is everything all right? Only you seem a bit upset.'

'Don't worry, Becca. Everything's fine.'

'If you're sure. You look fantastic, by the way.'

'Thank you.'

I run my fingers over the white flowing fabric that's caught with a gold belt at my waist before cascading to my feet. I wasn't going to take part in the parade until Luna persuaded me to close the shop and café for an hour. She offered to make my costume, which is why I'm currently dressed as a goddess in what was once a bed sheet. A spray-painted gold wreath of leaves is on my head and I've borrowed Luna's silver flip-flops.

I'd feel a bit of a prat, to be honest, if I wasn't surrounded by the great and the good of Honeyford, all dressed in a variety of outlandish costumes – from animals and superheroes to ballerinas and pirates.

We're all clustered around the war memorial, steaming gently in the hot lunchtime sunshine and waiting for Alan to start the parade. I crane my neck, trying to spot the book club through the milling crowd. There they are, ambling towards me and looking fabulous!

Stanley has ditched his loincloth, thank goodness, and is dressed as Biggles in a battered leather jacket and huge goggles. Dick has opted for Harry Potter, complete with a cloak, round glasses and a scar on his forehead that looks a lot like lipstick. Mary is a white-faced zombie in ragged clothes, and Millicent looks very Jo March in a long dress and a bonnet. Phyllis, being pushed in her wheelchair by Mary, is bonneted up too as Elizabeth Bennet and is carrying a large photo of Colin Firth's head on a stick.

Behind them, Luna is wandering along with a huge smile on her face. She's dressed as a goddess from the Greek myths too – she had two spare bed sheets. And, with her long silver hair flowing down her back, she looks far more other-worldly than me. Caleb, in his Spider-Man costume, is clasping her hand. He looks adorable and gives me a shy grin.

'Are you up for this then, Flora?' asks Dick, swishing his cloak as he reaches me. 'The whole town's gone mad and you know what they say – if you can't beat 'em, join 'em. There's a man over there dressed

as a gorilla who's never going to last in this heat. And have you seen
that Alan bloke on his float yet?'

When I shake my head, Dick chortles. 'Then you are in for a right
royal treat and, speak of the devil, here he comes.'

The crowd ripples back as a flatbed lorry pulls up next to the
war memorial. The back has been covered in what looks like gold
tinfoil and there, in pride of place, is Alan. He's sitting on a throne
that's really a chair covered in gold tissue paper, and he's waving at
everyone. Let's just hope no one notices the chocolate cake stains on
his lavish costume.

Katrina is seated next to him, now wearing a long silver lamé dress
and looking bored. She gives me a very non-regal wave and yawns,
before pulling a mobile phone from under her right buttock and having
a shifty look at the screen.

The lorry starts trundling slowly along the High Street and the
fledgling samba band falls in behind, along with local Brownie and
Cub packs, and people in fancy dress.

'Come on, everyone,' yells Stanley, grabbing the sign made by
Daniel that says: *Cosy Kettle Afternoon Book Club & Luna's Magical
Emporium.* 'It's time to par-tay!'

Honeyford Samba Band might be newly formed but it's brilliant.
The musicians dance and weave their way along the street and the raw
tribal beat lightens my heart and my mood as we follow them. Bystand-
ers are cheering and waving flags and I feel a sudden overwhelming
rush of affection for this tiny town and these people who have come
into my life when I needed them most.

As we go past the bookshop, I spot Becca, who categorically refused
to dress up. And there's Daniel standing next to her. He calls out to

Caleb and gives him a big thumbs up before the parade snakes past and turns into Weavers Lane.

By the time we arrive at the Memorial Park twenty minutes later, Dick is grumbling that his corns hurt, Millicent is overheating in her bonnet and Phyllis has almost had Mary's eye out with her Colin Firth stick. But everyone seems glad we took part in the parade, which is now starting to disband.

I'm about to hurry back to the shop when Daniel's voice suddenly sounds in my ear. 'That looked like fun.' He laughs when I jump, and waves at Luna, who's sitting on the park wall with Caleb.

'It was more fun than I expected. What are you doing here?'

'I need to collect Caleb so Luna can get back to her tarot reading. She's in demand.' He smiles at Stanley, who's ditched his Biggles goggles and is tucking into an ice-cream cornet. 'Everyone looked amazing and seemed to be enjoying themselves. It was great publicity for the book club.'

'It certainly was. Thank you for making the sign – it did the trick perfectly.'

We're back to being ultra-polite to each other and our earlier spat hangs in the air between us.

Suddenly, the crowd around us shifts and Daniel moves closer, until his arm is brushing mine. 'Look, Flora, I need a quick word. I've spoken to Caleb and he told me that he threatened to run away if you told anyone his secret. I still think you made the wrong call, but I can see that you were in a difficult position, and I'm sorry if I went over the top in the kitchen. I can be a bit… in your face with people sometimes.'

He winces as people around us cheer for local newsagent Ivor, who's dressed up as a giant bee and has just removed his costume head.

'It's all right. I should have told you,' I shout, trying to be heard above the cheering.

'Maybe, but you cared enough to try and do something to help Caleb and it sounds like Jemima's on top of the situation now so there's no harm done.'

'Except you don't trust me.'

Daniel shrugs. 'Like I said, I can be over the top. I was upset when I said that.'

'But I don't blame you for saying it. I don't trust myself either, right now, when it comes to making decisions. Everything's a bit of a muddle.'

'You've got a lot on your plate and you could have done without taking on my son's problems.'

'I didn't mind because I care about Caleb.'

'I know. That was very apparent when I saw you both in the café earlier. You're good for Caleb, Flora.'

'Even when I'm keeping important stuff from you and feeding him chocolate cake off the floor?'

Daniel's mouth twitches. 'Did you abide by the five-second rule?'

'Hmm, not quite, but the cake had been on the floor for less than five *minutes*, if that counts?'

'Yeah, as long as it's less than five something, that's fine.'

The bee has buzzed past, the crowd has quietened down, and Daniel's last sentence reverberates along the road.

'Oops.' When he grins, lines fan out from his brown eyes. 'Everything might seem like a muddle, Flora, but you're doing a grand job in the shop and the café. Your Charter Day is a great success.'

'Do you think? What about World War Three in The Cosy Kettle – a war fought with chocolate frosting, sponge fingers and crème pat?'

Daniel throws back his head and laughs. 'That sounds delicious. And from what I've heard, you dealt with the situation admirably.' He swallows. 'You look lovely, by the way, in your goddessy get-up. Really lovely.'

The sound from the crowd seems to fade away and it's suddenly quite hard to breathe. The skin of my arm is against the warm skin of his and my nerve endings feel as though they're on fire.

The spell is broken by the shrill ring of my mobile, which is clipped onto my belt. Daniel steps back as I unclip the phone and glance at the screen. It's Malcolm.

'Flora? Where the hell are you? It sounds like you're at the circus.'

'We've just finished the Charter Day parade and everyone's gathered at the park.'

'Oh yeah, I'd forgotten about that. Look, this is a quick call to let you know that Mr Kinsley has just finished his lunch so we'll be with you on time.'

'That's wonderful. Thank you for doing this, Malcolm. I appreciate it.'

'Of course. Like I said, I want to help make sure that my wife's event is a great success and her dreams come true. We'll see you soon.'

I'm about to end the call when Malcolm says, 'And I'm looking forward to speaking to you later—'

'About? Oh, about my decision.'

'Yes, of course, your decision.' Malcolm sounds cross. 'I hope you hadn't forgotten.'

'Of course I hadn't forgotten.'

I definitely had, momentarily. Daniel's arm pressed up against mine had completely pushed the fact that today is D-Day out of my mind.

'Hmm. Well, Mr Kinsley and I will see you soon.'

As soon as the call has finished, Daniel says, 'I'd better go and grab Caleb because Luna will want to get back to her shop. I'll see you later,

Flora. Congratulations again on a successful Charter Day and I hope all goes well with your famous author.'

'Thank you. I'm sure it'll be fine.'

We're back to being ultra-polite again. But a sudden thought strikes me as he walks away. 'I've been meaning to ask – what did you want to speak to me about in the kitchen, before Jemima came in?'

Daniel keeps on moving away from me. 'Nothing important. It doesn't matter.'

He weaves his way through the crowd towards his son and I watch him go.

Chapter Twenty-Two

Becca has opened up the shop by the time I get back and people are starting to gather for our VIP visit. We've cleared a large space at the front of the store and set up displays of S.R. Kinsley's bestsellers plus a couple of comfy chairs and a microphone borrowed from Alan. Now all we need is our special guest. I change back into my blue chinos and cream linen top and head outside because Malcolm texted a while ago that they were on their way.

Five minutes later, Malcolm's Jaguar purrs into view and draws up beside me. Our famous guest is here and I can finally relax because everything is going to be OK. Grinning broadly, I nip round to the passenger side and open the door.

I've never met a proper big-name author before – one who sells gazillions of books and is photographed at posh hotels in Sunday newspaper supplements. I'm expecting S.R. Kinsley to be debonair and charming, with an air of creativity surrounding him like a cloak.

I am certainly not expecting him to be drunk. But here he is, clambering out of Malcolm's car, pissed as the proverbial newt.

'You must be Flora,' he drools, dropping his leather briefcase on my toes and swaying alarmingly. He stares at me, jerking his head backwards and forwards in a bid to focus. 'How perfectly marvellous to meet you and you're so damned attractive too. No one mentioned that.'

When he lunges forward, I step back sharpish because the fug of alcohol fumes coming off him is making my eyes water. But I'm too slow and he plants a big, wet smacker on my right cheek.

'Ooh, you smell absolutely divine, sweetheart,' he slurs, 'and how gorgeous is this teeny tiny little town? Look at all the flowers and the tiddly houses. Tell me, how many pubs does Honey… Honey…?' He gives up. '…this place have?'

'A couple, Mr Kinsley,' I mutter, grabbing hold of his arm as he stumbles over the kerb. If he goes head over heels, he'll never get up.

'That's marvellous, and please do call me Sebastian,' he mumbles. 'I can try out both of 'em. Actually, talking of pubs, I quite fancy a cheeky pint and a whisky chaser right now.' He belches and giggles. 'Oops, I do beg your pardon.'

'What the hell?' I mouth at Malcolm, who's out of his car and leaning against it with his arms folded. He shrugs.

'Here he is, at last!' declares Millicent, bustling up behind me. 'Mr Kinsley, how magnificent to make your acquaintance once more. You came to my house a while back for dinner and… oh.' She stops and claps a hand to her mouth as our star speaker, her VIP dinner guest, sways back and forth with a stupid grin on his face.

'Is he…?' she asks, recoiling from the alcohol fumes. 'He appears to be—'

'Yep, Millicent. Mr Sebastian Kinsley, our VIP speaker, is absolutely bladdered.'

'But you shouldn't have let him anywhere near alcohol,' she splutters.
'I didn't.'

'Well, someone has, even though everyone knows he has no control after he's had a few.'

'I didn't know. Why didn't you tell me?'

'I didn't think I needed to spell it out,' she huffs. 'There are so many stories online about his fondness for drink. Why do you think he threw up in my flower bed?'

'I don't know. Food poisoning?'

'Food poisoning?' squeaks Millicent, aghast. 'At my dinner party?'

'It doesn't matter,' I say, as Mr Kinsley slumps against me. Malcolm is still standing by the car, doing absolutely nothing. 'The most important thing right now is working out what the hell we're going to do with our esteemed, rat-arsed author?'

'And with the crowd that's waiting for him. There are loads of people in the shop and they're expecting to hear from a famous writer. It's going to be really bad publicity for the bookshop if you let everyone down. No one will ever forgive you.'

'Cheers, Millicent. That really helps.'

'Just telling you the truth.' She purses her lips as though she's sucking on a lemon.

I take a deep breath and try to keep the drunken man, who weighs a ton, upright. 'OK. First things first. We need to get Mr Kinsley inside.'

'Definitely, and before people I know spot us together,' hisses Millicent. 'I don't want to be seen in the street with a drunk – even if he is a celebrity.'

She grabs his arm, which he's waving around as though he's conducting an invisible orchestra, and I put my arm around his waist.

'Aw, are you giving me a cuddle?' slurs Mr Kinsley, slumping against me with his head on my shoulder. 'Do you wanna kiss? Ooh, I wanna kiss you, biggish-like.'

Biggish-like? This is the man who's expected to talk eloquently about his love of the English language in ten minutes' time.

'Move yourself, Malcolm,' I snap. 'We need to get this sorted out.'

Together, with Malcolm's help, we spirit Mr Kinsley in through the back door of the café. Fortunately, everyone is gathered in the shop, waiting to greet our esteemed author, so the only person we bump into is Becca. Her mouth opens wide at the sight of our almost unconscious guest being hauled along.

'Is that him?' she asks, giving a nervous giggle. 'What's going on?'

'This is Mr Kinsley, who is… well, he's pissed and we need to get him upstairs, pronto. Please don't say a word to anyone. Not until we've worked out what we're going to do.'

Millicent, Malcolm and I manage to half-push, half-pull Mr Kinsley up the rickety wooden stairs and into the attic room. He stumbles into a huge cobweb that's hanging between the beams, before falling, face first, onto Ruben's camp bed. A large puff of dust rises into the air.

For a few moments, we all stand at the foot of the bed, staring, until I realise that someone needs to take control of the situation.

'Millicent, would you mind going downstairs and holding the fort? People are expecting to hear from Mr Kinsley any minute and we need to buy some time.'

'What shall I tell them?' she asks, frowning at our author, who's snoring loudly. His shirt has rucked up, exposing a roll of flabby white flesh above the belt of his trousers.

'Tell them anything but the truth. Say he's been delayed by… I don't know, traffic, diarrhoea, aliens? And in the meantime we can work out what we're going to do.'

'Let me get this straight,' says Millicent, who's not really being terribly helpful. 'You want me to lie to a shop full of people?'

Grasping her by the shoulders, I stare deep into her eyes. 'Absolutely. I want you to lie through your teeth because now is not the time to get on your moral high horse, Millicent.' When she looks equally doubtful and affronted, I sigh. 'Just apologise profusely and say that Mr Kinsley is indisposed at the moment. That's true enough.'

He gives a huge, foul-smelling belch to verify this fact as Millicent, pale-faced, descends the stairs. The moment she's gone, I round on Malcolm, who's leaning against the wall watching what's going on.

'What the hell happened? How did this go so wrong?'

'What do you mean? It's not my fault,' he blusters.

'You offer to pick up our author and give him lunch, and he turns up at my shop totally off his head. You're the only person who's seen him so whose fault is it?'

'Certainly not mine. I offered him a *glass* of Burgundy at lunchtime. *One* glass. That's just being a good host. I didn't know he was going to order a bottle when my back was turned, did I?'

'One bottle?'

Malcolm pushes out his bottom lip so far he looks like a big baby. 'Maybe two. We were busy and I didn't have the time to police his alcohol intake. I didn't think he'd take advantage of my free hospitality.' He emphasises the word 'free' as though I should be falling over myself to thank him.

But I'm still reeling from this extra information. My VIP guest, the man a crowd downstairs is expecting to talk sensibly to them about writing, has consumed two bottles of wine in the last couple of hours. What on earth am I going to do?

There's the sound of a steady tread on the wooden staircase and, even before his dark hair comes into view, I know it's Daniel.

'Is everything all right up here?' he asks, shooting me a quizzical look. 'Becca's downstairs in a bit of a flap and finally said there was "a bit of an issue" when I grilled her.'

He swiftly takes in the scene before him – Mr Kinsley is now half-on and half-off the camp bed, singing a filthy song involving a sailor and a prostitute in Plymouth; I'm running my hands through my hair over and over again; and Malcolm is still leaning against the wall, doing what can only be described as sulking.

'Right,' says Daniel. He gives a soft, low whistle. 'This is, indeed, a bit of an issue.'

'Lover boy's here and stating the bleeding obvious. That's all we need,' hisses Malcolm, puffing out his chest.

Daniel ignores him and walks over to the bed. 'I presume this is the great novelist S.R. Kinsley? What happened here, then?'

'Malcolm picked him up at Oxford Station and gave him lunch,' I tell him, trying to smooth my hair back into some semblance of style.

Daniel gives Mr Kinsley a prod on the shoulder and winces when the author launches into another verse of his song. 'A liquid lunch, was it?'

'It was honey-glazed veal escalopes with a summer vegetable medley, if you must know,' says Malcolm, speaking loudly to be heard above the singing. 'Plus a glass of Burgundy.'

'One glass? Our bestselling author might have a way with words, but when it comes to alcohol, he's a bit of a lightweight.'

'He had one glass of Burgundy – plus another two bottles,' I tell Daniel, with a sigh.

'Ah, that'll do it every time.'

'Two bottles of which I had no knowledge,' insists Malcolm. 'I was busy in—'

'Yes, you've already said,' I snap. 'Forget how it happened. The important thing is what happens now? I've got a shop full of people downstairs including a host of book lovers and the entire committee of Honeyford Heritage Society who are expecting to spend an interesting hour with an author they've heard of.'

I walk to the bed and give the author's leg a none too gentle nudge with mine. 'Shush, will you? Heaven knows what people will think we're doing up here.'

He stops singing and closes his eyes.

'Maybe we could fill him up with strong coffee,' I suggest. 'Or douse him in cold water to sober up. Becca's place is nearby and she's got a shower. I bet she wouldn't mind.'

'There's no way I'm stripping S.R. Kinsley naked and getting him into a shower,' huffs Malcolm. 'He's too far gone, anyway. There's nothing for it, Flora. You'll just have to cancel the event.'

'This event has been billed as the highlight of Charter Day. There must be *something* we can do.'

But when my VIP guest emits a loud, grunting snore and his head lolls back against the pillow, I realise it's all over. I sink onto the edge of the bed and put my head in my hands.

'I'm trying to be a part of this community. If I call things off at this stage, I'll look like an idiot who can't organise a simple event, let alone successfully run a local café and bookshop. The locals will organise a petition to get Ruben back.'

'Don't be so hard on yourself,' says Malcolm. He perches on the bed next to me, his arm snakes around my shoulder and I feel so miserable I let him pull me against his chest. 'Running a business is really hard and I'm proud of you for having a good stab at it,' he says, into my hair. 'But your place is with me. We can carry on running the restaurant together.'

'Good grief, it was you,' says Daniel, suddenly. He hits his forehead with the heel of his hand. 'Of course it was you. Of all the dirty, low-down tricks—'

'What are you talking about?' I mumble into Malcolm's chest.

'Your husband got this bloke drunk on purpose so you'd have to cancel the event and you'd lose confidence in your ability to run the shop and be more likely to go running back to him. To go back to your safe, sensible life where he can control you.'

'How dare you!' cries Malcolm, jumping to his feet. 'As if I'd do such a thing. I was trying to help Flora by feeding Kinsley – it's not my fault that he turns out to be an idiot when it comes to drink. And that wine he polished off – without me knowing – wasn't cheap, you know. I'm severely out of pocket.'

'Oh boo hoo! Flora's got a real problem here but you're still thinking only of yourself.'

'Boo hoo, indeed. We're not all working in boring finance and getting a set monthly wage.'

Hell's teeth. Just when I think things can't get any worse, an argument kicks off between my husband and my… my whatever Daniel is. They're both behaving like children. I drag myself wearily to my feet. 'Please stop arguing. Malcolm can be unkind, deceptive and a pain at times—'

'Um, I can hear you,' grumps Malcolm, his face like thunder.

I silence him with a wave of my hand. 'But I'm sure he wouldn't set out to sabotage my event.'

'Of course I wouldn't, and it's slanderous to say so.' He stands square in front of Daniel and juts out his jaw. 'You seem to know an awful lot about Flora's situation.'

Daniel bristles. 'I simply take an interest in her and her business.'

'What sort of interest? Exactly how well do you know my wife?'

'We live together,' says Daniel.

Which really doesn't help. Our rubbish guest carries on snoring loudly behind us as Malcolm starts quivering all over. Luna would tell me that negative energy is coming off him in waves. I can feel it, like a damp, suffocating blanket wrapping tightly around me.

But Daniel just stands there, seemingly unconcerned that my husband might be about to land a punch. Probably because he's almost a head taller and far more wiry. I don't fancy Malcolm's chances, to be honest.

Before I can step in, there's a shout up the stairs from Millicent. 'Can you lot hurry up? It's getting ugly down here. Alan has started regaling us with tales of his acting prowess and everyone's heard them many times before.'

'I'll be down in just a sec,' I shout, before turning back to Malcolm and Daniel. 'Look, I need to go down and announce the winner of the Best Loved Book survey and tell the crowd that the author event is off. Let's be realistic. There's nothing else I can do. Can you go down and keep things calm, Malcolm? I'll be right behind you.'

Malcolm moves towards the stairs but stops with his hand on the bannister.

'I'm not leaving you and lover boy alone up here.'

'Oh, for goodness' sake!' Daniel points at the bed, which is being rattled by seismic snores. 'That's hardly mood music, is it?'

'Both of you, just go downstairs. Please. I want to make sure Mr Kinsley's all right and then I'll be right behind you.'

Malcolm starts trooping down the stairs, but I grab Daniel by the arm before he can follow him. 'Hang on a minute,' I whisper. 'You don't really think that Malcolm planned this, do you?'

He shrugs. 'I wouldn't be surprised.'

'I know you don't like him much but I can't believe he'd do that. He's still my husband.'

Daniel sighs and shakes his head. 'No, I guess not. I just think Malcolm's a total arse for almost losing you.'

Almost losing me? Does he think I'm going back to my old life? My sensible, ordered life that seems very enticing all of a sudden, particularly after the bake-off punch-up and now with S.R. Kinsley in a drunken heap behind me. Maybe I should go back to helping out in the restaurant and not overreach myself.

'I'm waiting!' yells Malcolm up the stairs. With a lift of his eyebrow, Daniel turns away and hurries down to him.

I look at our author, who's flat out on the bed, and drape the thin sheet over him. Luckily, his snoring has reduced in volume to a rhythmic snuffling. My anger and panic are morphing into general resignation and I can't help feeling sorry for someone who feels the need to drink two bottles of wine at lunchtime. He's caused a huge problem, but I wonder what problems of his own he's trying to blot out.

We'll keep an eye on him for a couple of hours and, when he's sufficiently sober, we can put him on a train back to London. Telling everyone downstairs the truth is an option, but I'd rather spare Mr Kinsley's blushes. It was kind of him to agree to talk for free in my little shop, even if his visit didn't turn out quite as I'd hoped.

As I get to the stairs, he shifts in his sleep and lets out a rumbling fart.

Chapter Twenty-Three

Millicent got it spot on. The crowd waiting for S.R. Kinsley are definitely not impressed by Alan's tales of life on the West End stage. And neither is Katrina.

'Oh, thank goodness. He might shut up now,' she groans when she sees me. 'He only had a few minor ensemble roles but he carries on as if he was best mates with Ian McKellen.'

Alan is holding forth in the makeshift stage area Becca and I sorted out earlier. He's bellowing into the microphone, though he definitely doesn't need it, with his arm draped across a plastic display stand packed full of S.R. Kinsley novels.

'She's here!' yells Millicent, wrestling the microphone from Alan's hands as a general sigh of relief goes up from the crowd. At the back of the room, Malcolm is standing with his hands in his pockets and a strange look on his face.

I gaze at all the people who've turned up for our special speaker and swallow. There are far more people here than I'd imagined. Lots of them haven't been into the shop before and I don't suppose they'll come back once they hear what I have to say.

Standing so I block the bestsellers display, I start speaking into the microphone. 'Thank you all for coming, and I'm so sorry to have kept you waiting. First of all, I'd like to announce the winner of the

Best Book I've Read survey. Local readers were asked to nominate the book that they've enjoyed reading the most over the last three months. We've had loads of entries and I'm delighted to announce that the overwhelming winner is *Day of Desire* by April Devlin.'

A collective cheer goes up from most of the women present, and a couple of the men, I notice.

'I'm delighted that this particular book won because I've really championed this gorgeous love story. It's set amid the minutiae of everyday life and touches on universal feelings but describes them almost poetically. It's a wonderful book, and I hope, if you haven't read it, that you'll buy a copy today. We don't know anything about the author, April Devlin. She's a bit of an enigma and, as far as I'm aware, she hasn't written anything else, which is such a shame. Anyway, let's see who's won a book token for nominating this novel.'

I reach into a black velvet bag that Phyllis has made especially for the occasion and pull out a folded sheet of paper.

'The winner is… Eileen Conway. Congratulations.'

Eileen, an elderly woman with snow-white hair, makes her way through the crowd and smiles as I hand over the book token. 'It's a fabulous book,' she mouths at me, before disappearing back into the crowd.

Right. Next comes the difficult bit. I clear my throat and raise the microphone as Malcolm gives me a thumbs up from the back of the crowd.

'Next, I was hoping to introduce our special guest, bestselling author S.R. Kinsley, but I'm afraid I have some bad news. Mr Kinsley has had to cancel at the last minute because of… um, ill health.' A murmur of disappointment and discontent grumbles through the crowd. 'I'm so sorry but I'm afraid it's outside of my control.'

People are leaving. Of course they are. And Alan, at the back of the room, is glowering at me as though I'm personally responsible for ruining Charter Day. Everything was going brilliantly and now I've chucked a huge spanner in the works. So much for hoping to be a valued part of this community. I bite my lip as an urge to cry bubbles up inside me.

As I stand there, lost for words, I spot Daniel at the side of the room and our eyes meet. He stares at me for a moment and then marches over and grabs the microphone. 'Don't go,' he says, pulling back from the microphone when there's a feedback screech that stops people in their tracks. 'Please don't go. You haven't heard what Flora has planned to take the place of S.R. Kinsley.'

People are no longer moving for the door but they're not coming back either. Daniel takes a deep breath. 'Flora is going to reveal the identity of mystery author April Devlin.'

Has he gone completely mad? People start taking their seats again as I hiss at him, 'What are you doing? I don't know who April Devlin is.'

'But I do,' he says, simply.

It *is* Emma! No wonder my sixth sense kept telling me so. And Daniel is about to spill the beans in order to salvage something from the remains of my wrecked event. He's going to tell everyone – even though it's obviously important to him that it remains a secret.

'Don't do it,' I blurt out.

'Don't do what?'

'Tell everyone if you don't want to.'

Daniel lowers the microphone and takes hold of my hand. 'Trust me, Flora. Do you trust me?'

Out of the corner of my eye, I can see Malcolm bearing down on us. When I nod, Daniel gives me a crinkly-eyed smile and swallows loudly. Then, he turns to address the people who have crowded back around the stage.

'Who is April Devlin then? Don't keep us in suspense,' calls Katrina. 'Who is the mystery woman?'

Daniel is gripping the microphone so tightly that his knuckles have turned white. 'She is actually a he. The author is Daniel Purfoot.' He shrugs. 'That's me. I'm Daniel Purfoot and I wrote *Day of Desire.*'

'Get outta here!' Oops, did I say that out loud? I think I did, but what the actual…? April Devlin must be Emma. She can't be Daniel.

Katrina's mouth has dropped open, along with the mouths of several other women in the front row.

'No, you did not,' snorts Malcolm, his face twisted in confusion. 'You're making it up to save the day and get into Flora's good books. You did not write that sissy potboiler.'

'A fantastic book that has just been voted Honeyford's Best Read,' I shoot back.

'I did write it,' says Daniel. His cheeks are flushed and I'm close enough to notice a tremor in his jaw. Mind you, I'd be bricking it if I was him, coming out as the author of a novel supposedly written by a woman. I *knew* there was something weird about his connection to the book, but it seems my suspicions were way off the mark.

'If you're the author, why didn't you publish the book under your real name?' calls Katrina.

Daniel half-smiles. 'Because I was worried that people might describe the book as a "sissy potboiler", as Malcolm so eloquently put it. Boring accountants don't write books about feelings. And, to be honest, I thought it might be rubbish.'

'It's wonderful,' shouts a woman at the back, as I try to look all calm and collected, while my thoughts are racing. Daniel, the man who I once thought was a bit of a cold fish, is actually a seething mass of emotions who really 'gets' women and their lives.

'You're Luna's boy, aren't you?' calls Vernon, pushing his way to the front. He's only just finished serving up dozens of hot dogs to people watching the parade, and there's still a faint whiff of cooked meat about him.

'That's right. I'm the son of Luna, who runs the magical emporium further along the High Street.'

'And you're an accountant, you say?' Millicent looks totally confused.

'That's my day job.' Daniel takes a seat and gestures for me to do the same. 'I wrote this book a few years ago, after my wife died and I was bringing up my young son on my own.'

News that a tall, handsome local man is the author of their beloved book has made many of the women present go gooey-eyed. And this latest snippet of information, that he's a vulnerable widower with a small child, sends them over the edge. They hang on his every word, and Katrina gazes at Daniel with unadulterated lust, as he explains how he wrote the book in the evenings, after Caleb had gone to bed, and published it himself, rather than send it out to agents and publishers.

'I didn't want anyone to know I'd written the book because it felt so' – he pauses and swallows – 'raw.' He looks at me. 'I guess it showed parts of me that I wasn't prepared to let anyone ever see again. But I didn't want it to languish in my desk drawer forever. So I published it under a pseudonym and forgot about it really. I kept one copy to prove to myself that it existed and that was that.'

'Until it was discovered by the people of Honeyford,' I say.

'Until it was discovered and championed by you, Flora.'

He gazes at me with such intensity, a shiver trembles from my head to my toes. I'm vaguely aware of Malcolm tutting nearby, before Daniel turns towards the crowd. 'And then I was outed. So much for being incognito.'

'Does… does Luna know that you've written this book?' I stammer.

'I've never told her. I've never told anyone until now. I've been too' – he breathes out slowly – 'scared to.'

That's it for Katrina. She sobs – actually gives a loud, gasping sob – as Daniel's emotions are laid bare. And I feel something inside me shift. I thought I was a good judge of character but my early assumptions about what lay beneath his brusque personality were so wrong. This man is as vulnerable as I am.

'Have you written anything else?' shouts Phyllis.

Daniel shakes his head. 'I poured everything into that one book and then I kind of shut down. It was easier to get through the days, that way. And I've only recently started opening up again.' He stops and bites his lip as though he didn't mean to share so much. This must be so hard for him. And he's doing it for me, to help me save face. To help me settle into my new life in Honeyford.

As questions come from the floor, thick and fast, and Daniel explains more about his writing, I scan the crowd for Malcolm, but he's nowhere to be seen.

Chapter Twenty-Four

Malcolm has popped up again. He's suddenly appeared in the café, while I'm clearing up with Becca's and Mary's assistance, though he doesn't seem to be in the mood to help. At the moment, he's loitering by the coffee machine with a hangdog expression, trying to catch my attention. And my heart sinks as I realise that decision time has well and truly arrived.

When Malcolm clears his throat for the third time, Becca and Mary take the hint and scurry off to wipe down tables at the other end of The Cosy Kettle.

'Are you all right?' I ask, resting my broom against the wall.

'Not really.' He gallops over, drops onto one knee in front of me, as though he's proposing, and grabs my hands. 'It's decision day, Flora, and I can't wait any longer for you to make up your mind. I've kept my end of the bargain so what's your answer? We've been married for twenty years and you owe it to me, to our time together, to come home and give us one more try. Or what were those years worth, Flora? What am I worth? I've given up everything for you.'

Hmm, that's not strictly true. I've done most of the 'giving up' over the years to fit in with what Malcolm wants – from getting married in a register office and moving away from my friends and family, to suppressing my ambitions in favour of his.

When I don't speak, Malcolm shifts and winces as his knee scrapes along the painted concrete. 'Flora, don't leave me in suspense. You know I'd do anything for you,' he hisses.

I should say something but I'm transfixed by a small shiny patch of scalp on the crown of his head. Malcolm is starting to go bald. He won't like that.

'Flora? Are you listening to me? I'm starting to feel like a right prat down here. People are staring.'

He's right. Becca and Mary are watching us with their mouths open. But when I glance over, they go back to furious table wiping.

'I don't quite know what to say,' I murmur, feeling panicky as, over the top of Malcolm's balding head, I spot Daniel coming into the café. I can't cope with another macho scrap. Not right now when I'm making a decision that will affect the rest of my life.

Luckily, Daniel takes one look at Malcolm on one knee and beats a hasty retreat back to his adoring fans. He was mobbed by them the minute his talk ended and this is the first time I've seen him since.

'Well, say something, for goodness' sake,' moans Malcolm. 'My knees are starting to seize up. Just make your decision and come home.'

'Which is where?'

'What are you talking about?'

'What I mean is… oh, do please get up!'

After Malcolm has staggered unsteadily to his feet and brushed smashed cake crumbs from his trousers, I take his arm and guide him out into the garden. The café's adopted stray cat is lying on the patio flagstones in the sunshine and the early evening air is heavy with pollen.

'We can talk more privately out here. What I mean, Malcolm, is that I'm not sure where home is any more.'

'It's in Oxford, with me, of course. Or wherever we decide to move on to next.'

'Even though you had an affair?'

Malcolm sighs and wipes beads of sweat from his upper lip. 'I've apologised for that already and ditched Marina. Please come back to your old life, Flora, and leave this new life behind. It really isn't you at all.'

Does Malcolm have a point? Am I shoehorning myself into a life that doesn't fit? As the cat stretches out in the hope of a tummy rub, my brain goes all Judge Judy and starts reviewing evidence for and against…

My new life is stressful and hasn't been an unqualified success. Running the shop and café is exhausting, I've no idea where I'll end up living, I screwed up with Caleb, the bake-off ended in a fight and, although Daniel saved the day this afternoon, some local feathers were ruffled by the change of plan. Alan was shooting me daggers from the back of the room, especially when Katrina got all fan-girly over our outed author.

When I think about it like that, going back to Malcolm seems very tempting. Perhaps giving up the shop and The Cosy Kettle and moving on to something new would be best too. And yet… I felt so connected to Honeyford as I marched in the parade this afternoon, and I like spending time with Luna and Caleb and the book club regulars – with Daniel too, when I'm not feeling awkward and out of my depth. Charter Day was mostly a success and championing April Devlin's book turned out to be a great business decision. Even though it was a decision that Malcolm would have vetoed.

Luna was right. It's like being at a crossroads with my safe, familiar life in one direction and, in the other direction, uncertainty and potential chaos.

'So what's it to be?' says Malcolm, side-stepping the cat, who's given up on tummy rubs and wandered over for a stroke. 'Just remember that, to me, you're the same wonderful woman I married twenty years ago.'

And just like that, my brain fog evaporates and the way ahead becomes clear because Malcolm is wrong – I'm not the same woman at all. When I promised to love Malcolm forever, I needed security and familiarity and a life without too many surprises. But what I need and want has changed over the years, as it has for Malcolm, too. And that's OK, I tell myself – even though I feel guilty at what I'm about to do.

Taking hold of Malcolm's hand, I draw in a deep breath of warm, summer air. 'I've thought long and hard about this and I'm really sorry but—'

'No, don't say it! I know I'm the only one for you and you're the only one for me. You always have been.' Malcolm suddenly stares past my shoulder and goes so ghostly pale, I think he's about to faint. 'Oh, good grief,' he whines. 'Not now! Is there another way out of here?'

'There's a gate in that back wall but we hardly ever use it. Why? Hey, mind the plants.' Malcolm has gripped my arm and is pulling me across the garden that's been so carefully cultivated. I wince as his big feet flatten a clump of Busy Lizzies. 'Phyllis will go mad when she sees what you're doing to her flowers.'

'Like I care,' snorts Malcolm, shoulder-barging the tall black gate that's set into the stone wall. As he pulls me through it, I glance back. A young woman with dazzling blonde corkscrew curls has just rushed out of the café and into the garden.

'Is that Marina?' I ask, as Malcolm pulls me through a narrow side passageway. A young couple, holding hands, have to do a nifty swerve to avoid us as we pile into Sheep Street. There are people everywhere, some of them still in fancy dress from the parade, out enjoying the sunshine and festivities.

'There are too many people in this stupid little town. Get out of my way! Where to now?' gasps Malcolm, who hardly knows Honeyford.

Before I can answer, he pulls me into a nearby lane. But Hangman's Lane leads down to the river, which means it's a dead end, unless he's planning on going paddling. Malcolm comes to an abrupt halt at the water's edge and stares at the fast-moving current in confusion.

'What the hell is that doing there?'

'That's the river and it's always been there. Are you finally going to tell me what on earth is going on?'

'Oi, Malcy!' echoes along the narrow lane that's edged with the high stone walls of people's gardens. When I turn around, Marina is advancing towards us, her high-heeled ankle boots clattering on the road. 'Are you running away from me?'

'Of course not,' blusters Malcolm. 'Flora and I were just going for a walk.'

'It looked more like a sprint. Anyway, it's Flora I want to talk to, not you.'

'It's all right, Marina. Don't bother if you're here to fight over Malcolm.'

'Aren't you going to fight for me, Flora?' whines Malcolm with his hands on his hips.

'I think our relationship has reached a dead end,' I tell him, recognising the irony of saying it while stuck in a cul-de-sac. 'I'm sorry, but that's the truth. So, if you're here to claim him, Marina, he's all yours.'

'I don't want him,' puffs Marina, grimacing as though the very thought is distasteful. 'I told him our relationship was over a week or so after you walked out.'

'Hang on, let me get this straight. You broke up with him?'

'That's not true,' huffs Malcolm, his forehead wet with sweat. 'I ditched her, Flora, for you.'

Marina twists her pretty face into a scowl. 'You're such a liar, Malcolm. You lied to me about your marriage when you said Flora didn't care about you any more, and you're lying now. I so should have listened to Emily.'

'Emily who used to work in the restaurant?' I butt in. 'What's she got to do with it?'

'She warned me Malcolm had been flirting with her and that he was a creep, but I thought she was jealous 'cos he was the boss and he was interested in me. I was dazzled by his charisma.'

Malcolm's charisma has definitely done a runner. In fact, he appears to be shrinking before my eyes as he sinks onto the kerb and puts his head in his hands.

'So let me get this straight. When you first came into the shop after I left you, Malcolm, and you begged me to come back home, you were still with Marina. You misled and lied to me.'

His muffled voice floats up. 'I was going to ditch her.'

'But you were waiting to see if I'd come home first – basically, you didn't want to burn your bridges and be left without either of us. But then she beat you to it by chucking you. For goodness' sake!'

When Malcolm stays silent, I turn to Marina. 'So why are you here to see me?'

'I couldn't believe what he was doing with the writer bloke this lunchtime. He kept encouraging him to drink – he was practically pouring plonk down his throat.'

'Plonk?' squeaks Malcolm. 'That was a vintage Burgundy.'

Blood starts pounding in my ears as Marina's words hit home. Daniel guessed the truth. My husband, the man who should want the best for me, was doing his best to sabotage my high-profile event all along.

'How could you do that, Malcolm, after you promised to support me?' It's only when he flinches that I realise I'm shouting. 'You knew how important today was to me but you took advantage of a man who obviously has alcohol problems to try and wreck my event. He's still upstairs, sleeping it off. Did you want me to disappoint people and look stupid?'

'I think you're overreacting horribly,' grumbles Malcolm. 'Being with me is what's best for you, Flora, and I was just trying to make you see sense.'

'Oh, everything makes perfect sense now.'

Marina clears her throat. 'Anyway, I thought you should know the truth 'cos, to be honest, I'm quite inspired by how you've taken on a business on your own. And I feel like a bit of a cow for going behind your back and everything.'

She stops, giving me a chance to leap in and say that of course she isn't a cow. But she's got a long wait coming. When I just stare at her, she sighs.

'I just wanted you to know about today before you decided whether to go back to him or not. Female solidarity and all that.' Marina realises the total inappropriateness of what she's just said, and sniffs. 'Whatever. I've got to go because my boyfriend's waiting.'

'I didn't know you had a new boyfriend.'

Marina's cheeks glow fuchsia-pink when she smiles. 'Yeah, Ben's the same age as me and really nice. He's got me a job in the garden centre where he works so I'm leaving the restaurant. Did you hear that, Malcolm? I'm leaving.'

My husband doesn't react. He continues sitting in the gutter with his legs splayed out in front of him.

'And he's not…?' I ask.

'Married? No. He's completely single *and* he's a rugby player.'

I nod, unsure how these two facts fit together.

'Anyway,' adds Marina, sticking out her arm to shake hands. 'Sorry, again.'

This is the woman who precipitated the break-up of my marriage – the reason Malcolm and I are no longer together. Or maybe she merely highlighted the fatal cracks in our relationship that we'd papered over without even realising it.

I don't take her hand but I do say, quietly, 'I wish you well, Marina.'

'You too, Flora.' After a final scowl at Malcolm, she turns and clip-clops back along the lane.

When she's out of sight, I sit on the kerb, stare at the crystal-clear water and wonder how we both reached this point. Two moorhens float past, carried along by the current, and the shouts of excited children reach us on the breeze. Honeyford is alive all around me, but my marriage is well and truly dead.

'Tell me why you deliberately tried to sabotage my event, Malcolm. After all I've done to support you over the years with your restaurants. After two decades of marriage.'

My anger has burned out and left bitter disappointment in its place. I thought I had the measure of Malcolm after so long together, but it turns out I hardly knew him at all. He shifts his backside on the kerb until we're face to face.

'You've always been so sensible, Flora – someone I could rely on. But you changed when you took a risk on the bookshop and opened that daft café. And I thought if things went wrong and you didn't feel

welcome in this stupid town you'd be more likely to see sense, give up
your business, and come back to me and the restaurant. But I hadn't
factored in that man.'

'Daniel isn't the reason I'm not coming back.'

'Are you sure?'

'I'm absolutely sure.'

'It's me, then, is it?'

'Yes, it is you. And me. If I came back, I could probably get over
your affair in the end. But don't you see we've reached a point where
we want different things out of life? Me taking over the bookshop and
you being unfaithful are symptoms of that and, to be honest, I'm tired
of living in your shadow. Tell me, why did you chase Emily and have
an affair with Marina?'

'I didn't chase Emily. That's a lie.'

Malcolm is either lying himself or he's in denial. I try again. 'Would
you have had an affair with Emily if she'd been up for it?'

Malcolm shakes his head but then puffs out his cheeks. 'I don't
know. Yeah, probably.'

'Have you had affairs with other women?'

'No. Absolutely not. No way, Flora. Definitely not.'

I decide to believe him this time, although he's protesting rather
too much.

'Have you come close to having other affairs?'

Malcolm hesitates, before giving a slight nod.

'Why do you think that is? Honestly.'

'I don't know. Don't all men have affairs?'

'No, Malcolm, they don't. So why?'

'I suppose I'm getting older and I don't much like it, and I needed—'

'Say it,' I urge him. 'What do you need out of life?'

'A bit more excitement, I suppose. I was a bit bored and in a rut, really.'

'Me too. I need more in my life than helping you to achieve your business dreams and being your oh-so-sensible wife. Can't you see that we've been growing apart for a while?'

Malcolm thinks for a moment. 'Yeah, I guess.'

It's time for the million-dollar question and, for once, I think Malcolm might answer me truthfully. 'Why do you want me to come back, Malcolm?'

'I love you,' he says, automatically, but then he shrugs. 'I do love you, Flora, but it's more—'

'Habit? And you like being in control of everything, including me?'

'Possibly, although I resent the implication that I'm a control freak. The bottom line is that I just don't fancy being on my own, Flora, and there's the restaurant, too. Who's going to help me run that?'

'You'll sort something out. I can't come back to you and my old life just because you're lonely and you need someone to help with your business. I deserve more, Malcolm. And so do you.'

Malcolm folds his arms and pouts. 'Are you and that Daniel bloke an item, then?'

'No. I don't know. I don't think so.'

'He's dreadful.'

'That's funny. He says the same about you.'

'And he wrote that stupid drippy book with the awful cover.'

'I admit it is an awful cover. But the book's not drippy. It's heartfelt and beautiful.'

'Huh, he's a total pansy and I'm never going to read it.' Malcolm slowly staggers to his feet and brushes grit from his backside. 'So is this the end of us? Are you going to change your mind?'

'It's the end of our road together. We've reached a crossroads and now we're heading along different paths. But chances are they're the paths that are best for us.'

'You've been living with that witchy woman for too long,' grumbles Malcolm, looking confused. 'She's zapped her weirdness into your head.'

I take a deep breath. 'To put it bluntly, Malcolm, I'm afraid our marriage is over. And I'm not going to change my mind.'

He nods and his lips tighten into a thin line. 'You'd better come and collect all your stuff then.'

'I will. We can make those sorts of arrangements later.'

'And I suppose you expect me to take that author bloke back to Oxford Station, even though he'll most likely vomit in my Jag?'

'I rather think he's your responsibility, if he's sober enough to travel. Don't you?'

Malcolm stares at his feet like a naughty child who's been caught out. 'Point taken. I suppose this is goodbye then, Flora.'

'I suppose it kind of is. Goodbye, Malcolm.'

When he turns and trudges away, I get an urge to run after him. My old life is walking away and it hurts and it's terrifying. But from beneath the pain and the fear, bubbles of excitement and relief are rising to the surface. I'm in control of my new, scary life, so I'd better make it a good one.

Chapter Twenty-Five

The whole of Honeyford has thronged to Memorial Park. Or that's how it seems. Vast expanses of grass, running down to the river, are jampacked with families, children eating mountains of pink candyfloss, and couples holding hands.

It's a perfect summer evening. A light breeze is blowing off the hills, bringing with it the scent of honeysuckle that's mingling with a smoky bacon smell from the huge hog roast. Poor, sweating Vernon – who ended his day handing out enormous rolls crammed with thick juicy slices of pork – will never shake off the whiff of crackling.

I wander down towards the river as the sun touches the horizon and the sky glows ruby-red and burnt orange. It'll soon be dark and a fireworks display will begin on the opposite riverbank. People are congregating near the water and listening to a local band playing Carpenters covers.

Close by, Alan – still in full monarchic regalia – is ordering three giggling children to obey his commands or risk being banished to the Tower of London. Katrina, sitting on a rug with him, swigs back a full glass of what looks like champagne and gives me a what-is-he-like eye-roll. But she also strokes his back in a rare display of affection. Maybe Charter Day has worked its magic on these two as well. I could stop and have a few words but I'm not in the mood for a chat because I'm looking for Daniel.

Malcolm is back in Oxford, Mr Kinsley – and his cracking hang-over – are on a train to London, and Becca is here somewhere with her housemate, Zac. But I haven't seen anything of Daniel since he spotted Malcolm kneeling in front of me in The Cosy Kettle. He'd finished signing books and had disappeared by the time I got back to the shop after the confrontation with Marina. It was only a couple of hours ago but it feels like so much has happened since then.

'Hey, Flora. What a fabulous event at your place this afternoon.'

Amy waves a half-eaten roast pork roll at me. She's sitting on a picnic rug with her teenage daughter, who's shunned her mother's more retro style for skinny jeans and a cropped T-shirt.

'Thanks, Amy. Glad you could make it.'

'Wouldn't have missed it for the world. Everyone's talking about it.'

I smile and wave back, feeling a warm glow inside. Amy is the fourth person who's greeted me since I came into the park five minutes ago. And every greeting has buoyed me up and made me feel as if I could truly belong here. It's a feeling I've not had since Malcolm and I left Yorkshire.

Oxford is historic and beautiful but it always seems to me that the city is for the young, or full of ghosts. Whereas, here… I look around me, at the dark shadows of hills rolling into the distance and the town's glorious stone buildings, and I thank my lucky stars that I took a chance on Honeyford Bookshop and The Cosy Kettle Café. It's going to take a while to get used to the new path my life has taken, but I'm confident that this wonderful little community will support me.

As the band belts out 'Top of the World' and the sky darkens, I spot a tall, familiar person at the water's edge. Daniel has Caleb on his shoulders and he's pointing across the river to where the fireworks will be lit.

Caleb's face breaks into a huge grin when he sees me, and Luna, who's with them, beckons me over. She's rocking a long cream kaftan that's embroidered with gold thread and sprinkled with sequins.

'Flora! We were wondering where you were. You haven't brought Malcolm with you?'

'He's working tonight, in the restaurant.'

'Of course. Don't you think this whole day has been absolutely wonderful? People have come together and my son has been revealed to be a writer of some repute.' She waves her arms around like a windmill. 'Honeyford is full of positive energy and there's magic in the air.'

Daniel swings Caleb off his shoulders and turns towards me, his face tired in the fading light. 'What happened to your drunk author?' he asks. 'I'm sorry I couldn't help sort him out but I got rather swamped by people after the Q&A.'

'That's OK. Mr Kinsley's all taken care of. Malcolm took him back to Oxford and put him on a train. He'd sobered up a fair bit and was very apologetic when he rang me. He's promised to come and do an event in the shop when his new book's published next month.'

'I should think so, too,' says Luna. 'He could have wrecked your afternoon if my wonderful son hadn't stepped into the brink.'

She looks up at Daniel with such naked affection that I suddenly miss my mum, who died so long ago. She lived a quiet life of domesticity and seemed happy enough, but I rather think she would approve of the new direction my life has taken. I'm not sure she ever much liked Malcolm, anyway.

Two middle-aged women are wandering past, and they whisper and nudge each other when they spot Daniel. He's become quite the local celebrity, and I really hope he's not regretting outing himself this afternoon. For me.

'Are you famous, Dad?' chuckles Caleb, pressing his head against his father's chest. 'Now everyone knows you wrote that book with the half-dressed lady on it?'

'Hardly,' says Daniel, his face in shadow so his expression is hidden.

'I don't know. You'll have loads of women throwing themselves at you now they know that beneath that austere exterior you're really a vulnerable old softie.' I smile to hide the emotions that idea has thrown up. 'I did appreciate you stepping in to save the day this afternoon. I know it must have been hard for you because you've been so secretive about the book.'

'It was rather terrifying, but I was happy to help. I couldn't bear seeing you so upset. I…'

When he leaves his sentence unfinished and shakes his head, Luna grabs her grandson's hand. 'Why don't you two take a walk and have a chat about things? Caleb and I are going to nab a ringside seat for the fireworks.'

'We'll come with you,' says Daniel, but Luna is having none of it. She literally pushes him towards me and pulls Caleb away before we can protest.

'Shall we?' asks Daniel. 'My mother seems determined that we should talk.'

His voice is distant and cold, again. Daniel Purfoot, touchy-feely author, has disappeared and the prickly man I first encountered is back. Disappointment lodges in my chest but I nod and we walk side by side, past the crowds to the edge of the park and into the town.

The streets, thronging with people just a couple of hours ago, are quiet now and lamps in shop windows are casting golden pools of light onto the pavements. Discarded rainbow-coloured streamers twist and dance in the warm breeze blowing off the hills.

'Charter Day seems to have been a great success,' I say as we walk past the church and along Parsonage Lane, which rises towards the edge of town. 'Don't you reckon? Despite the fighting, the bake-off went well and the cakes were delicious. Dick had so many slices, he had a sugar high and started behaving as inappropriately as Stanley.'

When Daniel laughs, it seems to break the ice. And for the next ten minutes we chat easily about drunken authors, Becca's amazing kettle sculpture and Henry VIII lookalikes as we keep on climbing, past tiny thatched cottages with dark windows. He doesn't mention *Day of Desire,* or Malcolm, and neither do I.

At last we reach the edge of the town, where the houses stop and the lane winds into the darkening distance. Daniel leans against the gate to a field and looks out over Honeyford, spread below us. His strong face is illuminated by beams of light from a lone street lamp. Above us, stars are twinkling as the sky turns midnight blue.

It's all very peaceful and soothing, or it would be if today's events weren't suddenly catching up with me. I guess that's not surprising – so far, I've taken part in Charter Day, talked to a million people, brokered peace in a cake war, helped a rat-arsed author into bed, discovered that Daniel's alter ego is April Devlin, and broken up for good with my husband.

It's been one hell of a day and I'd quite like to sleep for a week. I stifle a yawn as Daniel asks calmly, 'When are you moving out of Starlight Cottage?'

Oh. It seems I might have outstayed my welcome. I do my best to keep my expression neutral, so the dismay I'm feeling won't show.

'Soon, I guess. Though I'll miss the cottage and that amazing view and your mum and Caleb and... you.'

'I doubt that,' says Daniel, coolly. 'You'll be far too busy helping your husband in his restaurant to miss any of us for long.'

'What do you mean? I haven't said I'm going back to Malcolm.'

'There's no need. I saw him on his knees in front of you and Dick spotted the two of you later, hand in hand in Sheep Street. It was pretty obvious what was going on and I'm happy for you, Flora. Honestly, I am. I know it's been a hard decision to make and I'm glad that you've made what you feel is the best choice for you.'

An owl, hidden in the dark trees behind us, hoots mournfully as it hits me that Daniel really doesn't seem to care that I'm going back to Malcolm. Though why would he? I'm the annoying house guest who barged into his bedroom, kept secrets about his son, and outed him as an author. It seems the frissons of… something that I felt between us at times were merely the ridiculous imaginings of a middle-aged woman in emotional freefall.

But if Daniel's keen to get me out of his hair why did he bother coming to my rescue this afternoon?

'Can I ask you a question?' I say, leaning on the metal gate beside him. 'Why didn't you tell me that you were April Devlin? Why didn't you tell anyone?'

Daniel stares at the firework display that's started far below us. Bursts of red, green and gold are blazing over the buildings of Honeyford.

'I suppose I was embarrassed. Look at me, Flora. I'm a blunt middle-aged accountant with a small child and no prior writing experience so I thought people would laugh at me if they knew I'd written a book like that. I thought you'd laugh at me. What was it that Malcolm called it – "a sissy potboiler"?'

'Malcolm wouldn't know a good book if it jumped up and slapped him in the face.'

'Although I've always wanted to write, it's not a sensible use of my time, is it, when I've got a young child to support on my own. That book flowed out of me while I was grieving for Emma and I was all over the place and, though I wanted it to be out there in the world, I wasn't brave enough to reveal that April was really me.'

'Until this afternoon.'

'Yeah, until then. And now my shameful secret is out.' He grins. 'And I thought it would be terrifying, and it was. But it was also quite liberating to say "I wrote this", and to hear how much people seem to like it.'

'They love it.'

'Thanks to you and your faith in it.' He catches my eye and only looks away when a rocket scatters silver stars above our heads.

'And now you're free to write another book, as Daniel Purfoot.'

'Is the world ready for that?'

'Definitely. You have real talent, Daniel, and insight. So why did you decide to let the cat out of the bag this afternoon?'

'Ah, Flora.' Daniel hesitates. 'You must know why. I did it to help you out. I did it for you. Oh, for goodness' sake, I can't do this.' He starts pacing as crackles echo across the hills, and an appreciative roar floats up from the Memorial Park.

'Can't do what?'

'Not say anything. I know it's a fait accompli and I'm trying not to be blunt.'

'Since when?'

'Since my mother told me, just before we set off for the park this evening, to tone it down if I saw you. Apparently some people find my bluntness off-putting. Hard to believe, I know.' He rolls his eyes and twists his mouth up in one corner. 'And I've tried to keep out of all this because it's none of my business. Not really. And I'm determined not to be overly blunt about it.' He takes a deep breath. 'But are you sure, Flora, about going back to Malcolm? You deserve more than a man who cheats on you and belittles your business and—'

'Gets an author deliberately drunk to scupper my big event?'

When Daniel's mouth falls open, I start massaging my temples to ward off the headache that's threatening. 'You were right. He admitted it, kind of. He was outed by Marina, the woman he slept with. She turned up in the café earlier and told me Malcolm was plying Mr Kinsley with wine like there was no tomorrow. That's why we ran out of the café. He spotted her, grabbed my hand and pulled me after him.'

'What a duplicitous, scheming little shit,' says Daniel, all good intentions to rein in his bluntness forgotten. 'He thinks he owns you, Flora. He wants you back under his thumb and doing what he thinks you should be allowed to do. He's not good for you.'

'I know. Which is one of the reasons why I'm not going back to him.'

Daniel stops pacing. 'You're definitely not going back?'

'Nope. I'd made up my mind before I found out about his scheme to wreck my event. My future is here in Honeyford. It's pretty scary, leaving a safe, predictable life behind and stepping out into the unknown. It may not even be the most sensible option, all things considered. But I've decided to do what your mum advised and follow my heart.'

'I see.' Daniel suddenly reaches out, grabs my hand and wraps his fingers around mine. 'And now you've properly decided to leave your husband, would it be all right if I kissed you?'

His question catches me off guard and I become aware of the thud of my racing heart.

'I'm not changing everything because of you,' I tell him. 'None of this is about you, Daniel. Not really. Leaving Malcolm is something I have to do for myself.'

'I know that.'

'And I need to move out of Starlight Cottage and find my own place. I've never lived on my own before and I need to try it.'

'That makes sense.'

I've explained myself and my whole body is screaming *just kiss him already!* But my mouth carries on talking. 'It's just that I don't want to live what someone else thinks my life should be. I've always been so sensible about everything and chosen the safe option, but now it's time to take a deep breath and step out from Malcolm's shadow into the light.'

OK, that sounds very over the top, but Daniel nods.

'Absolutely.'

'So I'm not leaving Malcolm and staying in Honeyford just because of the feelings I have for you.'

Aargh! Me and my big mouth and *getting everything out into the open.* I've just admitted out loud that my feelings for Daniel are not purely platonic. But he wants to kiss me, so that's OK, isn't it? Good grief, I'm so flustered and my heart is hammering and Daniel is standing so close.

'I get it,' he says, his breath warming my cheek. 'And I'm not trying to muscle in or take over where Malcolm left off, Flora. Heaven knows, I'm as scared about my life changing as you are. But please, can I kiss you now, before I go crazy trying to hide how I feel about you?'

'How you feel about me?' I still appear to be talking, rather than kissing.

Daniel rakes his free hand through his hair. 'I almost kissed you when you came into my room after the book club evening. But it would have been a mistake because you were so vulnerable and you still had to decide for yourself whether to go back to Malcolm. So I've tried to back off. But can I kiss you now that…?'

A rocket bursts above our heads, scattering golden filaments across the inky sky and drowning out the rest of Daniel's question. But I've got the gist.

When I nod, he cups my cheeks in his warm hands and pauses for a heartbeat, his lips a fraction from mine, before our mouths touch. I slip my arms around his waist and pull myself tight against him as he kisses me more urgently, one hand pushing through my hair to the base of my neck. His other hand slips down my spine and comes to rest in the small of my back. Oh, boy, this kiss has been a long time coming and it's all the sweeter for the wait.

When we eventually pull apart, my breath is coming in short gasps and Daniel splutters, 'Wow.' He laughs and I laugh too, caught up in the joy of this moment. Making a new life for myself in Honeyford won't be easy, and who knows what will happen between me and Daniel, but things have certainly got off to a wonderful start.

Daniel hooks his arm around my shoulder and I snuggle into him as the fireworks display builds to a crescendo and lights up the golden-stone buildings of Honeyford. As another roar drifts up from the crowd far below us, I think of the people who have become dear to me in such a short space of time: Luna, Caleb, Becca and Callie, the members of the book club – and Daniel, of course. They've welcomed me and made me feel as though I belong here.

They are the living, breathing heart of this town that's now my home. The town that I've come to love.

A Letter from Liz

You've reached the end of the book which means I now get a chance to say a very big thank you for reading *A Summer Escape and Strawberry Cake at the Cosy Kettle*. I'm delighted that you chose to spend time in Honeyford, and I really hope you enjoyed Flora's story.

Life goes on in Honeyford and I'm back there at the moment, writing about Christmas at The Cosy Kettle – the café is strewn with tinsel and fairy lights, and looks gorgeous. This time, I'm telling Becca's story – and what happens to her, and the people she loves, when she decides to reinvent herself. You can find out when that book will be published by signing up at the following link. Your email address will never be shared and you can unsubscribe at any time.

www.bookouture.com/liz-eeles

If you had fun reading *A Summer Escape and Strawberry Cake at the Cosy Kettle*, I'd really appreciate it if you could spare the time to write a review. It doesn't have to be a long review – just a line or two is fine – and it might help a new reader to discover my books. Thank you.

I look forward to seeing you again soon in Honeyford. And, in the meantime, if you'd like to get in touch or check out my latest news, you can find me loitering on Facebook, Twitter, Instagram and my website.

Liz x

 lizeelesauthor

 @lizeelesauthor

 lizeelesauthor

 www.lizeeles.com

Acknowledgements

This is my fifth published novel, and I'm still pinching myself. Just three years ago, I didn't have a publisher, the first romcom I'd tried to write was languishing in a drawer and I wasn't sure I had another book in me. My writing dreams were slipping away – and then along came Bookouture.

The Bookouture team gave me an amazing opportunity, and have been brilliant ever since. As well as being super-talented, they're really nice people. And that counts for a lot when you're a writer not over-endowed with confidence who's pretty new to publication. A special thank you goes to my wonderful editors Ellen Gleeson and Abigail Fenton for being my #CosyKettleDreamTeam. This book is all the better for their wise suggestions and support – plus their gentle encouragement when writing and editing deadlines were looming.

I'm blessed with fabulous family and friends. And I'm ever grateful to the bloggers who write about books and are supportive of so many authors, including me.

Writing makes me happy. It also makes me very distracted at times, and occasionally slightly grumpy (did I already mention deadlines?). Thank you, Tim, for being understanding when I'm on a writing roll, and for making me happy too.